LOVE AT
COOPER'S CREEK

What Reviewers Say About
Missouri Vaun's Work

Crossing the Wide Forever

"*Crossing the Wide Forever* is a near-heroic love story set in an epic time, told with almost lyrical prose. Words on the page will carry the reader, along with the main characters, back into history and into adventure. It's a tale that's easy to read, with enchanting main characters, despicable villains, and supportive friendships, producing a fascinating account of passion and adventure."—*Lambda Literary Review*

The Time Before Now

"It is just so good. Vaun's character work in this novel is flawless. She told a compelling story about a person so real you could just about reach out and touch her."—*The Lesbian Review*

Birthright

"*Birthright* by Missouri Vaun is one of the smoothest reads I've had my hands on in a long time. It is a romance but its subgenre is action/adventure which is perfect for me since romance tends not to hold my interest. …This story was so pure."—*The Lesbian Review*

Jane's World: The Case of the Mail Order Bride

"This is such a quirky, sweet novel with a cast of memorable characters. It has laugh out loud moments and will leave you feeling charmed."—*The Lesbian Review*

Visit us at www.boldstrokesbooks.com

By the Author

All Things Rise

The Time Before Now

The Ground Beneath

Whiskey Sunrise

Valley of Fire

Death By Cocktail Straw

One More Reason To Leave Orlando

Smothered and Covered

Privacy Glass

Birthright

Crossing The Wide Forever

Love At Cooper's Creek

Writing as Paige Braddock

Jane's World The Case of the Mail Order Bride

LOVE AT COOPER'S CREEK

by

Missouri Vaun

2018

LOVE AT COOPER'S CREEK

ISBN 13: 978-1-62639-960-0

THIS TRADE PAPERBACK ORIGINAL IS PUBLISHED BY
BOLD STROKES BOOKS, INC.
P.O. BOX 249
VALLEY FALLS, NY 12185

FIRST EDITION: FEBRUARY 2018

CREDITS
EDITOR: CINDY CRESAP
PRODUCTION DESIGN: SUSAN RAMUNDO
COVER DESIGN BY JEANINE HENNING

Acknowledgments

This book is set in an area of North Carolina where I attended high school. I have such fond memories of that time and place. However, the area has changed since I lived there, and input from Paula about present day Hendersonville was invaluable.

Several of the story threads in this book were taken from tales I heard as a child about people who were contemporaries of my grandparents and parents. After all, some of the best fiction finds its source in truth.

Special thanks to D. Jackson Leigh, Jenny, Alena, Rad, Sandy, and my editor, Cindy. And to my wife, Evelyn, your love and support save me every day.

I think for those of us who've left the Deep South because of the necessities of career there's a part of us that always longs for home. The initial idea for this book possibly started because of a brief bout of homesickness, but then, as with all character-driven stories, this novel took on a life of its own. I love these characters and I fell in love with their journey.

Welcome to Cooper's Creek.

Dedication

For my grandmother, Birdelle.
Most of this story is yours.

CHAPTER ONE

She was suspended in warmth and darkness. Floating. The muscles in Shaw's arms and shoulders relaxed. Then space opened up. Everything dropped away. She was in a free fall. Shaw lurched, flailed her arms, and hurled the bottle of water against the console in the seatback in front of her. The half full plastic bottle thumped loudly against the black video screen, then rolled under her reclined sleeper and was lost in the darkened compartment.

It had only been a dream.

Shaw Daily had been having the same dream off and on for weeks, but she had no idea why or what it was supposed to mean. Why couldn't the subconscious speak plainly? It was probably a stress dream. And every time it happened she was certain she was falling. The dream always frightened her. She'd panic and thrash herself awake, breathing hard, her heart drumming so fast it threatened to break through her ribs.

The seat belt loosely fastened over the blanket held fast as she tried to get up. She relaxed against the reclined seat and unclipped the seat belt. Passengers around her had eye masks and noise canceling headphones. The guy next to her snored softly, completely unaware of the terror she'd suffered in the seat next to him.

Surrounded by people yet utterly alone.

Shaw glanced at her watch, tilting it to catch soft ambient light from the galley. They still had five hours of flight time. She stood, braced her arm against the overhead luggage compartment, and took deep, slow breaths. The lights in the cabin were off so that passengers could sleep. It was always strange on long international flights, easy to forget that you were in an aircraft somewhere over the seemingly limitless sea. The blinds were down for the comfort of sleeping passengers, blankets and pillows strewn about. They could be anywhere. They could just as easily be on a train, or in a submarine. But they weren't. They were at thirty thousand feet, somewhere over the northern Pacific Ocean.

Shaw headed toward the faint light visible beneath the galley curtain in search of something stronger than water.

She brushed the curtain aside to discover a flight attendant reading in the jump seat. She was very pretty and Shaw instinctively ran her fingers through her hair to smooth it down. Short hair with a bit of product in it could get unruly if you slept on it for too long or at the wrong angle. Which Shaw figured had just happened. Sometimes her hair looked cavalier or carefree; sometimes it just ended up looking like she'd fallen asleep and forgot to check the mirror.

"Can I get you something, sir?" The crewman smiled and set her book aside. She had blond hair that was neatly pulled back into a clasp. Her uniform was a perfect fit, hugging every curve, and her skirt showed just the right amount of shapely leg. Shaw cleared her throat. As the attendant stood, her nametag reflected the overhead reading light.

"Your name is Carmen?" Shaw was still recovering from the falling scare so she was feeling a bit vulnerable and in need of conversation.

"I'm sorry I called you sir." It seemed Carmen had realized Shaw wasn't a man when she heard her voice. That happened a lot. Shaw was used to it. It didn't bother her. She figured it had something to do with her height, broad shoulders, and short hair. A preference for tailored men's clothing probably added to the gender confusion she frequently encountered, especially in women's restrooms.

"No worries." Shaw didn't want Carmen to feel bad.

"I just glanced up and in the dark, well, I'm sorry. What can I get you?"

"Bourbon and Coke?"

"Can't sleep?"

Shaw shook her head. Carmen poured soda into a glass and then held up a single serving bottle of bourbon as if silently asking *how much*?

"You can just fill the glass with it." Shaw peered out the small window in the exit door. The surface of the water was black and choppy, reflecting the moon in a stucco texture.

"Here you go."

"Thanks." Shaw took a few sips and again looked out the window to see if she could spot the moon. When she turned back, Carmen was casually studying her from a few feet away. Carmen poured the rest of the soda into a glass and sipped it.

"How is it to work such a long flight?" asked Shaw.

"It's not so bad. It goes faster if you can sleep, but I guess that's not working for you."

"I think I dozed off, but...bad dream."

They were quiet for a moment. Shaw had probably said too much. Acknowledging a bad dream was kind of a personal detail and she'd known Carmen all of six minutes. She was about to return to her seat when Carmen spoke.

"Is this your first trip to Japan?"

"No. I go at least twice a year."

"Really? What sort of work do you do?"

"I'm in sales and marketing." That sounded so boring.

"I have a layover for twenty-four hours in Tokyo."

Was Carmen flirting with her? She didn't really give off a lesbian vibe, but the tilt of her head, the direct eye contact as she regarded Shaw, definitely could be flirtation.

"You can do a lot in Tokyo with twenty-four hours." Shaw decided to play along. Bantering with Carmen was much better than trying to decipher the dream.

"Really? Perhaps you could give me some ideas about how to spend my time." Maybe Carmen wasn't flirting; maybe she simply found Shaw more interesting than the thick-waisted suits, snoring, in sock feet all around them. Working in the business class compartment on an international flight had to be tiresome.

"Sure, if you've got something to write on I can jot some things down for you."

Carmen handed her a napkin. "Why not start with your phone number?"

❖

A high-pitched clanging echoed through the dark house. No, wait, it wasn't completely dark. Kate Elkins leaned up on one elbow and squinted toward the light seeping in from the hallway. The distinctive sharp sound of metal pots banging against each other was coming from the kitchen. The clock on her nightstand read three a.m.

She tottered down the hallway in flannel pajama pants and a T-shirt, rubbing her face; the wood floor was cool against her bare feet. Blinking to chase the sleep from her eyes, she paused to take in the scene. It looked as if her mother had pulled every cooking pot in the house out of the cabinets and put them on the tiled counter.

"Momma, what are you doing?" For a moment, Kate wondered if her elderly mother was sleepwalking.

"I've gotta get the ham in the oven and then start the biscuits."

"It's three in the morning, Momma. Who are you cooking for?"

"Well, darlin', it's Christmas isn't it?" The elder Mrs. Elkins hoisted a large broiling pan onto the stovetop. Her thin gray hair fluffed around her head like wisps of fine silver feathers. Her nightgown and robe hung slightly askew. "I need to have everything ready for when Ned gets home with the ham."

The mention of her father's name was like a punch in the stomach. Her father had been gone for more than five years from a massive heart attack. Kate swallowed the knot rising in her throat as she watched her mother fuss with a large spoon for basting.

"Momma, it's not Christmas." She put her arm around her mother's slightly stooped shoulders. "It's the middle of the night. Let's get you back to bed."

"It's not Christmas?" Large doe eyes, innocent and confused, darted to meet Kate's.

"No, Momma, it's almost summer." She eased her mother toward the bedroom and helped her back into bed.

"Where's Ned?"

"Daddy's gone, Momma." Tears gathered at the edge of her mother's lashes. Kate pulled the covers up and tucked them around her frail shoulders. "I'll sit with you for a little while if you want me to." She sank onto the side of the bed and stroked her mother's hand.

"No, sugar, I'll be fine. I'm sorry I woke you." Her mother's mind seemed to be catching up with where they were in the present. "I swear I don't know what got into me. I must have been dreaming."

"It's okay. You just try and get back to sleep." Kate switched off the bedside lamp and returned to the kitchen. She'd deal with the pots in the morning. It would be too noisy to restore order even though she was now wide-awake.

There was a small crocheted throw over the back of the couch. She stopped mid reach as she glanced at the photograph on the nearby lamp stand. She held the photo up and studied it. It was a photo of her mother and father shortly after they'd married. At this young age her mother looked more like Kate's twin, with shoulder-length brown hair, an oval face, and girlish figure. Kate imagined her mother's youthful hazel eyes dancing with hope for the future that awaited her. She lightly traced the outline of her mother's face with her fingertip.

Kate replaced the photo and plucked the throw from the couch. She draped it around her shoulders and walked out onto the long porch across the front of the house. The whole world seemed asleep. The wind stirred the treetops. She could hear the rustling but couldn't really see the movement because it was so dark.

It was early summer, but the nights in the mountains were still chilly, despite the warmth of the days. Misty fog settled into the hollows and didn't burn off until late morning, softening the valleys between the rolling blue ridges.

Light from the kitchen extended a few feet past the edge of the porch. Beyond that point was absolute darkness. Kate stepped off the porch into the cushioned carpet of thick damp grass. Looking up toward the crest of the ridge in front of the house, she could see the faintest moonlit sky through the trees. In the utter silence of the woods surrounding the house she heard the distant sound of running water. It had rained two days earlier, and Cooper's Creek was running high as it wound its way down from higher elevations.

The sounds, the smells, the soft crush of tender grass under her feet and the dark outlines of the hardwoods, all of these things were a comfort to her. All of these things felt like home.

It was strange to be back home again with her mother. Their roles had reversed and she was now the caretaker. Caretaking had always been a part of her nature, whether she was mothering a kitten, or heartbroken friends, or children in her classroom, but mothering her mother was an entirely different thing. The next few months would no doubt test her patience and challenge her ability to deal with her mother's accelerating frailty. Not to mention that to do this for her mother meant putting her entire life on hold.

But that's what it meant to be a family. Her mother needed her, so here she was.

She pulled the blanket up to her chin and let out a long sigh. It wasn't as if she had some huge thing in her life at the moment aside from her job. It wasn't as if she had a family of her own or even a steady girlfriend. In general, her life wasn't where she'd thought it would be by now.

Kate started to head back in the house. She decided to look for the moon one more time, but she couldn't find it through the thick smattering of broad leaves. She returned to the house and settled back into bed. Her mother was getting worse and that worried her. Worry would make it hard to sleep.

Chapter Two

Shaw scanned the empty hallway of the elegant hotel that seemed to curve to infinity. Mahogany doors at regular intervals paced away in both directions. The ornate pattern of the carpet contrasted sharply with the serenely stark walls. This was one of those moments when where you stood versus where you started felt surreal. Twelve hours ago, she'd been in San Francisco; now she was in Tokyo.

The door lock flashed green and clicked. Shaw leaned into it with her shoulder, pulling the rolling bag along across the threshold. Two sliding bamboo doors stood on either side of the unadorned entryway. She left the bag and chose the door to the right.

Should have gone left.

In Japan, things were always opposite of what you expected them to be. Magazines were read back to front from a Western perspective. Cars drove on the other side of the road. Hotel rooms were organized differently as well.

The bath and shower were to the right. She circled through the space walking counterclockwise through two more sliding doors, one to the bedroom suite and the next to the sink area that featured a complicated electric tea kettle, coffee accessories, and bottled water.

Shaw chugged water for a full minute before she took a breath. International flights made her incredibly thirsty. Probably the dry air or too many roasted nuts during the flight. Plus, the bourbon and Coke had taken the edge off but had just made her thirstier. She took another long swig as she stood in front of the floor-to-ceiling windows overlooking the lights of the city. Tokyo Tower skewered the sparkling skyline. She was on the twenty-seventh floor, and from this vantage point the lights seemed to reach all the way to the edge of the earth.

It might have been fun to show Carmen around Tokyo, but Shaw had politely returned the napkin with a few tourist spots, but without her phone number. She wasn't sure why. The timing just didn't seem right, or her mood. Shaw wasn't feeling quite herself lately.

After finishing the bottle, she circled back to the entry and retrieved her bag, tugging it into the bedroom. The dress linen suit jacket she'd worn for twelve hours looked like she'd slept in it. Shaw tossed it onto the bed and went into the small room off the bath area where the toilet was tucked discreetly away from the rest of the living space.

After relieving herself, she reached to flush the toilet and was greeted with seven buttons labeled with Japanese text. The eighth button on the far right was red. Her hand hovered over the complex panel of functions as if waiting for her brain to translate. Some she knew were discreet noisemakers, one was for the bidet, but what were the others for? Did red mean flush? Shaw pressed it and stood watching the toilet bowl. Nothing.

Within twenty seconds, there was a rapid knock at the door.

Oh shit. Red doesn't mean flush. Shaw moved quickly to the door. A dark-haired woman with an anxious expression on her face looked up at her when she opened the door.

"Ms. Shaw, is everything okay?" The nametag on her dark, tailored jacket read Kyo.

"Sorry. Daijoubu." Shaw used the Japanese word to communicate that things were *okay* and bowed slightly at the waist.

"May I assist you?" Kyo bowed back and gestured toward the water closet. Shaw felt her cheeks warm as she nodded.

Shaw stood next to Kyo in the small space feeling even taller than she was at five feet ten inches. She towered over Kyo, who couldn't have been more than a little over four feet and was extremely petite. Shaw always felt as if she stood out when she visited Japan. She worried that her height intimidated Japanese women and maybe even some of the men. She kept her hair short; that detail alone was enough to make her stand out, but along with her height and then paired with blue eyes and her preference for masculine fashion, Shaw looked unmistakably foreign. In a culture that tended to be racially homogenous and held to strict gender norms, Shaw must have seemed like a strange anomaly. Yet as was their custom, locals were incredibly polite and never made Shaw feel unwelcome.

Kyo paused, smiled, and indicated the appropriate button to push for flushing. Then she bowed several more times as she backed toward the exit.

Apparently, the red button was for emergency situations. *The red button is not for flushing. Got it.*

This was a different hotel than she usually stayed in, and every hotel seemed to have their own system of buttons, in different orders. A college degree combined with fifteen trips to Asia and she still couldn't figure out the toilet functions. Shaw shook her head, walked to the bed, and tumbled facedown into the heap of pillows. A shower, room service, hopefully a good night's sleep, and then she'd feel almost human again. She rolled over, hugging one of the cushions against the front of her rumpled shirt.

The ceiling fan stirred the air. It brushed across her face lightly as she watched the blades slowly circle. Shaw closed her eyes and exhaled. The hazy contours of the Blue Ridge Mountains rose from her memory and flashed across her eyelids. If she stilled her mind she could almost hear the birdcalls and smell the damp air in the hollows.

Shaw opened her eyes and sat on the edge of the bed, feeling suddenly homesick.

Kate stood at the front of the classroom waiting for the chatter to subside. When it didn't she clapped her hands.

"Eyes up!"

"Hands empty!" the children called back to her.

She gave them another minute to settle. Kate smiled at the roomful of hopeful and excited faces. They were on the verge of graduating from first grade and were about to leave her for the summer.

"I still have a fire engine on my desk." Jacob held up his hand as he announced his circumstances to the room.

"Thank you for telling me, Jacob. Please put the truck in the toy bin." In first grade, children were old enough to know the rules but young enough to turn themselves in for breaking them. Kate was enchanted by their vulnerability and openness. If only she could bottle that and share it with the world. She loved working with children and hoped someday to have a few of her own. That hadn't happened yet, and given her current personal situation, motherhood might not happen anytime in the near future.

She waited for Jacob to stow the toy and return to his desk.

"Now, in a few minutes the bell will ring." This was the last day of class and only a half-day, prior to the beginning of summer vacation. "I will miss all of you this summer. I hope you take some time to practice your letters and the words you learned this year. So that next year Mr. Garner will have the smartest group of second graders he's ever seen."

Samantha, seated on the front row, grinned up at Kate. Her two front teeth were missing. By the end of their first year, several in Kate's class had lost their front teeth, but she was proud that most could now tie their own shoes. These small instances of personal growth were huge milestones for kids and she gladly celebrated with them.

The bell rang and the children scrambled to collect their things and make tracks for the door.

"Walk, don't run!" Kate felt a tug at her waist. She looked down to see Samantha's slender arms around her. She patted Samantha's back. "Thank you, sweetie."

"I love you, Miss Elkins." Samantha's face was buried in the folds of her dress.

"I love you too, Samantha. Have a great summer." Samantha clung to her for another moment and then trotted out the door.

Kate was tidying up her desk when Hank Garner spoke from the doorway.

"We're going to Never Blue for lunch and drinks. Are you coming?"

"Absolutely."

"Do you want me to wait for you?" Hank had a hopeful expression on his face.

"No, thanks. I'll just meet you there." Kate collected a couple of spiral-bound notebooks and her desk calendar and tucked them into her messenger bag.

Within ten minutes, Kate was easing her vintage Honda into a space along Main Street. Never Blue was located in the historic district of downtown Hendersonville, North Carolina. And despite its moniker, featured a bar that was bright cobalt blue. Obviously, the name referred to the mood of the establishment and not the color.

Kate paused and searched the lunch crowd for her friends. Emily waved from a spot in the corner. Hank stood as she neared the table. Melanie, Roy, and Crystal were already seated. Hank pulled out a chair. He was such a gentleman.

"I took the liberty of ordering you your first drink." Emily seemed happy. She'd clearly already taken several sips of hers.

"Here's to us." Melanie held her glass aloft. "Here's to shaping young minds. We survived another year!"

Everyone touched glasses. Kate had a slight sinking sensation as she sipped her drink. She hadn't told her friends that she was taking a leave from teaching. Well, she'd talked with Emily about it, but she hadn't let any of the other teachers know she'd made her mind up for sure.

Emily shot her a look as if to say *tell them*.

"I have some news to share." Kate's voice cracked. She cleared her throat and tried again. "I have some news to share."

The chatter around the table subsided and everyone looked at her.

"I'm taking next year off." No one said anything. They were all just watching her with surprise on their faces.

"Why—" Hank's question was interrupted by a thump under the table and a grimace. Emily had probably kicked him. "I mean, congratulations." His tone was sheepish.

"I'm taking time off to help my mom out." Kate loved her mother dearly. She thought back to when she'd been in grade school and was upset because she'd fallen and skinned her chin. The whole underside of her chin had a big red raspberry on it. Her mother had allowed her to stay home, and they'd baked sugar cookies and then eaten most of them hot right out of the oven, only waiting long enough for the sprinkled sugar on top to melt.

Her mother needed her. If she didn't take the time to care for her now Kate knew she'd have regrets. "It's just for a little while. Then I'll be back, shaping our country's future leaders. Or at least teaching them to read."

"I think you're doing the right thing." Crystal reached across the table and touched her hand.

"Thank you." Kate hoped she was doing the right thing. Good teaching positions were hard to come by. She'd arranged to take a leave of absence for a year, but if her mother's condition required more care she worried she might not have a job to return to. It didn't matter. There was no money to hire full-time care, and Kate and her sister had decided to try to keep their mother at home for as long as possible.

"Can I take your order? Just let me know if you need more time." The waitress stood at the end of the table. No one responded right away. "Or would you like another round of drinks first?"

"Yes!" Emily jumped at the offer grinning over the top of the cocktail list at Kate. "I'd like to order a Prickly Bitch for myself, and my friend here will have a Fifty Shades of Delicious." She winked at Kate. "Or does Tiki Bar Romance sound more up your alley?"

"Fifty Shades does sound delicious." Kate smiled, and just like that the mood shifted and the conversation around the table switched to summer vacation plans.

Kate listened to the chatter, a little lost in her own thoughts. Summer vacation was usually her time to get away, take a trip to Pensacola for a week on the beach, basically, she'd treat herself to a week somewhere warm and lazy to regroup after the end of the hectic school year. This summer would be different. She sipped her drink and tried to imagine how her life might change in the coming weeks.

CHAPTER THREE

S haw skimmed the document Akari had circulated to the
meeting attendees.

"On the second page of the ideation brief you'll find the top line
of key milestones and the expectations for each milestone." Akari
was seated at the far end of the long conference table in her tailored
dark skirt suit and perfectly straight black hair, trimmed to just brush
her shoulders. The sterile windowless off-white walls reminded
Shaw of some scene in a futuristic science fiction movie where *the
corporation* was about to confront the hero with their sinister plan for
world domination.

In the narrative Shaw imagined, the villains would bury their
evil plot beneath jargon like *ideation* and *market activation. Strategic*
would actually be a code word for the demise of civilization as we
know it.

The screen at the other end of the conference room came to life,
and as if choreographed, the overhead lights dimmed.

"I have some data to share. These are the dashboards that
illustrate where the brand is positioned in the market at the moment."
Akari clicked through slides, each with a well-designed pie chart and
bar graph. "I think these numbers show that our strategic planning is
beginning to pay off."

Wait for it. The next slide would be key dates for market
activation, which would be referred to as a holistic approach, as if they
were discussing organic vegetables or something more meaningful
like child development. Shaw had heard it all before, hell, she'd said

it all before, and at some point she'd even thought there might be some truth to it. Before she realized it was all empty, meaningless. They were simply selling things to people, things that no one really needed. Her job was to sell a lifestyle through product placement. Her job was to sell happiness. She was good at it. And so was Akari Nakamura, her counterpart in the Tokyo office.

But before Akari could reveal the next slide, alarms began to sound on every cell phone in the room. There were ten people in the room; all reached for their phones to silence them. Ever since the tsunami hit Fukushima, cell phones now signaled in advance of an earthquake. Shaw was from San Francisco, so she was experienced with tremors, but every phone in the room ringing in unison was completely unnerving.

The gentleman in the navy suit seated next to her spoke in Japanese.

"He said an earthquake will hit in thirty seconds." Akari was kind enough to translate.

Thirty seconds? How was anyone supposed to prepare in thirty seconds? Everyone was silent. Shaw sat stone-still in her chair. Seconds later, the tremor rocked the floor, but only barely. Water in the pitcher in the center of the table rippled like the scene from *Jurassic Park* when the T. rex was moments away from chasing that Jeep through the jungle. After another minute, everyone seated around the table visibly relaxed, except for Shaw.

She white-knuckled the arm of her chair and fought the urge to rage at the room. Blood pounded in her ears. She squeezed her eyes shut and tried to focus on breathing. In. Out. In. Out. Heat seemed to radiate down her neck past her collar. Was she having a heart attack? Or was this what a panic attack felt like? Akari was talking about the slide on the screen but directed a look of concern at Shaw as she excused herself quietly from the meeting. Air was what she needed. Akari could handle the meeting without her.

In the hallway, she concentrated on taking slow, deep breaths as her long, deliberate strides took her farther away from the conference room. What was the world coming to when everyone sat calmly through an earthquake and then just carried on with a meeting about a marketing strategy?

This particular office was a bit of a labyrinth of nondescript hallways and unmarked doors. It took her a few minutes to remember where the coffee machine was. The employee kitchen was small but had a nice espresso machine.

As if on cue, a young office girl scurried into the room and, using hand signals, offered to make Shaw a coffee. After a moment, she delivered a perfectly fashioned cappuccino and then bowed as she backed out of the small tidy kitchen space leaving Shaw alone. Her heart rate had slowed while she'd waited for her coffee. She didn't want to make a scene or literally run from the building. She just needed to be alone for a few moments and let her mind wander to calm her nerves.

Shaw took tiny sips from the steaming cup while studying employee forms posted on a corkboard. Of course she wasn't able to read them because all the text was in Japanese. But she found the pictogram illustrations fascinating. They seemed to be instructions for worker safety and were pretty fun to decipher, especially the causes of various falling hazards.

"Did you get lost?" Shaw wasn't sure how long she'd been lingering in the kitchen when she heard Akari's voice behind her.

Maybe hiding was more accurate. "Uh, no, sorry."

Akari rested her manicured fingers on her hips and frowned. What she lacked in height she made up for in attitude.

"Well, don't rush your coffee break. I can handle the pitch alone." Sarcasm was normally outside Akari's comfort zone. Clearly, she'd been practicing.

Shaw turned to face Akari as a moment of clarity struck her. Life was short and she was wasting hers. That hadn't been a panic attack. It was a wake-up call sounding in her head.

In that instant, Shaw knew exactly what she needed to do. And she was going to do it right now. "I'm going home."

Kate faced the glaring fluorescent-lit interior of the storage space stacked with boxes. One of the lights flickered on the left.

"This is the last one." Her brother-in-law, Greg, placed the box of random kitchenware on a small bit of open floor space.

Without her teaching income, Kate had decided to sublet her apartment, and that meant storing all her worldly belongings while she stayed at her mother's place. Greg had helped her take a few personal things over to her mother's, but everything else was now in storage. That felt oddly unsettling. Kate liked her things. She was a nester. She'd furnished her apartment for optimum coziness, and now all of it was in boxes in this cold concrete space.

A splash of blue and white caught her eye. She lifted the lid of one of the boxes nearby. It was a box of treasures from high school. A couple of yearbooks, her journal, and the sweater she'd gotten when she'd lettered as a cheerleader. She picked up the journal and thumbed through the pages before gently stowing it on top of the folded sweater. Kate took one last look around before joining Greg.

The retractable door screeched like fingernails on a chalkboard as he tugged it down. Kate secured the padlock and shoved the key in her pocket. Her sister, Miriam, had taken the kids to Chuck E. Cheese while Greg helped her move.

"Can I buy you lunch at least?" Kate placed her hand on Greg's shoulder as he rolled the ropes they'd used to tie down the mattresses and stowed them in the tool compartment right behind the cabin of his pickup.

"I should probably get going."

"Grass to mow and all that?" Kate smiled up at Greg. Her sister had married well. Greg was a terrific guy, with all-American good looks and a kind-hearted spirit.

"More like laundry to do." They both laughed.

Miriam looked the part of the quintessential Southern belle, but she expected equality at home. Greg was an old-fashioned guy, doted on by three sisters, but he seemed to take Miriam's feminist streak in stride. Kate had even heard rumors that during their ten years of marriage he'd learned to cook.

"Well, thank you again. I really appreciate it." Kate could have asked Hank to help. He had a truck and would have been more than willing, but his assistance would further complicate things since she already knew he had a terrible crush on her.

No matter how many times she reminded Hank that she was a lesbian, he just didn't seem to believe her. Maybe if she dated more her lesbianism might be more convincing. She and Karen were involved for three years and had broken up over a year ago. It wasn't that she hadn't had opportunities to date women since the breakup. It was just that she was…well, picky sounded so negative, but she was. Sex just for the fun of it wasn't really her thing. And dating led to sex, so before she'd even gone on the first date her mind would spin forward, playing the whole scenario out. Which meant she'd usually shut things down before they even started.

This probably had something to do with the fact that Karen had cheated on her. She'd known Karen had a slight reputation for being a player, but she'd thought their relationship would be different. She'd been stupid or naïve or possibly both. So maybe she did have a wee bit of a trust issue; maybe that's why she intellectualized a possible dating situation into nonexistence before it even happened. Greg spoke, snapping her out of her mental spiral.

"I was happy to help, Kate." Greg turned to face her, standing in the open door of his truck. "This is a generous thing you're doing. I hope you know that Miri and I know the sacrifice you're making for the whole family. And we're here to assist in any way we can."

"I appreciate you saying so." With two young children at home and a husband who had to sometimes travel for work, Miriam had her hands full. It would have been impossible for her to take care of their mother. When they'd discussed their options at the first signs that their mother's dementia had worsened, Kate had known she was the logical choice. After a few weeks of deliberation, she'd agreed to put her life on hold and move in with their mother, for as long as it took. Greg and Miriam would help as best they could. But most importantly, they would all support each other, as a family.

Kate hugged Greg.

"Well, all right then." Greg slammed the door and spoke to her through the open window. "We'll come check on you in a few days. In the meantime, call me if you need anything." He waved as he pulled away.

Kate sat in the parking lot for a moment. When she'd finished grad school this wasn't what she'd seen as her future. But that was life, right? Life happened and you dealt with it. She had always assumed she'd be married with kids by now. That thought made her laugh.

In order to get married you might have to go on a date now and then.

She eased her Honda out through the main gate and onto the winding road toward her mother's place.

Her cell buzzed on the car seat next to her.

"Hello?"

"Hey, Kate." Emily sounded just a wee bit frazzled. "I'm sorry I couldn't help this morning. How'd it go?"

"It was easy. We're all done." Emily had offered to help pack boxes, but then her youngest had woken with a fever.

"Okay, good. Well, let's meet for a drink later in the week. I don't want you to feel stranded out there in the wilderness." Her mother's place was on twenty-six wooded acres. It was secluded, but not what Kate would call remote. But then Emily was more of an in-town girl. She lived in Hendersonville proper, about twenty-five minutes away. Her litmus test for *wilderness* was the radius for call-in pizza delivery.

"It's not really the wilderness, you know. It's only a half mile to the highway."

"If I can't see the paved road from my front porch it's too far for me."

Kate laughed. "You're *so* funny."

"That's good to know. If this teaching career doesn't pan out I can always fall back on doing stand up." Kate heard a wailing child in the background. "I gotta run. Motherhood beckons."

"Bye." Kate clicked off and tossed the phone onto the passenger seat, smiling.

She rested her elbow on the doorframe and rubbed her forehead. Would she get to have children of her own someday? She wanted them, plural, but she'd settle for one. At thirty-four, her biological clock was chiming loudly.

But she did have time. When the timing was right, it would happen. Not before. And timing was something you just couldn't rush.

The damp smell of the recent rain blew across her face through the open window, and she took a deep breath. The wind pulled a wisp of hair loose from her ponytail and she tucked it behind her ear. The curvy mountain road was walled in on both sides by dense hardwoods. The sun was out now and the pavement nearly dry. Sunlight broke through the bright green of the late spring foliage and splattered the roadway with undulating sunny shapes and patterns.

Kate pulled on her sunglasses and turned up the music.

Chapter Four

The black town car pulled up to the center median outside the international terminal a few feet from where Shaw was standing. The sun was bright in the cloudless sky. The brisk breeze cut right through her rumpled suit jacket, but it felt good. The damp, sea-scented chill in the air was like a refreshing splash of cool water on her face.

"Did you have a nice flight, Ms. Daily?" The driver, a portly fellow in a dark suit and sunglasses reached for her luggage.

"I did. Thanks for asking." She slid into the backseat just as her phone began to vibrate in her pocket. She checked the screen and for a moment considered not answering.

"Hi."

"Where are you?" Raisa Finch's tone was terse.

"At the San Francisco airport."

In the moment of silence that followed Shaw swore she could hear Raisa tapping her always perfect, always red nails on the sleek glass top of her desk.

"When Akari told me you'd left Tokyo I thought you'd had a breakdown or something, but you sound so...normal." There was an edge to her voice. Was that worry or anger? "It would almost have been better if you'd had a breakdown."

Definitely anger.

"I'm sorry to disappoint you."

"What the hell is going on, Shaw?"

"Look, I'll be at the office in twenty minutes. I'd rather talk to you in person." The driver eased into moderately heavy traffic, heading north toward downtown San Francisco.

"That sounds ominous."

"It's not ominous. It's just…" Shaw took a deep breath. "Listen, I'd rather talk about this in person." She clicked off.

Shaw sank into the leather seat and tried to relax. She needed to enjoy this brief moment of peace before the storm.

"There's heavy traffic on the 101. If it's okay with you I'll take an alternate route." The driver glanced at Shaw in the rearview mirror.

"That's fine with me." Taking the scenic route would give her a bit more time to adjust to this time zone. According to the clock, she'd arrived in San Francisco one hour before she left Tokyo on the same day. Traveling east to west was like time travel, with a lot more jet lag.

Tall, narrow row houses in pastel colors swept past her window as they traveled down Nineteenth Avenue. They crested the hill and the red-orange trusses of the Golden Gate Bridge punched up past the dense treetops of Golden Gate Park. At the edge of the park they turned right and headed in the general direction of downtown.

What was she going to say to Raisa? Maybe she'd had a breakdown after all. No doubt the person having a breakdown was the last to realize it.

How would she explain her sudden sense of urgency? Her phone vibrated again, a text from the vice president of marketing in LA. She ignored it.

Connectivity was supposed to be liberating, enabling people to work outside the confines of an office. But what it really meant was that you could never get away. Instead of liberation, connectivity had just inspired a whole new set of anxieties. Every problem required a solution, right now, regardless of what was happening in the rest of your life.

Shaw turned her phone completely off and shoved it in her jacket pocket. She couldn't remember the last time she'd done that. It felt scary but good.

"Can you wait for me?" The driver pulled into one of the executive spots on the first level of the parking garage beneath the building. "It should only take me about fifteen minutes, maybe twenty."

"Of course, no problem."

"Thanks." Shaw left her briefcase and angled toward the elevators. Her phone was off. Her heavy laptop bag was in the car.

She felt almost naked, unarmed. Her first steps toward freedom felt awkward, like some wallflower at her first high school dance.

Red Rock's offices were on the ninth floor. Shaw had originally noticed the company because of the name. She was even more intrigued when she discovered that the marketing start-up was named Red Rock because of the founder's love for the desert of southeastern Utah. Raisa Finch, a rock climber in a power suit, strong, feminine, and fierce. She and Shaw had clicked immediately, and over the past ten years, they'd built a strong company.

Red Rock had the reputation of identifying trends before they were trends and helping brands draft on those trends. It was a gift. Really, it was mostly instinct and the skills required to do it were hard to quantify. Hard to quantify, but valuable, lucrative even.

Shaw had been a senior at UCSF, doing an installation for her senior show, when she and Raisa first met. Raisa's father had put up the capital for Red Rock, and Raisa was just getting the company off the ground. She needed help staging an event, and something about the sculpture installation Shaw was doing caught her eye. Maybe it was nothing more than finding a woman who knew her way around metal works and power tools.

Raisa contracted Shaw for the event. It was the first time Shaw had actually made money putting her art degree to work. Three months later, they collaborated on another fund raising event, which led Raisa to solicit Shaw's help with a campaign presentation. One thing led to another. For some unexplained reason, Shaw had a knack for pitches and presentations. If Raisa could articulate something, then Shaw could bring it to life visually and stage it in a physical setting, whether that was through model construction, concept drawings, or brand identities. Raisa and Shaw simply clicked. They were like two halves of the same brain. The money was good, and with student loans to pay, Shaw had needed the money.

As Red Rock grew, Shaw moved further and further away from hands-on creation. She'd become more of a director. Maybe that was part of what contributed to her recent malaise related to her work. The work she was doing seemed to no longer enrich her life.

The better she'd gotten at her job the more she'd risen in the company, the further she'd gotten away from what she actually enjoyed doing—metal work and sculpture. It wasn't as if she'd ever dreamed she'd become this financially successful as a sculptor, but she never even really tried. Corporate life had lured her in, hook, line, and sinker.

Shaw exited the elevator and angled toward Raisa's office. Bethany, the receptionist, looked up sheepishly as she approached.

"Hi, Bethany, is she in her office?"

Bethany nodded. "Can I get you some coffee or water?"

"No, thanks."

Raisa looked up from her keyboard when Shaw entered. The click of the door closing seemed to echo loudly around the sleek, sparsely appointed office. She took a seat in a chair on the opposite side of the desk, facing Raisa who looked pissed. But to her credit she waited for Shaw to speak first. Shaw let her attention drift to the photo of Raisa's husband and their son. Somehow Raisa had managed to have it all, a demanding career and a life.

"My mother died."

"What? Today?" Raisa looked as if the oxygen had suddenly been sucked out of the room.

"Six months ago." Shaw never talked about her mother or her family or much of anything personal. It was all too embarrassing so she tried to hold herself apart from it as much as possible.

"I had no idea." Raisa's voice softened.

Shaw offered her a weak smile.

"I know."

"Is that what this is all about?" Raisa leaned forward with her elbows on her desk. She swiveled the monitor aside so that there was no barrier between them.

"Yes and no."

Shaw could tell that Raisa wanted to pelt her with questions. Intensity radiated from the other side of the desk. But Raisa held back.

"Raisa, I'm feeling very...on edge. I need to take some time away."

"This isn't like you."

"I know." Shaw was the executive vice president over international marketing and sales. She knew that she would be leaving Raisa in a bit of a lurch. Raisa depended on her, trusted her. "Akari can run things for a few months—"

"A few months?" Raisa cut her off. "Shaw, a few days is one thing, even a couple of weeks, but a few months—"

"Raisa, I'm not asking permission."

Raisa bristled. "Excuse me?"

Shaw's words had sounded terser than she'd intended. "I'm sorry, I didn't mean that the way it came out."

Raisa sank back in her chair. "Do what you need to do."

"Akari can handle things. You probably won't even notice I'm not here." She considered for a moment the truth of that statement. She was taking a chance letting Akari step in. Akari was quietly ambitious. Shaw knew she'd jump at the chance to prove she could handle more responsibility and the opportunity to earn a larger bonus would only fuel her drive.

Shaw felt a twitch of uncertainty, just for an instant, a shiver traveled down her arm. It felt like she was making some big, course-altering decision and she wasn't even sure what the consequences would be. Was she having a breakdown? If she were sitting where Raisa was would she consider this a crazy move? Probably.

"I hope you know what you're doing."

Shaw stood and moved to the window looking out at nothing. *I hope I do too.*

When she turned around Raisa was standing next to her. Not one for public displays of affection, Raisa surprised her when she wrapped her arms around Shaw's waist and pulled her into a hug.

"I'm sorry that I didn't know about your mother, Shaw."

Shaw held her arms awkwardly at her sides. When Raisa didn't release her after a moment, she hesitantly returned the embrace. It felt good to be held, even if it was by her straight, furiously competitive boss.

"What are you going to do?"

"I'm going home."

"Um, you are home."

"San Francisco is where I live, but it's not home." That was maybe the truest thing she'd said in a long time.

❖

Forty-five minutes later, Shaw was booked on a flight to Asheville, North Carolina, and almost packed for departure. She rolled a few more T-shirts and placed them in the suitcase. She'd decided to take one large bag filled with only her favorite T-shirts, jeans, shorts, and a couple of shirts nice enough for a night out. Oh yeah, and her favorite red ball cap, broken in and frayed at the edges along the brim.

What was she forgetting? She looked around and spotted the urn containing her mother's ashes. She unzipped the bag and wedged the simple brushed silver urn in between her jeans and a flannel shirt and then closed the bag again. She wasn't sure why, but it seemed weird to leave her mother's ashes behind.

She'd left instructions for the property manager to collect and forward her mail. She owned the building, but only occupied the apartment on the top floor. The two lower floors were rented out to tenants and managed on her behalf. She was out of the country too often to be a decent landlord, so the management company had taken that off her hands. There wasn't much else to take care of. No pets, no plants, no girlfriend, Shaw traveled too much for that sort of maintenance.

She realized now that she was remarkably untethered. She'd been an ambitious workaholic, who wanted to create a life as far from the one she'd had in her childhood as she could. Her mother had dragged Shaw from place to place as if she was continually searching for something and never finding it; new towns, new schools, and always barely scraping by. The one ambition Shaw had after graduating from high school was stability. She wanted to be her own master and in control of her own life. Red Rock had provided that, and until now, she'd been satisfied. But something was nagging at her, rippling the smooth surface of her carefully constructed contentment. She was thirty-eight, a well-adjusted adult with a thriving professional career, a six-figure salary, real estate holdings, and the strongest urge to just chuck it all and disappear.

CHAPTER FIVE

Kate turned onto the lengthy dirt and gravel driveway that led to her parents' place. The Honda heaved and bounced on the rutted drive. It was definitely time to grade the road now that winter had passed. As soon as the spring rains let up she'd talk to Greg about the best person to call for that task.

The road dipped and she slowed the car as she crossed the weathered culvert over the creek. The culvert was basically three large galvanized steel pipes with a thin layer of concrete over them. This allowed the creek water to flow unhindered but also created a makeshift bridge that you could drive across unless the creek flooded. Then you could easily get stranded on one side or the other until the water receded. That rarely happened, although precipitation seemed to be heavier and more sustained in duration in recent years, so maybe a proper bridge should be considered. Weird weather patterns happened more frequently and with more ferocity. *Welcome to climate change.*

Kate always crept slowly when she crossed the creek in hopes she'd get a glimpse of the ancient snapping turtle that made his home in the mud near the oversized drainage pipes. She'd seen him a few weeks ago. His ridged shell was the size of a manhole cover. He looked like a holdover from prehistoric times. She wondered how old he was. He'd probably seen some things in his life. Oh, the stories he could likely tell. That thought made her smile.

He was elsewhere today. The Honda lumbered up the hill toward the house. Her mother was in the flowerbed out front when she arrived.

"Hi, Momma." She popped the trunk. She'd brought one last box with her.

"The deer are eatin' all my flowers up." Her mother stood with hands on her hips.

"I suppose the deer have to eat something." She hoisted the box onto her hip so she could balance it with one arm and closed the trunk.

"We should put some corn out for them so they leave my flowers alone."

"I'll pick some up at the feed store next time I'm in town."

"Do you need help with that?" Her mother seemed herself today.

"No, I've got it." They walked toward the porch together. "Greg helped me move everything else into the storage unit."

"Who's Greg?" Maybe she wasn't quite herself after all.

"That's Miriam's husband, Momma." Kate had been reading some books about dementia and most had advised to simply answer questions but not to argue about details the person affected couldn't remember. She didn't want to make her mother feel bad about forgetting so she tried to gently remind her of things without any judgment in her voice. Memories seemed to come and go more often since the small stroke her mother had suffered a few months ago.

"Oh, yes, that's right."

Kate carried the box to her bedroom on the far end of the house. She'd considered taking over the bedroom upstairs where she'd have more privacy, but then she was afraid she wouldn't be able to hear if her mother got up during the night.

"Have you had lunch yet?" Kate asked.

"I reckon it's that time isn't it?"

"Yes, shall I make us some soup and sandwiches?" Kate checked the options in the cupboard. She needed to make a trip to the grocery. That had been on her *to-do* list, but she'd forgotten. After a quick lunch she'd have time to run back to Hendersonville before dinner. "How about tomato soup and grilled cheese sandwiches?"

"That sounds nice, sugar, thank you." Her mother sank into a faded floral print upholstered chair in the den. "Maybe I'll just rest here a minute."

She closed her eyes and Kate knew her mother would be asleep almost instantly. She stirred the soup and then heated the cast iron skillet for the sandwiches. Iron skillets made the best grilled cheese, especially if you didn't skimp on the butter.

Shaw took a cab from the Asheville airport to her grandparents' place. The drive took forty-five minutes. Unincorporated Cooper's Creek wasn't much more than a three-way stop, a post office, and a general store. Cell service was spotty heading through the mountains that ringed the small rural community.

In autumn, outsiders streamed along the winding two-lane road, sheltered by hardwoods. Leaf lookers would pack the parking lot at the general store in hopes of an espresso and find only twenty-five-cent coffee of the gas station variety. But as with many other rustic communities along scenic byways, the tourists kept things afloat so locals tried their best to remain friendly and accommodating.

Growing up, she'd lived at different addresses, but "home" had always been in the mountains. Abandoned by her husband, her mother was always chasing the next new thing, whether that was a man or a job. She dragged Shaw along with her on her journey to *anywhere but here*. Her strict Southern Baptist grandparents frowned on Shaw's mother, Iris, bringing any of her boyfriends home to the mountains. So usually, she'd just drop Shaw off. Those were the happiest times of her childhood.

Her attachment to this place was powerful and could be called forth by a sound, scent, or a kind word spoken in a melodic Southern accent. A birdcall or the scent of fresh cut grass would bring Shaw right back to that time in her childhood. She'd wake up to the sounds of the mountain coming alive to greet the day, a soft breeze wafting through the open window. There'd be real breakfast waiting for her when she got up, not the cold cereal variety she usually made for herself.

Shaw always wondered why her mother didn't just leave her with her grandparents for good. It wasn't as if they ever got along, and raising a child alone had to have been a burden. Shaw half expected, no, hoped was more accurate, that her mother might just decide not to come back and get her. It seemed to Shaw more often than not that she was the adult and her mother was the child. If it hadn't been for Shaw would her mother have remembered to pay the rent or get groceries? As she got older, Shaw took on more responsibility just to benefit from the stability of it. And to her frustration, her mother let her. Iris treated Shaw more like a peer than her child, except when it suited her, of course. When Shaw crossed her or made any attempt to rebel as a teen, her mother was quick to reestablish her authority. Or try to.

Iris wanted to be the adult when it worked in her favor.

Shaw tried to talk to her mother about why she'd left Cooper's Creek, but Iris was tightlipped about what exactly had lead to her departure from her North Carolina home. Shaw had also tried to get the story from her grandparents, but every time she'd brought up the subject they'd shush her as if she'd asked an impolite question at the dinner table in front of guests. As a result, Shaw learned by example to deal with uncomfortable truths by avoiding them. That was as much a part of her Southern heritage as her deep love of anything battered and fried.

It was difficult to find anything covered in batter or deep-fried in San Francisco. And if they did fry something they'd have to put some strange twist on it, like adding a sprig of lavender. Some things were perfection and needed no improvement. Like buttermilk fried chicken or pecan pie. Shaw figured she'd live longer on the West Coast. Left to her own devices, she'd surely eat a lot less locally sourced organic greens.

Now she'd done it. Just thinking of her favorite Southern specialties had her craving chicken fried steak with sawmill gravy. She'd have to drive into Hendersonville one night to satisfy that.

The cab turned onto the gravel and dirt drive, then climbed the steep approach to the simple, whitewashed frame house. As the car pulled away, she surveyed the place from the side yard. It looked as if Jimmy was doing a good job of keeping things up for her. Since her grandparents had passed, Shaw'd been sending a little cash every month to Jimmy Ludlow as a caretaker's fee. She could only get back to the mountains once or twice a year, and even then she didn't stay long enough for any real maintenance work.

The springhouse at the back corner of the yard was cool and dark when she stepped down onto the dirt floor. The spare key was under a mason jar of blackberry wine. She wondered how long the wine had been there and if it was still even drinkable. Maybe homemade wine aged like all other wine, but she wasn't sure.

The back porch looked as if it might fall away from the house in a stiff wind. The unpainted boards were sagging in places and curled up at the ends from years of exposure to the damp, humid air. An old oak table with faded hints of ancient green paint stood at the far end of the porch, piled with planting pots, a chipped ceramic basin, glass jars, and a decrepit soda box. It looked as if none of it had been disturbed since her grandparents lived there.

The screen door squeaked and the linoleum in the kitchen creaked as Shaw dragged her rolling bag along behind her. First things first, open some windows. The air inside smelled of old wood and forgotten things. Shaw moved from room to room investigating and fighting with the swollen wooden windows. She stood and looked out the last window she opened. It was late in the afternoon. The breeze was cooling off, and as it drifted past her it brought with it the smell of grass and honeysuckle. The sun started its afternoon decline behind the ridgeline bathing the room with orange.

The refrigerator was empty. Shaw lowered the temperature on the dial inside and chided herself for not thinking to have the cab driver stop at the grocery in Hendersonville before they drove up the mountain. She'd traveled from Japan to the West Coast to the East Coast and her stomach still wasn't in the right time zone. Which meant she'd likely wake up at two in the morning starving.

Oh well, the general store would probably have some canned soup and maybe a loaf of bread to get her through the night. The leather key fob for her grandpa's old Jeep CJ5 was hanging inside the cabinet next to the sink. She headed out toward the barn hoping that Jimmy had kept the Jeep running for her. She slid the heavy barn door aside and was greeted by the Jeep's smiling grill. Maybe she imagined it, but she felt sure the vintage Carolina blue CJ5 was happy to see her. Climbing into the short-backed bucket vinyl seat, she felt sixteen again.

Maybe she was having some sort of pre-midlife crisis. It didn't matter. It felt good to be home. The engine roared to life after the second try and Shaw blinked into the sinking sun as she eased it out of the dark interior of the barn. The vinyl soft top and doors had long since disintegrated and had never been replaced. She'd purchased a bikini top that offered only the front seats cover.

A churning bank of dark clouds rolled over the ridge in the distance, opposite the setting sun. It looked like a storm was coming, but she'd be back long before the rain arrived.

Chapter Six

Kate decided to walk to the store instead of driving into town. It was a little more than half a mile, and the walk would do her good. She wasn't used to having such an unstructured schedule. Not going in to work every day was going to take a little getting used to. Tomorrow, she'd drive into Hendersonville for a more complete grocery excursion, but for now she'd just pick up milk and bread to get them through until breakfast. After spending the better part of the day moving her stuff into the storage unit, she was tired and didn't feel like driving back across the mountain.

As she crossed the culvert, she slowed and once again looked for the old snapping turtle. He was nowhere to be seen. It was dusk and it smelled like rain. Kate quickened her pace and jogged along the paved road toward the post office. She cut across the neatly trimmed grass in front of the small brick structure toward the back of the store. There was a screen door at the rear entrance, and it banged loudly when she didn't catch it in time.

"Good Lord, child!" Edwina was seated behind the register. A vintage black-and-white countertop TV was on just behind where she sat perched on a high padded stool. She covered her heart and squinted her eyes in Kate's direction. Edwina was in her sixties, full-figured and matronly, her large bosom acted as sort of a plump shelf upon which she rested her hand. "You scared the life out of me. That sounded like a gunshot!"

"You say that every time I come through the back door."

"That's 'cause most paying customers don't try to sneak up on me. They come in the front door like normal folk."

"I'll take that under advisement." Kate was looking in Edwina's direction as she reached for the handle of the refrigerated glass milk case. When she turned back, what appeared to be Shaw Daily's face regarded her through the fogged up window of the glass door. Was that Shaw Daily or a ghost? She flinched, let go of the handle, and fumbled the half-gallon jug of milk she'd just reached for. It hit the hardwood floor with a thunk.

Kate reached for the milk at the same instant that Shaw did. They bumped heads.

"Oh, sorry!" Shaw dropped a can of soup and it rolled loudly toward the front of the store.

"Shaw, that was my fault. I'm so sorry."

"It's okay." Shaw rubbed her forehead and took a step back.

"You surprised me. I didn't know you were in Cooper's Creek." Kate hadn't seen Shaw in a long time. Years, maybe. Those years had been good to her. Shaw was still tall and lanky with devastatingly blue eyes that made you want to believe in love at first sight. Her dark hair was short, in the sort of cut that said *I'm not from around here*. It looked lightly tousled as if she'd just gone for a drive in a convertible or recently rolled out of bed. Kate's cheeks flamed hot and she cleared her throat. "You didn't recognize me at first, did you?"

"Of course I did. It's nice to bump into you, Kate. Pun intended."

Kate laughed. Shaw was the same age as her older sister, Miriam, and Kate had had a crush on Shaw for…well, forever. They'd never hung out that much as kids. Kate had been the annoying younger sister, six years Shaw's junior. By the time Kate was old enough to understand why she'd been so drawn to her, Shaw was attending college on the West Coast. Their lives had taken different paths on opposite sides of the country.

"Wow, how long has it been since we've seen each other?" Shaw juggled a loaf of bread and a six-pack of beer with one arm and retrieved the fallen jug of milk.

"Years. Maybe since your grandfather's funeral?" She'd spoken briefly to Shaw at the gravesite and then Shaw had flown back to California the following day. It wasn't as if they'd actually talked for real.

She accepted the bright yellow Mayfield milk jug from Shaw. "Thanks."

"Did someone back there lose a can of chicken noodle soup?" Edwina craned her neck to see past the rack of potato chips near the front of the store.

Shaw managed with some effort to pull her gaze away from Kate long enough to respond to Edwina.

"Yeah, sorry. That's mine." Shaw opened the refrigerated case for a small carton of milk and then recovered the runaway soup can. She fished in her pocket for cash and tried inconspicuously to watch Kate as she moved around the small country store interior gathering a few more items.

Edwina was taking her sweet time, not that Shaw was in a particular hurry. Kate joined them at the counter before change was tendered. Kate was standing a respectable distance away, but Shaw still felt as if their proximity was making her body temperature rise. Sporty, femme women like Kate were her weakness. A fluttery sensation upended her stomach, and her cheeks felt suddenly warm. She gave Kate a weak smile while Edwina continued to ring her up.

Kate was younger than her sister Miriam, probably in her early thirties now. And still as pretty as ever, with an easy confidence that some probably found intimidating. But Shaw was drawn to confident women. In fact, she found that trait alluring.

Kate tucked a silky errant strand of brown hair behind her ear and glanced sideways at Shaw. Her hazel eyes were teasingly soft. Shaw let her gaze follow the landscape of Kate's firm girlish curves, down and then back to her slender fingers that rested on her hip. *Hmm, no wedding ring.*

There was no way Kate was single. Shaw made a mental note about that curious discovery. Kate's legs were toned, tanned, and smooth, extending temptingly from tailored khaki shorts to pink Converse tennis shoes. She realized Kate had caught her checking out her legs. She cleared her throat and made a big show of bagging her groceries while looking everywhere but at Kate. The brown paper sack crinkled loudly in the awkward silence. She should have brought a cloth bag, like Kate had astutely thought of, because the paper sack would probably last no more than five minutes in the rain. Edwina just stared at her from over the top of her bedazzled cat-eye glasses. Busted.

"Well, it was nice seeing you, Kate." Shaw gathered up the bag and backed toward the door trying to regain a few cool points along the way. "Tell Miriam I said hello."

"I will." Kate had an amused expression on her face. If she was at all embarrassed about being so overtly checked out in the Cooper's Creek General Store she showed no signs of it.

Shaw had parked under the carport next to the single gas pump, and it was a good thing because the rain was pelting the ground with quarter-sized drops. As she pulled the Jeep onto the main road, she saw Kate leave through the back door of the store. The rain was really starting to come down, and even though the Jeep had only a partial top, it offered more cover than walking. Shaw eased onto the grassy shoulder.

"Can I give you a ride?"

"You don't mind?"

"It's not like this will be a completely dry ride, you might still get wet." Her cheeks flamed again. Was Kate making her nervous? *You might still get wet?* She couldn't believe she'd said that out loud.

"I'm staying up at my parents' place at the moment."

Kate launched herself gracefully up into the passenger seat, holding the sack of groceries on her lap. Shaw pulled back onto the paved road, then turned left just past the post office and followed the gravel road that lead along the back side of her grandparents' property, across the creek, and up the mountainside to the Elkinses' place. Memories came rushing back. She'd spent a fair amount of time over at their place during summers at her grandparents'. She and Miriam would go for hikes, try to find salamanders under moss-covered stones near the stream, and they even played house. Shaw was always cast as the husband, which now made total sense. Those were fun times. She hadn't seen Miriam in years either. It would be nice to catch up with her.

"How's Miriam doing?" They approached the house from the last curve, and the pitch of the road steepened.

"She's doing great. She and Greg have two kids. Maybe you already knew that."

"No, I didn't. I mean, I knew she and Greg were together but not the kids part."

"They have two girls. The youngest, Emily, is three. And Lara is five. She'll start first grade next year." Shaw pulled as close to the porch overhang as she could because the rain was still coming down pretty good.

Kate hesitated and Shaw thought she might invite her in, but she didn't.

"Well, thanks for the ride." Kate had an expression on her face that was hard to read.

Shaw nodded, uncharacteristically at a loss for words. Kate jumped out and waved from the porch with her grocery bag on her hip before disappearing into the house.

CHAPTER SEVEN

K ate leaned against the closed door. Her pulse beat a quick staccato cadence. Shaw Daily was in Cooper's Creek.

Shaw was as gorgeous as ever, with that boyishly androgynous style that made Kate think things she probably shouldn't be thinking about her childhood crush. What a surprise to run into her out of the blue. Damn, she looked good. California must agree with her. Shaw had to be close to forty, but she looked as if she was still in her early thirties.

Why hadn't she thought to ask how long Shaw would be staying? She could have invited her over for dinner or something. Although, maybe that wasn't a good idea. Kate's current situation wasn't exactly ideal for entertaining. She sighed and walked to the kitchen to put away the items she'd picked up at the store.

She joined her mother on the high back porch that faced the slope overlooking the woods. The rain was falling in sheets. The heavy drops made a muffled thudding sound as they hit the broad-leafed maples that surrounded the porch railing. Kate settled into the rocker next to her mother.

"Did the rain get you?"

"Almost. I ended up getting a ride."

"From who?"

"Shaw Daily."

"Do I know them?"

"The Daily place is just over the creek." Her mother and Faye Daily had been close friends and neighbors. She hoped to jog her mother's memory.

"Faye Daily?"

"Yes, her granddaughter."

"Well, I'll be, I didn't know Faye had a grandchild."

It was as if thirty years of her mother's life had gone missing. She could call forth details of her childhood and her early marriage, but details from the last few decades seemed to be out of focus or just not there.

"Maybe I'll invite her over for dinner so you can meet her. Would that be okay?"

"Of course, sweetheart. You invite anyone over you want. I enjoy the company."

Kate smiled and looked out at the rain. If she were going to have Shaw over for dinner she'd definitely need to stock up on more than milk and bread. Tomorrow, she'd drive into Hendersonville for groceries or maybe even to Fresh Market for something a bit more highbrow. That'd probably be more what Shaw was used to.

Recipes ran through her mind as she rocked slowly and relaxed under the tin porch roof to the light drumming sound of rain.

❖

It rained all night and all the next day. Steady, torrential at times. And then it continued to rain the following day. Shaw leaned against the doorframe and sipped her coffee. It was dusk and rain and fog made the mountain ridges soft gray against the darker sky. She shuffled barefoot back into the house but left the door open so that she could listen to the sound of the rain. She heard the cricket sing again. He'd moved inside sometime during the late afternoon, probably through the open door. And he'd apparently decided to stay.

"I don't blame you. I'd stay indoors too."

Shaw climbed the narrow stairs slowly, taking time to revisit things she found stacked along the ledge to the left of the stairs. There was a thick ancient Bible, the cover curled from years and humidity. There was an unsigned 1970s era post card from Florida and a couple of battered editions of Nancy Drew. Shaw set her coffee down and thumbed through one of them. She must have read this book a hundred times during her youth. Her grandparents weren't big readers. Her grandfather had only finished grade school and her grandmother only up to the ninth grade. They spent all their time working. She supposed that was the habit of anyone who'd spent their youth surviving the depression. They saw work as essential to survival. They'd farmed a few acres to supplement groceries purchased. And her grandfather was a part-time mechanic to add to what he earned working on a road crew for the state.

As a kid, Shaw had known that her grandparents disapproved of her mother's choices. They'd also been less than encouraging about Shaw pursuing a degree in art. Aspiring to be an artist of any kind simply wasn't a practical career. At least that's the impression she'd gotten from her grandparents. Despite her grandfather's pragmatic dismissal of her art career, he'd given in to her and taught her how to use a welding gun when she was in high school. In a way, he'd shown her the path while at the same time discouraging her from following it.

It was getting dark so Shaw pulled the cord to light the naked bulb at the top of the stairs. When she was a kid she'd made her grandmother climb the stairs ahead of her and turn on the light. The cave-like upper floor could be harboring any sort of creature that only electric light would scare away. She had to laugh now. This frame house was tiny, probably no more than twelve hundred square feet, but as a kid the place had seemed huge and the upstairs a cavernous space not to be entered alone.

The second floor was basically one long room with attic storage on either side that you could access through something that looked like a square hobbit door. Twin beds were set at opposite ends of the room, both covered with sheets, and a simple nightstand and dresser sat between them against the far wall.

She preferred the room downstairs behind the chimney. That was her grandfather's room. Despite being married for more than fifty years, at some point there'd been a row, as her aunt Treva described it. Row being Southern for big damn argument that no one ever gets over. At any rate, afterward, they took separate rooms. Her grandmother had the room at the front of the first floor and her grandfather took the cozy room, with the slanted roof, just behind the chimney. With no central heating, that was the smartest choice in the wintertime.

It was so strange to walk through the simple dwelling and compare this life to the life she had on the West Coast. She hadn't intentionally left them behind, but in the end she sort of did. The five-star hotels, city living, fine meals, and town cars. If her grandparents had ever come to visit her they'd have no doubt found her lifestyle unnecessarily extravagant. Maybe it was. Because certainly she had everything she could possibly want for and more, and yet, something was missing.

Shaw returned to the kitchen and put her mug in the sink. It was fully dark now. The black glass window over the sink reflected the interior. She allowed her eyes to refocus beyond her reflection to the darkness outside. A light pierced the black spaces between the trees. Someone must have stopped by the creek crossing. She waited for the lights to move on, but they didn't. And then she had a thought. That maybe the elder Mrs. Elkins was stalled in the rain. She decided to investigate.

Chapter Eight

Kate saw the headlights approach through her foggy rear window, but still she jumped when Shaw rapped her knuckles against the driver side window. Kate pulled the hood of her raincoat up and got out. They stood facing each other in the downpour. Kate had to lean closer to hear what Shaw was saying.

"What?"

"I said, are you okay?" Shaw repeated the question.

"The creek is too high. I don't think my car has enough clearance." Kate had gone into Hendersonville to run errands, but she'd met Emily for coffee first and clearly, she'd waited too late to drive home. It had been raining for almost two straight days and the creek was out of its banks and well over the culvert. She'd been stupid to take so long getting back. "The water wasn't even up to the road when I left this afternoon."

Shaw was wearing a ball cap and a denim jacket that was quickly absorbing water. "I would drive you across in the Jeep, but I can't even see the edge of the culvert now so I don't think we should chance it."

Kate squinted into the wind. Shaw was right. It was impossible to be sure of the culvert's exact location, and driving off the edge of it would dump them into deeper water.

"I really need to get home." Kate shielded her eyes and glanced from her car back to the rushing water.

"I guess destiny has other plans for you tonight."

If that was a pickup line it was a good one. Shaw smiled broadly from beneath the dripping brim of her ball cap.

"I have groceries in the car and some of them won't keep."

"Come to the house and we'll put them in the fridge."

They were practically shouting at each other above the wind and rain. Kate felt foolish to have gotten herself stranded with her mother at home alone. She hesitated, weighing her options. She considered for an instant that she'd subconsciously sabotaged her return trip to have a chance to see Shaw. If that were the case then she owed her subconscious a heartfelt thank you.

"Just leave your car and we'll take my Jeep. It has better traction in the mud."

Kate nodded. They made quick work of loading the two bags of groceries into Shaw's open Jeep. Luckily, she'd remembered her cloth shopping bags because paper bags would have been useless and soaked to disintegration by now. Shaw took a shortcut through the woods along a wide trail, heading straight up the hillside toward her grandparents' house. It was a quick but rough ride, and more than once Kate had to grab the roll bar to keep from getting tossed into Shaw's lap.

They carried everything into the house, dripping water with every step. Finally, Kate shook off her raincoat and hung it over a chair on the porch. Shaw was soaked through. When she peeled off the jacket it was plain she wasn't wearing anything under the drenched T-shirt that was now suctioned to her chest and torso. Kate tried not to notice the contours of Shaw's body and instead busied herself putting a few things into the refrigerator. This simple act of putting food in the fridge in Shaw's kitchen seemed oddly intimate.

"Um, I'll go put on some dry clothes." Shaw looked down at her clinging white T-shirt probably just then realizing it was practically see-through at this point. "Can I get you anything?"

Kate's shirt was dry thanks to the rain gear, but her pants were wet and cold below where the hem of her jacket had covered.

"If you have some sweat pants I wouldn't turn them down."

"I do. I'll be right back." Shaw tossed her cap on a chair in the living room and swept her fingers through her damp hair as she disappeared into a nearby bedroom. Shaw returned wearing a nicely broken in navy T-shirt casually tucked in only at the front of dry jeans, which hung low at her narrow hips, offering just a hint of the boxers she was wearing underneath. She held some sweat pants out to Kate. "I think these might fit. Although they might be a little long."

"I'm sure they'll be fine." Suddenly feeling bashful, Kate ducked into the bathroom to change and check the state of her hair and makeup. Her mascara was a bit of a mess because of the rain. She dabbed at it with a tissue and then finger combed her hair before returning to the kitchen.

Shaw was rummaging in the bag in the center of the bright yellow Formica table. Shaw's grandparents had probably owned that table since the fifties. And it had chairs to match. She hadn't been inside the Daily house in a long time. It looked like a house filled with remnants of a life. A twinge of sadness constricted her throat, but she wasn't sure exactly why. Was she sad for Shaw's loss or the looming loss that she had yet to face? Maybe all of it.

"Is there anything else that needs to go in the fridge?"

"No, I think I got everything." Kate didn't want to reveal that most of what she'd purchased was for the dinner she'd planned to cook for Shaw at her mother's house. Oh well, best laid plans and all that. "I should call my mother."

"Sure."

They regarded each other across the kitchen like two awkward teens on a first date. The phone rang several times. Depending on where she was in the house, it would no doubt take her mother a little while to reach the phone.

"Momma, I'm over at the Daily place."

"You're not driving in this weather are you?" Her mother forever cautioned against driving in any kind of weather. A light sprinkle had always been all it took to abort a day out and stay at home.

"I was bringing home groceries, remember?"

"Oh lordy me, I plumb forgot already. I'm fine over here. I already had a ham sandwich for dinner. You just stay over there until the rain stops. I don't want you crossing the creek in this."

"Okay, Momma. You call my cell number if you need anything. I wrote it on the pad next to the phone."

"Okay, sugah, don't worry about me. I'm just fine."

Shaw watched Kate from across the room. Kate somehow managed to make casual cotton sweat pants look sexy. Shaw averted her eyes. She couldn't really offer privacy because the house was too small.

"Is everything okay?" Shaw didn't want to pry, but it seemed from the expression on Kate's face that she was worried about her mother.

"Yes, she's okay at the moment." Kate offered Shaw a weak smile. "My mother had a minor stroke a few months ago and she hasn't quite recovered. That's why I'm staying with her."

"Oh, I'm sorry. I didn't know." Now she understood Kate's urgency to get home.

"She's not terribly ill quite yet. It's just that the stroke has affected her memory. She can remember things from her youth, but her short-term memory isn't good at all. She sometimes forgets to eat or she'll forget to turn things off, like the stove." Kate placed her phone on the table and surveyed the kitchen. "Have you eaten dinner?"

"Um, no, actually. I had a coffee a little while ago, but I hadn't really thought of dinner. I've been traveling a lot. I'm not sure I'm quite in this time zone yet in terms of proper meal times."

"Well, we have groceries and we won't get across the creek in the next few hours. Maybe I could make us something. Stir-fry?"

"Wow, yes, that would be great." Shaw opened a cabinet near the stove. "I hadn't really had a chance to stock up." She brandished a large skillet. "Will this work? I'm afraid I haven't had an opportunity to expand the culinary equipment in the kitchen either."

"If you can manage to boil water and simmer the rice then I think that skillet will work just fine for the rest." Kate took the heavy pan from Shaw. "Is there a cutting board?"

"Um...let's see." Shaw rummaged in a few cabinets. "I think this is supposed to be a cutting board, but it looks like it's seen better days."

"I can work with that."

The eat-in kitchen was small so as they prepared dinner they were frequently sidestepping each other. At one point, Kate reached around Shaw for the salt and brushed against her. Even the faintest touch from Kate spider-webbed through Shaw's nervous system. The smell of Kate invaded her senses as she brushed past her, vanilla and the fragrance of roses. The sweetest, sexiest scent Shaw had stumbled across in a long time.

They sat at one corner of the table. They'd only sampled the food when the lights flickered and went out. Lightning flash lit the room. Only a barely audible distant rumble followed.

"Hang on." Shaw felt around in the pantry and returned with a thick candle of the Christmas variety. It was red and smelled like cinnamon. The match flame danced in Kate's eyes and the candle highlighted the contours of her beautiful face with a warm radiance. If Shaw had conspired to plan this she couldn't have created a more magical ambiance. She'd blundered into it, the accidental romantic.

"This is nice." Kate took a moment to chew her food. "Unexpected, but nice."

"Yeah, it is." Shaw was having a hard time not staring, and she had to keep reminding herself that this wasn't a date. For all she knew, Kate was in a relationship or possibly even straight. Kate was only being kind by making dinner for her in return for being rescued from a rain-swollen stream.

CHAPTER NINE

Shaw looked downright edible by candlelight. Kate was grateful for the power outage. Not only because candlelight vastly improved the ambiance of the room, but also hopefully the low light hid the heat she felt rising to her cheeks every time Shaw made eye contact. It was unnerving. It was as if they were having a conversation out in the open, but at the same time there was some other conversation inaudible to the human ear. While she couldn't hear it, she felt it tingle all the way up her spine to the small hairs at the back of her neck.

"I was surprised to see you at the store yesterday." Kate wanted to ask a hundred questions, but tried to pace herself.

"Yeah, there was no food in the house. I forgot to have the cab driver stop on the way from the airport."

"Did you fly into Asheville?"

"Yes, via Atlanta."

"I guess what they say is true."

"What's that?"

"That even if you're en route to heaven you have to connect through Atlanta." That was dumb and she was sure Shaw had heard that joke before. However, she was polite enough to laugh. She needed to up her game. She didn't want Shaw to think she was overly provincial. She'd been places and she'd seen things. There'd been the semester abroad during grad school and an ill-conceived romantic getaway to Paris with her ex. That one probably didn't count.

"The Atlanta airport is sort of a city unto itself."

"How long will you be in Cooper's Creek?" Kate tried her best to sound nonchalant.

"I'm not sure." Shaw looked down at her plate.

"Really?"

"Does that answer surprise you?"

"A little. I was under the impression that you had some big career on the West Coast." Kate leaned forward, resting her elbows on the edge of the table. There was still food on her plate, but butterflies in her stomach were making it hard to eat.

"You know the kind of work I do?" Shaw seemed pleased that Kate knew something of her life in California.

"People talk." Kate took a bite.

"Do they now?"

"Well, there aren't many who hail from Cooper's Creek who not only leave, but go on to travel the world for work. I think your grandparents were proud of you."

Shaw averted her eyes as if she didn't want to give away whatever emotion she was feeling.

"So, you're going to stay for a little while then?"

"Yeah. I needed a break. I decided this was the one place that I could relax and get away from my work."

That sounded a bit vague. She'd assumed Shaw was some sort of power lesbian on the West Coast, with a successful career and all the trappings that went with it. Something wasn't adding up.

"What did you need a break from? I mean, if that's not too personal a question."

Shaw looked down at her plate. She took a few bites before answering.

"My life is boring. Let's talk about yours."

Wow, that wasn't even a subtle deflection. Shaw clearly didn't want to talk about whatever made her want to come back to the mountains. Now Kate was even more curious. But she'd allow Shaw a reprieve for the moment.

"I teach first grade in Hendersonville. And I love it."

"And now you're staying with your mother."

"Summer break just started and I took a leave of absence for next year."

"How does your...significant other feel about that?"

"Are you trying to find out if I'm single?" Kate couldn't help giving Shaw a bit of a hard time. "You could just come out and ask, you know."

"Are you seeing anyone?"

"No."

"That's all I get? A single-syllable answer?"

"What would you like to know?" Kate smiled and leaned forward again with her chin in her hand. This had definitely moved from get-to-know-you small talk to flirtation. Shaw matched her pose, putting less space between them. The soft glow of the candle danced along the wall behind Shaw casting a larger than life shadow of her profile.

"I'd like to know what you'd say if I asked you out."

The intensity of Shaw's gaze warmed Kate and in almost the same instant gave her a chill of anticipation. "Are you asking me out?"

Shaw couldn't help smiling at the teasing expression on Kate's face. Shaw hadn't intended to flirt with Kate. She hadn't meant to take advantage of her in a situation where she had no other choice but to wait out the storm. But Kate was so damn cute that Shaw couldn't help herself.

"Yes, I'm asking you out." Shaw leaned back in her chair.

"That didn't sound like a question." Kate grinned playfully and twirled her fork.

"Wow, you're tough."

"I feel confident you can handle it."

Shaw laughed. It felt good to laugh. Then she leaned forward and hoped the expression on her face telegraphed the sincerity she felt in her heart in that moment.

"Kate Elkins, will you go on a date with me?"

"Yes. When?"

"I wondered if you might be free tonight?"

"Hmm, that's sort of short notice. I'm having an unexpected dinner with someone. But who knows how that will go."

Shaw laughed. "Is that a challenge?"

"Do you need a challenge?"

"Not really." Shaw lightly brushed her fingers across the back of Kate's hand resting on the table. Kate turned her hand over and lightly stroked Shaw's sensitive palm. The fleeting contact transmitted a surge through Shaw's body. She looked at Kate's face, softly lit by the candle, feeling lightheaded and hopeful.

❖

Shaw glanced sideways at Kate. They stood elbow to elbow as they rinsed the dishes and left them in the sink. She was standing close enough that she could smell the rose scent of Kate's hair. It smelled like summer.

"What are you smiling about?"

"Um." Shaw had given herself away. "Just your hair…your hair smells good."

"Thank you."

It was still raining, but not as hard, and the wind had died down almost completely. Every now and then a flash of distant lightning lit the soft contours of the mountain ridge visible from the kitchen window.

"Could I interest you in a drink?"

"There's alcohol in this house? I thought your grandparents were strict Baptists?"

"They were, but there's a pint jar of blackberry wine in the spring house. I noticed it was still there yesterday." Shaw casually leaned back against the counter top. "I'm sure my grandmother only kept it for medicinal purposes. Should we sample it?"

"Why not."

"Mind if I borrow your rain jacket?"

Kate shook her head.

Shaw pulled the jacket on as she crossed the porch. It was a bit small and a tad short in the sleeves, but it had a hood and it kept her mostly dry as she trotted across the side yard to the springhouse. She should have brought a flashlight with her. Not much light filtered in from the partially cloud covered moon. Keeping the door open with her foot, she felt around for the glass jar of wine on the middle shelf. Found it.

Back inside, it took her a minute to loosen the lid. It still had a good seal on it, which boded well for the wine. She poured a small sampling and tasted it.

"Well?" Kate looked at her expectantly.

"Not bad. A little on the fruity side, as you'd expect, but not bad at all." Shaw poured two glasses and handed one to Kate. "Should we sit in here?" She motioned with her head toward the couch.

Kate enjoyed the view as Shaw ambled toward the sofa. She kicked off her shoes and crossed the hardwood floor barefoot. Kate couldn't help but appreciate how good Shaw's ass looked in Levi's; the faded square from her wallet was outlined on one pocket. She followed Shaw's lead and slipped out of her shoes as she neared the couch. Shaw had carried the candle from the kitchen table and put it on the mantel over the fireplace. It cast barely more light than a nightlight.

They settled onto the couch at opposite ends. Kate curled her legs under her while Shaw slouched and stretched her long legs in front of the couch. She had the strongest urge to climb into Shaw's lap. Maybe wine was a bad idea. She didn't really want to allow herself to get carried away the first evening they were around each other. Even though Shaw had teasingly suggested it was a date. Kate wasn't going to take that too seriously. For all she knew, Shaw was a player. She certainly was good-looking enough to play the field if that's what she wanted. This thought reminded her that she hadn't followed up with questions to find out whether Shaw was even single. She'd only assumed as much. Assumptions had gotten her in trouble before.

"Is there anyone back home that I should know about?" She might as well find out now before she let her libido get too carried away.

"Funny that you said home. California is where I live, but I've always felt like Cooper's Creek was home." Shaw was looking out the living room window. Then she turned toward Kate. "And no, there isn't anyone you should know about."

Kate felt a little embarrassed for thinking the worst of Shaw just because she was so attractive. She averted her eyes and sipped the sweet wine.

"You know, I wasn't sure you were into women until I asked." Shaw studied her from the far end of the couch.

"Why? Because I went out for cheerleading instead of softball?"

"Maybe."

"I've made assumptions about people, too, and sometimes I'm way off."

"Does it cause any issues with your family?"

"Being a lesbian?"

"Yeah."

"Not really." Kate relaxed a little. Her foot was going to sleep so she straightened her leg so that her toes were only inches away from Shaw. "Of course, there was tension and arguments at first, but the bottom line was that my parents loved me and they wanted me to be happy. I know I'm lucky. Not everyone who comes out in a rural area finds the same acceptance."

Shaw set her wine on the floor and reached for Kate's foot. She pulled it against her stomach and began to gently rub with her fingers. Kate moaned softly.

"You probably shouldn't do that." Kate said the words aloud, but she wasn't sure she meant them. Shaw didn't respond as she continued to massage her foot.

The rain kept a soothing cadence on the tin roof of the old frame house. The candle flickered in the damp breeze that wafted through from the open window and the wine was going straight to Kate's head. Or maybe Shaw's touch was the intoxicating factor. Kate was acutely aware of Shaw's caress along the arch of her foot with her thumb. Did she slow the movement when she saw that Kate was looking at her hands or did Kate imagine it? She forced herself to change her focal point from Shaw's strong fingers caressing the contours of her foot to Shaw's face. Only, staring directly into those eyes didn't seem to help cool the heat radiating through her body.

"What sort of work do you do in California?" Kate hoped to steer the conversation to a neutral topic as a distraction for herself, despite the delicious disturbance of the foot rub.

"Sales and marketing."

That was a vague answer. Kate had no doubt that Shaw was good at what she did. Given what she'd experienced so far she felt certain that Shaw Daily could sell an open flame to the Devil himself.

Shaw's fingers drifted up her ankle past the hem of her sweat pants. It felt good to be touched, and especially by someone she was so attracted to, but she wasn't sure she was ready for where this might be headed. She drew her foot slowly from Shaw's grasp.

"You want me to stop?" Shaw seemed reluctant to release her.

No, which is exactly why you should. Kate sipped wine and didn't answer immediately.

"Did I do something wrong?"

"No, it's…too much." That sounded silly. Had she become someone who couldn't handle a foot rub from a sexy woman? That was just plain sad, but it was the truth. Kate didn't do casual, and she had the distinct impression that Shaw did. She should stop this before it went any further.

To her credit, Shaw didn't press her or try to make a pass. Shaw exuded quiet confidence as she reclined into the corner of the sofa with her arms outstretched across the back. They regarded each other. Shaw had an expression on her face that seemed to signal something. Kate waited for what that something might be, but nothing came.

Kate rotated, shifting her legs off the couch.

"I suppose it's getting late." Whatever had started between them, whatever spell had been cast during dinner, she'd ruined it by pulling away. Shaw seemed completely shut down.

"I doubt the water level has receded enough to drive you home. I think you should stay."

The invitation surprised Kate, but then she realized that invitation had been inevitable regardless of anything else. How had she thought she'd get home? She hadn't. Clearly, they'd have to wait until morning.

"Sorry, I should have thought of that." Kate looked at Shaw. "If you have a blanket I'll just sleep here on the couch."

"No way." Shaw stood up. "You take my room and I'll sleep on the couch."

"That doesn't seem fair. Is there another bedroom I can use so that I don't take your room?"

"Well, there are beds upstairs, but I can't vouch for the condition of them. I haven't really changed sheets or taken stock of things. Please, sleep in my room." Shaw held out her arm motioning toward the room just off the living room.

"Is this some chivalrous butch thing?" Kate had her hands on her hips. She hoped she was giving Shaw her best playful smile. She wanted so badly to recapture the casual banter they'd shared earlier.

"It most certainly is. So there's no point arguing with me." Shaw seemed to visibly relax. "Seriously, I'm sleeping on the couch."

"Okay, I surrender." Kate held up her hands and sidled past Shaw on her way to the bedroom. Even the most fleeting contact with Shaw sent electricity through every nerve ending. Wow. This sort of physical reaction to someone hadn't happened in, well, maybe forever. She'd been attracted to women and excited by women, but this, this was something new.

"Why don't you take the candle with you?"

Shaw handed her the candleholder and their fingers brushed.

"Thank you, Shaw." She wanted to say more, but what could she say? "Sleep well."

"You too."

Chapter Ten

Shaw waited until the orb of light cast by the candle disappeared along with Kate. She stood in the center of the room for a moment and then sank onto the couch with her head in her hands. What the hell? Why had she pushed things with Kate? It had been like a compulsion or something. She couldn't stop herself. Kate was so beautiful and unguarded, and the attraction she'd felt sitting across the table from her during dinner was so powerful and so surprising. How had she not noticed Kate before this? To be honest, she had noticed her. She'd occasionally run into Kate when she'd visited Cooper's Creek in the past, but when they were younger there'd been their ages. When you're kids six years is a lifetime of difference. And in recent years, as they'd gotten older, well, she'd sort of assumed Kate was straight. That was obviously not the case and she felt stupid for not figuring that out sooner.

She pulled a light cotton blanket out of the hall closet and returned to the sofa. Sleep would likely be hard to come by. Her body was still on California time, and her nervous system was humming from the brief contact she'd had with Kate.

The foot massage had been an impulse. If she'd pushed it, things could have gone even further. Should she have pressed Kate? No.

Shaw squeezed her eyes shut. She was here to get away from responsibility not step into more. And Kate's life was all about responsibility right now. Kate was clearly focused on her mother's care. Shaw's distant, sometimes volatile relationship with her mother had been very different from Kate's with hers.

She'd give Kate a ride home in the morning and then get back to her mission statement for this little sabbatical. Relax. Reboot. Figure out what she wanted to do next.

Kate wasn't sure how long she'd been lying in bed looking at the ceiling. She'd feigned fatigue, but the truth was she'd just needed space from Shaw. Lying in Shaw's bed wasn't really helping because the pillow smelled like Shaw, along with the sheets. She sighed and rolled onto her side. The pillowcase was suffused with deep base notes of amber, oakmoss, and vetiver, with just a hint of vanilla. The rich, earthy fragrance invaded her senses. She gave into it, buried her face in the pillow, and inhaled deeply.

Crafting perfumes using essential oils was a hobby of Kate's. Whatever cologne Shaw was wearing it was a good one and it just left Kate craving more contact.

She shifted onto her back and exhaled. She actually was tired, but she just couldn't sleep. Her mind couldn't help conjuring up *what-if* scenarios. What if she'd met Shaw at another time when she hadn't just quit her job to care for her mother? She was not exactly a catch. Her life was complicated and she needed to focus on her mother, not on some hot butch who was probably only in the area for a week or two and then jetting back to the West Coast. Flirtation was harmless. Kate coached herself to draw a firm line. What she needed to establish with Shaw was a clear boundary. Any physical involvement would no doubt leave her feeling used and lonely. That would be a vulnerable place to be while dealing with her mother's decline.

Flirtation and friendship, that was all she had to offer Shaw.

It wasn't the intense sunlight that woke Shaw, although now that her eyes were open she was acutely aware that at some point during the night she must have fallen asleep and left the drapes open because the sun was streaming across the sofa in full force. What woke her was banging, a loud hammering sound from the front porch.

Groggily, she staggered outside in the rumpled T-shirt and jeans she'd slept in.

"Jimmy? What the hell are you doing?" Jimmy Ludlow was on a ladder, hammer poised mid air, and he looked as if he'd just seen a ghost. He dropped one of the nails that had been dangling from his lips. Jimmy was a wee bit taller than Shaw, but just as lanky. His shaggy blond hair was hidden beneath a seasoned Tractor Supply cap, except for a few unruly curls, and it looked as if he had two weeks of scruffy beard growth.

"You scared the shit out of me. I didn't know you were here." He put the remaining nails in his pocket and climbed down.

"Yeah, I got in a day or so ago. I was going to call you, and I would have had I known you'd show up hammering at this unholy hour." Shaw rubbed her eyes with the palms of her hands.

"It's seven a.m."

"Which is four a.m. in California."

"Oh, sorry. I always forget about the time difference."

"Yeah, you and everyone else on the East Coast." She squinted at Jimmy. "So, what are you doing?"

"Oh, I've been keeping an eye on this spot." He pointed toward the roof near the ladder. "And I thought, well, with so much rain the roof might be leaking. Some of these shingles need to be replaced. I was gonna call you about it."

"Thanks for paying attention to that."

"I'm sorry I woke you, but it's not like you've got a woman here. Where are you gonna find a girl in Cooper's Creek unless you imported one from—oh…"

"Hi, Jimmy." Kate stood in the doorway, still wearing Shaw's sweatpants, her hair adorably tousled from sleep. She self-consciously finger combed it to smooth it down.

"It's not what you think." Shaw knew the way Jimmy's mind worked well enough to know she should defend Kate's honor.

Jimmy and Shaw had been close as children, building forts, racing go-carts, and hunting imaginary bears. Actually, one time they found one rummaging in someone's discarded lunch sack off the side of the highway not far from the house. They hightailed it home in a panic. As a preteen Shaw had been envious of the freedoms that Jimmy's gender allowed him. In high school she'd even probably wanted to be Jimmy, but then she'd gone away to college and discovered that she didn't have to actually be a guy to sleep with girls. That discovery rocked her world. That discovery changed everything. She'd been chasing girls ever since. Sometimes she even caught them.

"I wasn't thinking anything." Jimmy was trying to keep his expression neutral, but she could tell he was about to laugh.

"The culvert was underwater so Kate couldn't get across the creek. I offered for her to stay here, in the spare room." She made sure to emphasize the room detail. "And now I should get her home."

Shaw followed Kate back into the kitchen, leaving Jimmy to his task.

"I'll give you a ride whenever you're ready."

"Thanks. Can I wear these home and wash them for you?" Kate tugged at the side of the sweat pants.

"You're welcome to wear them, but you don't need to go to the trouble of washing them, really."

Shaw helped Kate gather the food out of the fridge that they hadn't cooked. The Jeep had been parked in the barn so it was mostly dry. Shaw wiped down the front seats with a towel. Jimmy waved as they pulled away and headed back down the trail to where Kate had left her car. The water was still up over the culvert.

"You might be able to make it with your car, but it's probably better not to chance it." Shaw leaned on the steering wheel and looked sideways at Kate. "I'll just drive you home."

"Are you sure?"

"Yes, I'm sure. The Jeep has four times the clearance of the Honda."

Kate nodded.

Shaw crawled across the culvert. She leaned out watching the edge to make sure she didn't drive off into the creek bed where the water was much deeper. As it was, the stream reached halfway up the wheel well.

"Hey, look at that."

"What?" Kate strained to see where Shaw was looking.

"That's the biggest snapping turtle I've ever seen."

"I look for that turtle every time I cross the creek. I rarely ever see him."

"Maybe the rising water chased him out of his usual hiding spot." Shaw eased forward a little and still the turtle didn't move. "Check out the ridge on his back and tail. He looks like a dinosaur."

"He's very old. Maybe he is a dinosaur."

"I wish I had my phone to snap a photo." Shaw had turned her phone off and thrown it into a dresser drawer to avoid work calls.

"Oh, wait…I have mine." Kate handed Shaw her cell phone.

The turtle continued to ignore them. He posed quietly, and after a few shots, Shaw continued up the muddy road toward Kate's house. The sun was bright. Only a few feathery clouds crossed the deep blue sky. Everything looked green and alive. Heavy drops fell from the leaves of the trees making it sound as if it were still raining as they continued up the hill toward the house.

The Elkins house was warmly appointed, nothing like the plain, neglected feel of her grandparents' place. Floral curtains hung in the window of the cozy kitchen. Kate's mother was dozing in an overstuffed armchair near the fireplace when they clamored in and set the groceries on the counter. Her mother started awake and swiveled to see who'd come in.

"It's just me, Momma. I didn't mean to startle you." They walked over toward where her mother was seated, and Kate made a motion with her arm as if she was about to announce that Shaw was with her when her mother spoke.

"Charlie Miller, if you aren't a sight for sore eyes. Yer as good-looking as ever." Mrs. Elkins's eyes practically twinkled with mischief. She took Shaw's hand in her fragile, aged hand.

"Momma, this is Shaw Daily. You know her grandparents used to live across the hill from us." Kate gently touched her mother's shoulder. Her mother's eyes seemed to refocus from some far off place. The smile on her face faded, replaced by confusion.

"Here, why don't you sit down?" Kate helped her ease back into the chair.

"I'm sorry. I thought you were someone else…" her voice trailed off.

"Who's Charlie Miller?" asked Shaw.

Kate shrugged and shook her head. She didn't know who her mother was talking about either.

"Mrs. Elkins, who's Charlie Miller?"

"Who?" She craned her neck to look up at Shaw.

Shaw sat on the ottoman in front of the chair. "You mentioned someone named Charlie Miller just now. I just wondered who that was."

Mrs. Elkins looked down at the floor shaking her head. "What they did to that boy, it weren't right. It left a hole in Iris's heart that she spent the rest of her life trying to fill."

The mention of her mother's name was like a punch in the gut for Shaw. A chill ran up the small hairs on her arm, and she instinctively pulled her hand away from Mrs. Elkins's grasp as if she'd been burned. Disconnecting seemed to break some sort of trance. Mrs. Elkins looked up and focused on Shaw's face.

"Tell me your name again, child?"

"Momma, this is Shaw Daily." Kate introduced Shaw again.

"Nice to meet you."

"It's nice to see you, Mrs. Elkins."

"We don't go on formality here. You call me Edith."

"Yes, Miss Edith." Shaw might reside in California, but she was Southern at heart. She'd never call an elder by only her first name.

Shaw moved to the kitchen while Kate spoke softly to her mother. Shaw couldn't really make out what they were saying. She was still reeling from what Miss Edith had said. Who was Charlie Miller? It seemed that Kate's mother had mistaken her for someone named Charlie. She rubbed her face with her hands. She realized she hadn't even had coffee yet and was suddenly feeling the fatigue of all the travel she'd been doing. Or was this a different sort of fatigue?

When Kate touched her arm she flinched.

"Sorry, I didn't see you there."

"Are you all right?"

"Yeah." But she knew that didn't sound very convincing.

"Let me make you some coffee." Kate busied herself filling the pot with water. She looked over her shoulder at Shaw while the water ran. "Why don't you sit down?"

"No, I'm fine." Shaw leaned back against the counter and crossed her arms in front of her chest.

Kate studied Shaw while she counted spoons of ground coffee and switched the coffeemaker on. Shaw looked shaken. Shadows ringed her eyes. She looked sad. Why hadn't Kate noticed it before?

"Please sit down." Kate put her hands on Shaw's arms and gently pushed her toward one of the kitchen chairs. While the coffeemaker purred she went to check on her mother. She was napping so Kate didn't wake her.

"Momma is asleep." Kate took the chair nearest Shaw. Shaw's hand was on the table and Kate covered it with hers. Shaw rotated her hand and their fingers entwined as if it was the most normal thing. As if it was something they did every day. The simple gesture caused Kate's heart to flutter like a hummingbird. "Hey, why don't I make you some breakfast?"

Shaw didn't answer right away. She wasn't looking at Kate; she was staring off, as if lost in thought, and then shook her head. "You made dinner last night. You don't have to keep feeding me."

"Are you seriously saying that to a Southern woman?"

Shaw laughed, which made the air in the room vibrate with lightness. It was good to see Shaw smile.

"Sorry, what was I thinking?"

"I'm sure I have no idea. But telling a Southern woman not to feed you is basically a cultural insult." Kate moved to the stove and pulled out a cast iron skillet. "You're gonna sit there and I'm gonna make you some breakfast. I have my Southern heritage to uphold."

"Yes, ma'am."

"That's more like it." Kate brought a cup of coffee over to Shaw. She put her hand on Shaw's shoulder as she leaned past. Even that casual contact kicked her heart rate into high gear again. She needed to settle down, but that seemed impossible around Shaw.

What was she just schooling herself about the previous night? Friendship. Clear boundaries. She probably should have sent Shaw home right away, but Shaw had looked so low and forlorn that Kate couldn't bear to send her back to that barren frame house alone.

"This tastes good." Shaw raised her mug in Kate's direction. "Thank you."

The scrambled eggs and toast were quickly prepared. For the second time in less than twenty-four hours, they shared a meal.

"Did you hear what your mother said? Who is Charlie Miller?"

"I don't know. I've never heard that name before." Her mother's condition was bringing up all sorts of random details from her youth. Some days her mother would talk to Kate about things she'd done in her teens or twenties as if she didn't know who Kate was. Her mother could suddenly remember what her sister had said to her in grade school but couldn't remember what she'd had for breakfast. It was a little unnerving at times.

"Maybe your mother would know." Kate sipped her coffee.

"She died about six months ago." Shaw's tone was flat, as if she were discussing the weather or some other mundane topic.

"I'm so sorry. I didn't know."

"Why would you?"

Shaw took a bite and didn't make eye contact.

"Shaw, I'm so sorry." She was repeating herself but she'd been so caught by surprise that she didn't know what else to say. Shaw's responses had sounded emotionless, but now Shaw looked at her with the most soulful expression. She fought the urge to cradle Shaw's head against her chest and caress her hair and tell her everything would be all right.

"Do you mind if I ask what happened?"

"Ovarian cancer."

"That's terrible."

"I'm sure there were signs, but she was probably in denial about them so she didn't go to a doctor. She never wanted to deal with reality. So it was near the end before she was even diagnosed." Shaw stabbed the scrambled eggs with her fork.

Kate couldn't imagine talking about her own mother with so little emotion.

"Were you and your mother close?" Kate tried to think back over the years. She didn't remember seeing Shaw's mother spend much time in Cooper's Creek. Usually, it was just Shaw, visiting her grandparents.

"Let's just say we didn't have the same relationship you have with your mother." Shaw pushed back her chair. "I should get going. Thank you for breakfast."

"Anytime. Really."

Shaw reached for Kate's phone on the counter. "If you unlock this I'll input my number so that you have it."

Kate wasn't sure how to take the offer.

"You know, in case the water doesn't go down and you need a ride somewhere. You can call me and I'll come get you in the Jeep."

"Yes, right, of course. Thank you." She entered her passcode and handed the phone to Shaw. Her mother stirred and spoke behind her so she went to check on her leaving Shaw with her phone.

"Momma, do you need something?"

"I think I must've dozed off. If you'll help me up I need the bathroom."

Kate supported her mother as she got to her feet.

"It was nice to meet you, Miss Edith." Shaw waved from across the room. "Thanks again for breakfast, Kate. I can let myself out."

And with that, Shaw was gone. What did she expect? A good-bye kiss? A plan for a second date? She wasn't sure, but Shaw's nonchalant departure left a cold stone in the pit of her stomach.

"That Charlie is a good-looking young man." Her mother chuckled.

"Momma, who is Charlie?"

"I don't know who you're talking about dear."

"You just mentioned him."

"I did?" Her mother looked completely confused. "Lord knows I'd forget my own head if it weren't attached."

Chapter Eleven

Jimmy's truck was still near the barn when Shaw parked the Jeep, but she didn't see him. She needed a shower, but first she wanted to check her phone. It took a minute for the screen to come back to life. There were several texts from Raisa, she should probably respond to at least one of those, and a few missed calls, but there was only one call she cared about. She'd dialed her phone from Kate's so she could save the number. Possibly a sneaky trick, but if Kate checked her recent calls list she'd see it.

Kate shut her down the night before, but still, she seemed interested. And she'd invited her to stay for breakfast. That had to mean something. Shaw wanted the option to at least be able to ask for a second date. It didn't mean she had to call; she simply wanted to keep her options open.

When she stepped back outside, Jimmy was loading tools in his truck.

"Well, what do you think?" Shaw rested her forearms on the scuffed tailgate of Jimmy's vintage Ford.

"Kate's gorgeous."

"Not about that, the roof."

"Seriously? You spent the night with Kate Elkins, THE Kate Elkins, and you want to talk about the roof?"

"Yes, I need a distraction." Shaw shielded her eyes from the sun. "And besides, I told you already it wasn't that sort of sleepover."

"Maybe your skills are slipping. Do you need some pointers?"

"No and no." She crossed her arms in front of her chest. "Does the roof need work or what?"

"Yeah, I was just about to head to town and pick up some lumber and a few other things."

"Give me the list and I'll go."

"Really?"

"Yeah, I need to find a spot with Wi-Fi and get food to restock the kitchen."

"Okay, if you insist, that'd be great. Then I could come back later in the week and do the repair. There's a chance of rain tomorrow, but I think I've done a good temporary fix." He offered her a rumpled piece of paper from his pocket. He stopped shuffling items around in the truck bed and gave her a serious look. "Hey, all kidding aside, Kate is special."

"I know that." The words almost got caught in her throat. She coughed. What was he trying to say? That she didn't deserve a woman like Kate?

"She's sort of a local treasure. Treat her right."

"Well, you don't need to worry. I made a pass last night and she totally shut me down. End of story." She didn't mean to sound defensive, but she was pretty sure she did.

Jimmy nodded and got into the truck.

"Hey, do you know someone named Charlie Miller?"

He rested his arm on the doorframe of the open window. "Doesn't sound familiar. Why do you ask?"

"Kate's mother mentioned that name today. When she saw me, for a minute, she thought I was someone named Charlie Miller. I just thought that was strange and it made me curious."

"That is odd. I only know one person named Miller. Addie Miller lives down in the flatlands."

Shaw knew the general area. It wasn't too far away. A green valley of bottomland spread out east and west along the county road on either side of Cooper's Creek farther south.

"Do you know where exactly?"

"Yeah, take the dirt road across from Clarence Hill's barn. Drive until you can't go any farther." He cranked the engine. "But be warned, Addie Miller ain't exactly what I'd call friendly."

❖

By late morning, Kate was restless. The pharmacy had called to say that her mother's prescription was ready. Maybe she'd walk down to the creek and see if the water was low enough to retrieve her car.

"Momma, I'm going to walk down the hill and see about getting my car."

"Okay, honey. I'll just be sittin' here when you get back."

A cooking show was on. Normally, Kate enjoyed watching cooking shows, but not this morning. She couldn't sit still to save her life. Maybe she should go for a run after she checked on her car and got her mother's meds.

Everything was good and soaked from the heavy rains. As the air warmed, steam rose from the ground and then hung in wisps in the air. No doubt the humidity would be high by the afternoon. Kate took her time strolling along the muddy road. Staying with her mother was going to be a challenge. She was used to having a lot of structure in her day during the school year, but she'd be on summer break anyway at this point. The difference was she usually planned a trip to celebrate the end of the school year. Or at the very least she had day trips planned with friends. Sometimes she did freelance writing for travel magazines that focused on western North Carolina. It was beautiful country, and she knew all the local spots. These writing gigs also gave her an excuse to investigate new restaurants. But she was afraid to schedule much. She didn't want to leave her mother alone overnight if possible.

The road made a turn through the garden patch that had been planted along the half acre of flat ground on the whole property. Greg had come over a month earlier, tilled and planted corn, tomatoes, and one row of potatoes. She figured keeping that up would help keep her busy.

Just past the hilled potatoes the road sank underwater. The creek was still running high and fast. Maybe six inches over the culvert, but maybe a little more, it was hard to tell. She searched the bank for the old snapping turtle, but he was gone. What were the odds that he made an appearance when she was with Shaw? Should she take that as some sort of good omen?

Stepping closer to the edge of the stream, Kate tried to gauge the depth. Possibly she could wade through the creek, but then she'd be a mess to go into town. Shaw had offered to help; she should give her a call.

Who was she kidding? Despite all her high talk about boundaries, she'd done nothing but think about Shaw every minute since she'd left. This was the perfect excuse to call without seeming too obvious.

Oddly, her cell phone rang just when she was about to reach for it in the pocket of her jeans. A 415 area code flashed across her screen. She considered not answering it, but then curiosity got the best of her.

"Hello?"

"Hi, Kate, it's Shaw."

How had Shaw gotten her number?

"That's so strange, I was just thinking of calling you." Butterflies appeared out of nowhere in Kate's stomach at the sound of Shaw's voice.

"Really?"

"Yes, but now I'm wondering how you were able to call me first when I didn't give you my number." Kate wasn't really angry, but she felt like at this point, she couldn't let Shaw get away with anything. For some reason she wanted to have some sense of control over whatever was happening between them.

"Yeah, sorry about that. You were talking to your mother and I called my cell from your phone so I'd have the number. You know, for emergencies." There was playfulness in Shaw's voice.

"I'll let that slide for now."

"Thank you." There was silence for an instant. "So, you said you were just about to call me?"

"Wait, but you called me for some reason. You rang first."

"I'm heading into Hendersonville to pick up some things for Jimmy to repair the roof so I thought I'd see if you needed anything. I figured the creek might still be up."

"It is. I'm standing right next to it."

"You are?"

"Yeah, I was going to try and get my car, but I think the water is still too high. The pharmacy called to say they have Momma's meds ready."

"I can pick them up for you and bring them over later."

"You're sure you don't mind?"

"It's no trouble, really. Just text me the address of the pharmacy and any other info I might need to pick it up for you." Shaw paused. "Is there anything else you want?"

The low, husky quality of Shaw's voice when she asked the question sent a delicious tingling sensation up Kate's spine. Was there anything else she wanted? That list was potentially long. And was probably just as much about need as want, although sometimes it was hard to tell the difference. She wanted a family of her own. She wanted a partner that loved to travel, but was soothed by the comforts of home. She wanted a blue house with ivory trim, with pink dogwoods in the front yard. She wanted a lover who made her feel cherished. *Is there anything else I want? You, on a platter.*

"I can't think of anything at the moment."

"Okay. Well, if you think of something, just call me."

"Thank you, Shaw. See you soon."

She held the phone to her chest, closed her eyes, and sighed.

CHAPTER TWELVE

The wind whipped through the open Jeep. Shaw had to grab her ball cap before it took flight. She tossed it onto the passenger side floorboard and swept her fingers through her damp hair. A convertible Jeep was nature's hairdryer. She smiled and shifted into second so that she could slow into the curve without relying solely on the brakes.

Her plan was to siphon Wi-Fi from Starbucks in Hendersonville just long enough to download email and contact Raisa. But first she was going to pay a visit to the Miller place. Miss Edith's words burned in her brain. They kept running in a loop inside her head. *What they did to that boy, it weren't right. It left a hole in Iris's heart that she spent the rest of her life trying to fill.*

Clarence Hill's barn came into view. Shaw eased off the gas and took a sharp left onto a rutted dirt road across a rickety one-lane bridge. The road traversed an overgrown pasture with an ancient barn set askew. The whole faded gray structure, which leaned sideways on its foundation, looked as if a slight nudge would push it over. Beyond the pasture, the road climbed gradually through a thick stand of poplar, sweet gum, and oak. At one point she passed by a small cemetery. The rough stone markers were barely visible, mostly overgrown and darkened by moss and age.

Shaw started to think she might be in her own version of *Wrong Turn*. Wasn't this how every one of those horror movies started? A hapless city dweller lost on a deserted road deep in the Appalachian Mountains. Nice. She checked the rearview mirror because now she was feeling good and spooked.

Just as she was about to try to make a three-point turn to head back, she saw what looked like the end of the road. Jimmy had said take the road until you couldn't go any farther, and this looked like where it stopped. A 1930s era truck marked the edge of the yard; its headlights broke through the tall grass like some sort of rusted out hillbilly gargoyle standing watch. Firewood was stacked at the edge of a long unpainted porch that looked as if it were about to pull away from the house and break into a million weathered splinters. There didn't appear to be another car on the place, although there was a barn off to the far left and the doors were shut, so maybe there was a vehicle from this era parked inside. Shaw was about to turn and go when the screen door banged loudly. A woman stood on the porch watching her.

"What'chu want?" The woman had a thick drawl. She looked to be in her seventies, but her face and clothing told of a hard life, so she might have been younger. She had gray-white hair that fluffed around her face like down feathers.

Steeling all her nerves, Shaw climbed out of the Jeep and approached the house.

"I said, what do ya—" Her words died in her throat and she regarded Shaw with a wide-eyed scowl, almost as if she knew Shaw and was pissed to see her.

Feeling the woman's intense blue eyes boring into her, Shaw cleared her throat and tried to keep her voice even. "I'm looking for the Miller place."

"Ya found it didn't ya?"

"I'm looking for Addie Miller."

"Ya found her too." Jimmy's warning that Addie wasn't exactly friendly now seemed like the understatement of the year.

"I'm Shaw Daily. I was wondering if—"

"Ain't nothin' good ever come from someone carrying that last name."

"Excuse me?"

"You turn around and get off my property before I feel the need for my shotgun." Addie took a step down off the porch. She was tall and thin like Shaw. Her faded flannel shirt two sizes too large hung loosely on her slender frame. She was wearing work pants cuffed above boots reinforced with gray duct tape around both toes. Addie bore down on her with an intimidating air. Shaw took a step back. She didn't want a feud with this woman, but she did want some answers. She squared her shoulders and mustered the confidence that had served her well in tough business negotiations.

"Look, I don't want to make any trouble for you, I simply wanted to ask if you knew Charlie Miller."

Addie stepped within a foot of Shaw. They'd have been the same height if Addie weren't stooped with age. Addie studied her. The laser focus of her gaze was unnerving.

"He were my brother. Charlie Miller were took from our family and forced to serve. He had no business bein' in that far off place." Rage fairly pulsed off Addie. Shaw could feel the unseen weight of it in the air all around Addie.

"I'm sorry. I didn't know."

"There's a lot you don't know." Addie turned her back to Shaw and stomped up the steps. "Don't come here again." Addie never looked back. The screen door banged loudly again behind Addie as her figure was swallowed up by the dark interior of the house.

Shaw stood in the uncut grass, weak-kneed. Her heart thumped in her chest. *What the hell?*

After a minute or so she climbed in the Jeep and headed back down the winding dirt path to the main road. She gripped the steering wheel in an effort to get her hands to stop shaking. Who the hell was Charlie? If that old woman thought she could intimidate Shaw into not finding out, then she was in for a surprise.

Forty minutes later, Shaw was in Hendersonville and had nested herself into a corner table at Starbucks. Laptop up and running, phone charging, Wi-Fi connected, now all she needed was to hear her name called so she could claim her drink. Starbucks wasn't her favorite coffee, they over roasted their beans a bit too much for Shaw's liking, but she'd overlook that for the ambiance and free Internet connection.

She'd heard some of her California friends bemoan the ubiquitous nature of Starbucks. There were positives and negatives, and Shaw was aware of both. One of the positives was getting a cappuccino when you needed it most. It was a first-world problem and she'd readily admit it.

The barista called her name. Shaw settled back into her corner chair with her ball cap low over her eyes and headphones to cancel out all the chatter. About two hundred emails downloaded while she sipped her coffee. A top line search for Raisa's name brought the most recent email to the top. That was the only one she planned to respond to, unless there was also a note from her building manager back in San Francisco.

Raisa basically wanted an ETA for Shaw's return. Unfortunately, at this point, Shaw had no idea of her return date. She sent a note back to Raisa with a promise to respond with an estimate of her return date by the end of the week. That would buy her a few days to figure out what the hell she was doing.

Her fingers hovered over the keyboard. She knew what she was going to do first. She closed her email and opened her browser to search for Charlie Miller. What had Addie said? That he'd been forced to serve? Did she mean military service? If Charlie was close to her mother's age then he was too young for WWII. Could he have been in Vietnam? Unlikely. Would he have probably been the right age for the Korean War? No, based on his likely age, the math didn't work for that either.

Lots of Charlie Millers came up along with "C. Millers." She refined her search to *Charlie Miller military veteran*. A couple of sites showed up with lists for veterans. Maybe this was too broad a search. Maybe she should use the more formal version of his name. He probably didn't go by Charlie on official documents. She altered the search to *Charles Miller, Cooper's Creek, NC*. Shaw sat back in her chair, staring at the screen. There it was, an obit for Charles Shaw Miller of Cooper's Creek.

Charlie's middle name was Shaw.

Her stomach lurched, and for an instant, she thought she might have to dash for the restroom. Shaw closed her eyes and pinched the bridge of her nose. She took a few deep breaths and opened her eyes.

The obit was short. Private 1st Class Charles Shaw Miller was stationed in the Philippines and had been killed during a bivouac training exercise. His unit formation was hit by a 105-mm howitzer shell fired beyond range units. *Friendly fire.*

She read the last line. *Charlie Miller is survived by his parents, George and Irma Miller; and his sister, Adeline, of Cooper's Creek.* Her mother, Iris, wasn't mentioned, which wasn't necessarily conclusive of anything. She texted the obit link to her phone and shut down the laptop. The music piping in from her phone's playlist drowned out the hum of noise and random chatter. Her mind wandered as she finished the coffee. The obit summarized the end of his life but told her nothing about who he was.

Was Charlie Miller her father? That was a radical thought, but there had to be some connection. She'd always wondered why her mother had named her Shaw. And why her grandmother seemed so annoyed by that fact.

Someone knew the truth.

Miss Edith probably knew but was possibly unreliable, although she'd delivered the first clue, and Addie, well, she no doubt knew the whole story, but would she share it with Shaw? The pharmacy was just down the street. She'd pick up the prescription and get some groceries. Maybe other memories would return to Miss Edith while she was there. It couldn't hurt to ask.

A quick stop at the pharmacy then a speedy turn through the market, and the things that Jimmy needed for the roof, then Shaw headed back toward Cooper's Creek through downtown. It seemed Mast General Store was still a highlight. That made her smile when she thought of all the candy she'd consumed from that place as a kid. The store had been open since 1883 and was basically a big general mercantile, her favorite kind of store.

She passed McFarland's Bakery, and if there hadn't been a line out the door she'd have considered circling back for something sweet to take to Kate and her mother.

And then there were the bears.

All up and down Main Street were life-sized painted fiberglass bears standing on their back legs. They each seemed to have a different artistic theme. Some were more understandable, like the one in front of the ice cream shop holding a heaping ice cream cone.

One of the locals seated on a bench in front of the ice cream shop waved. She nodded and gave him a small wave. She'd probably been staring. The friendly thing to do was wave back.

Chapter Thirteen

Kate pulled sheets from the washer and shoved them into the dryer. Her mother had been sleeping off and on all day in her recliner so it seemed like a good time to freshen all the bedding. Back in the kitchen, she poured water from the kettle over a tea bag. She watched a deer skirt tentatively through the trees as she waited for the tea to steep. If the doe made a move for her mother's flowerbed, she'd run out and shoo her off.

As it turned out she needn't have worried. The deer's ears twitched at the sound of tires on gravel, and in the next instant, the doe shot up the hill, white tail flashing as she went.

Kate stepped out on the porch expecting to see Shaw's Jeep. Her stomach sank. Her disappointment was instantaneous when she saw it was her brother-in-law, Greg. She chided herself. She wasn't supposed to care, remember? She and Shaw were just friends. *Yeah, keep telling yourself that and maybe you'll believe it.*

"Hey, Sis. How's it going?"

"Hi, Greg. All is well." Kate leaned against the porch railing. "Miriam and the kids aren't with you?"

"No, Lara picked up something at vacation Bible school and brought it home to Emily. The whole house is sick with some twenty-four-hour bug." He propped a foot on the edge of the porch but didn't step up. "She sent me over to make sure you didn't need anything."

"We're good."

"I'd sort of worried that the creek was out of its banks, but it wasn't over the culvert when I drove up just now."

"That's good to hear. It was still high when I checked this morning."

"I wondered if that's why your car was parked down at the crossing. I'm sorry you got stranded. You should have called me."

"As it happened, Shaw Daily was at her grandparents' place. She rescued me in her grandad's old Jeep."

Greg arched his eyebrows and looked as if he was about to give her a hard time when they heard gravel crunching. Shaw's Jeep crested the hill, and she pulled up next to Greg's truck.

"Speak of the devil." Kate smiled and waved as Shaw climbed out and ambled over to where they were standing.

"Hi." Shaw seemed sheepish. She looked adorable in her worn ball cap and perfectly faded jeans.

"Hi, Shaw. Hey, you remember my brother-in-law, Greg."

"Sure. How are you, Greg? It's been a long time." Shaw extended her hand in greeting. "Oh, here, I picked this up. I hope you weren't in a hurry for it. I had a few other things to pick up in town for Jimmy, and the hardware store took forever." She handed the small white paper bag from the pharmacy to Kate.

"There was no rush." She tilted her head toward the front door. "Won't you come in? I just made myself a cup of tea."

"Uh…I don't want to intrude."

"You ladies enjoy your tea. I'm on a mission for 7 Up and soda crackers." Greg trotted back to his truck. "Good to see you, Shaw. And, Kate, call me if you need anything."

"Tell the kids I said hello and I hope they feel better soon." Kate waved as he pulled away. Then she turned to Shaw. "So? Join me for tea?"

"Sure."

As she followed Kate inside, Shaw couldn't help noticing that Kate had the cutest ass. And the way the cutoff denim shorts hugged her curves only perfected the view. Kate glanced back, and she averted her eyes quickly. She wasn't completely sure that Kate hadn't caught her looking. *Damn.* She used to be subtler than this. She was obviously slipping.

Just as they crossed the threshold, the sound of breaking glass greeted them. It came from the bedroom. Instinctively, Shaw followed on Kate's heels. Kate's mother was on the floor near an overturned bedside table. A lamp with a ceramic base lay in pieces on the floor. Shards of the shattered light bulb spilled out of the half crushed lampshade.

"Momma, are you all right?" Kate was on her knees beside her mother. Shaw hovered nearby not sure how best to help.

"I had a dizzy spell, but I didn't make it to the bed in time."

She had probably tried to grab the edge of the small nightstand and taken it to the floor with her. Shaw knelt down so that she could move Miss Edith's hand away from the sharp slivers of the broken light bulb.

"Let's get you up." Kate looked at Shaw. "Can you help me move her to the bed?"

Shaw nodded. She stepped over Miss Edith so that she was opposite Kate, and the two of them gently helped Miss Edith to her feet and then onto the bed. Shaw held onto her hand. Miss Edith sat at the edge of the bed while Kate rotated and lifted her mother's legs up onto the bed.

"I'm sorry I made such a mess." Miss Edith seemed fragile and shaken. Her eyes darted around the room and then back to Kate.

"It's okay, Momma. You just rest now. Do you need some water?" Miss Edith nodded. Kate tugged the drapes open to allow more light into the room. "Shaw, would you get her a drink of water while I get the broom?"

"Sure." Shaw felt self-conscious of the fact that she was bearing witness to the indignities of Miss Edith's frailty, the realities of the failing flesh. She returned with a glass of water. Miss Edith's hands were shaking when she covered Shaw's fingers still holding the glass, so Shaw didn't let go. She cradled Miss Edith's head and helped her take a few sips.

Behind her, broken glass clattered lightly onto the metal dustpan.

"Do you need help, Kate?"

"No, I think I've got it. You can close the drapes now if you don't mind."

Shaw looked back to discover that Miss Edith's eyes were closed. She drew the drapes to darken the room and followed Kate to the kitchen. Neither of them spoke. Kate put the kettle on and then slumped back against the edge of the countertop with her face in her hands.

Shaw touched Kate's arm. "Are you okay?"

Shaw was standing close so Kate didn't have to move far to lean into her, resting her cheek against Shaw's shoulder. Instinct took over. She encircled Kate in her arms.

"Hey, your mom is okay. She just fell. That could happen to anyone."

"I'm not ready." Kate's voice was muffled against her shirt. She felt Kate's arms tighten around her waist.

"Not ready for what?"

"I'm not ready to lose her."

"That's not going to happen any time soon." She tightened her embrace.

"How do you know?"

"I just know." She kept one arm around Kate and with the other, caressed her hair. She felt guilty for thinking about how cute Kate looked in cutoff shorts earlier when Kate had real life stuff to contend with.

She couldn't really relate to the bond that Kate had for her mother. If Shaw had known how sick her mother was, would she have made the same sacrifice to care for her? Probably not. Acknowledging her own selfishness turned her stomach.

Being around Kate and her mother cast in stark relief the relationship she'd had with hers. The hurt of Shaw's relationship with her own mother came back to her like some phantom pain that remains after a damaged limb has been removed.

She felt Kate shift in her arms, pulling her back to the moment. Reluctantly, Shaw released her.

"Thank you." Kate wiped at a tear with the palm of her hand.

"For what?" She didn't feel like she'd done much.

"Just for being here. It's nice to have a hug when you really need one." Kate smiled weakly.

Shaw hesitated. She wanted to say something comforting but couldn't think of anything. The kettle whistled like a train in the distance, intruding on the silence between them. She'd missed the moment. She should have said that she needed the hug as much as Kate had, but that discovery bothered her and she wasn't sure why.

Somehow Shaw had made things awkward after the embrace. She took a seat on one of the stools next to the counter and watched Kate pour water for their tea.

"I went to see Addie Miller earlier today." A subject change seemed like the safest course.

"Who?" Kate set a steaming mug in front of her and took the stool next to hers.

"Remember how your mother mentioned Charlie Miller?"

"Yes."

"Well, I asked Jimmy if he knew anyone by that name and he mentioned Addie Miller so I drove over to her place."

"And?"

"She didn't exactly invite me in for tea, but she said enough for me to track down Charlie Miller's obit. His full name was Charles Shaw Miller."

"His middle name was Shaw?" Kate regarded her with wide eyes.

She nodded. She took small sips of her tea. "He knew my mother, Iris, according to your mom. And his middle name was Shaw." Her hand started to shake. She set the mug on the counter to stabilize it. She wasn't sure she could say the words out loud, but she pushed through. "Do you think it's possible that he was my father?"

"Oh my God."

"Yeah."

"All this time you've never known who your father was?"

"No."

"Why didn't someone ever tell you?"

"I don't know, but I'd really like to find out why."

"I can ask my mother more about Charlie when she wakes up."

"I'd appreciate that. I'd sort of like to be here when you talk to her about it. If you don't mind." Not that she didn't trust Kate to relay the conversation accurately, but there were nuances sometimes lost if you didn't hear something firsthand. The tone of voice, the expression on someone's face, body language, all those things added a supporting narrative to any story.

"Of course." Kate sipped her tea and glanced at the wall clock. "Why don't you come back and have dinner with us? Momma will likely nap for another hour. Let's see, it's four now..." Kate looked as if she were doing math in her head. "Would dinner at six work for you?"

"Considering my schedule at the moment is wide open? Yes, six will work." Shaw stood. "I'll let you have some time to yourself."

Kate had the strongest impulse to stand and pull Shaw into a hug. Shaw seemed suddenly so sad and forlorn. Kate couldn't imagine losing her mother or having no idea who her father was. That must make a person feel unmoored. Knowing whom you came from was part of how you came to know who you were in the world. Obviously, that wasn't a person's entire story, but as least the foundation of that story.

"Is there anything I can bring over for dinner? Is there anything you need?"

Kate shook her head. *Just you.* She stopped herself from saying it aloud. *All I need is you.* Good Lord, her internal dialogue was beginning to sound like a romance novel.

The house seemed strangely empty after Shaw left. Kate carried her tea out to the porch and settled into a rocker to finish it. She'd had such good intentions of setting firm boundaries with Shaw, but regardless of what her brain told her she kept finding reasons to spend time with Shaw. Intellectually, she'd put boundaries in place that her emotions were choosing to ignore. If she allowed herself to act on her attraction for Shaw who could blame her? So what if it turned out to be only a fling? Maybe a fling was just what she needed. It wasn't as if she currently had the physical space or the emotional bandwidth for a serious relationship. She was living with her mother. Not exactly a recipe for hot romantic nights. Shaw was here for the short-term and short-term was all she could handle. As long as she managed her expectations and didn't let herself get carried away, everything would be fine.

She was a grown-up. She could have a fling if she wanted one.

Then she thought of Shaw. The hurt expression on Shaw's face when she'd told her about the discovery of Charlie's middle name. And she felt suddenly guilty for objectifying Shaw into a fling. Who was she kidding? She should stick with her original plan and just be Shaw's friend. Except now she'd asked her over for dinner. It was as if her subconscious was conspiring against friendship. Maybe her subconscious knew better than she did what she really needed.

Kate finished the tea and then stepped inside to retrieve her laptop. She hadn't checked email in two days, which had been a nice mental break, but she was hoping to hear back about a freelance piece she'd pitched to *Blue Ridge Getaways*, a monthly travel magazine published out of Asheville. As she waited for her email to download, she ran through recipes in her head. She had at least an hour to decide what she'd make for dinner.

Chapter Fourteen

Shaw waved to Jimmy sitting on the porch as she drove up. She had two bags of groceries, one in each arm, as she walked past him.

"Don't you have a home to go to?" she called to him from the kitchen. She'd left the door open on the way in.

"Anne was afraid you'd starve all by yourself. She sent me over with a casserole. It's in the fridge, second shelf."

"Tell your wife thank you. I can fend for myself, but I'll never say no to a home cooked meal." She leaned out the doorway. "Do you want a beer?"

"Is a frog's ass watertight?"

"I have no idea, but now, unfortunately, I'm visualizing a frog's ass. Do you want a beer or not?" Shaw stood in the doorway with her hands on her hips.

"Yes, I want a beer." He accepted the bottle from Shaw and took a long swig. "Seriously? You never heard that saying? I'm worried about your cultural education out there on the left coast, in the land of fruits and nuts."

"You know I live in California too, right?"

"What? That's where they grow oranges and almonds, right?"

"Nice save."

Shaw tipped the chair back so that it rested against the wall and propped her foot up on the porch railing. The sun was low and the ridge looked hazy in the humid evening air. Cicadas were singing, no doubt perched in the dark shadows of the hardwoods that surrounded her grandparents' property. By dusk, if she squinted into the shadows she'd see fireflies. Warm nights and fireflies, two things Northern California couldn't offer. No matter how hot it got during the day the Pacific marine layer brought with it evening temps that dropped into the fifties most nights. There were lots of places to watch the sun set or sit and have a drink along the coast, but you couldn't do it without layering a light coat over a sweater even in August.

It was warm here. The sun was on its way to bed and the air held no chill.

It was nice to sit with Jimmy and feel no obligation to talk, although she did want to tell him about her encounter with Addie.

"I drove out to the Miller place."

"How was it?"

"Rundown, except for the barn."

"Yeah, that's about the size of it."

"And Addie Miller is a real peach."

"I told you she wasn't friendly."

"She threatened to pull a shotgun on me."

"Did she actually get the gun?"

"No."

"Then she must have liked you."

Shaw laughed. "I'm not sure I'd bet my life on that." She took a few swallows of the microbrew she'd picked up in town. Luckily, she'd thought to take a cooler so the beer was nice and cold. "What's in that barn anyway?"

"Not sure. She hired me and another fella to do some repairs to the outside, but she got really steamed when I made a move to open the door."

"That's a little odd."

"I thought so too, but I wasn't going to argue with her about it. Whatever it is, it's her business."

They sat quietly as Jimmy finished his beer.

"Well, I guess I better get to the house." He stood, leaving his empty bottle in a wooden crate near the edge of the porch. "Say, did you get the things on that list I gave you?"

"I did. I paid for everything, but the lumber wouldn't fit in the Jeep. You'll have to go back with your truck." She handed him the receipt.

"All right then. You take it easy." He gave her a small salute as he trotted down the porch steps.

Shaw got another beer. She sat for a while mulling over the events of the day. She'd possibly stumbled across her father's identity, and yet she couldn't begin to come to terms with that. She'd wanted to have a father her entire life. If Charlie was her father why hadn't her mother just told her the truth? Why hadn't she told Shaw that he was dead? Instead of hinting around that he was out in the world somewhere, alive, but not wanting to be with them. Wasn't that worse than thinking someone was dead?

When you're dead you can't be held accountable for desertion. You're just dead and that's the end of it.

There had to be more to the story. What details she did have so far only brought lots more questions. Why had Charlie not married her mother? Did he not know her mother had been pregnant? Did her grandparents not approve of the match? Is that what had happened?

What they did to that boy, it weren't right. Miss Edith's words were seared in her gray matter. Who was *they* and what had they done?

Kate decided not to make a big deal out of dinner. Spaghetti would be simple. She didn't want to do something fancy and have Shaw think she was making more of the visit than she was. Friendship. That was the word for the night. Friendship, and hopefully some insights about Charlie. Her mother seemed to be feeling better following her afternoon nap. There was a bruise on her arm from the fall, but otherwise she seemed without injury, except perhaps to her pride.

Shaw looked edible in a faded red T-shirt and jeans. Every time they made eye contact across the table she swore she could feel the heat of Shaw's laser focus. Kate had decided not to change out of her sleeveless blouse and cutoff shorts. She was determined that this was not a date. Although, she couldn't completely ignore that the looks Shaw was giving her meant she might think it was.

Kate made a simple vanilla sheet cake for dessert. She scooped fresh strawberries over it and then added a dash of whipped cream. This was an informal version of strawberry shortcake. She liked her version better because the cake had more flavor.

Her mother murmured something as she and Shaw sampled the dessert.

"What d'you say, Momma?"

"How long will you be here, Charlie?" Kate's mother directed the question to Shaw. Her eye's had lost their focus and it seemed she was thinking of the past again.

"I'm not sure." Shaw put her fork down and looked across the table at Kate as if she were asking permission to lead her mother through this memory.

"It ain't right that them other boys got off without punishment."

"No, it wasn't right." Shaw echoed her mother's words.

"You shouldn't leave Iris, not now. I know you think you'll be back and everything will pick up where it left off…but, son… sometimes the world has other ideas. You best not take this girl for granted."

"What would you do if you were me?"

"I'd marry her. I'd get far away from here."

"Why do you think we should leave?"

"You know Iris's daddy ain't ever gonna come around. He'll never give his blessing."

"Why do you think we should marry?"

"Because you love each other. You can't choose who you love, son. The heart has its own designs on these matters." Her mother took a bite of the strawberry-soaked cake. "Kate, this dessert sure is good."

And just like that the spell was broken. Her mother was back in the present. Shaw sat at the other end of the table in shocked silence. The color was gone from her face and Kate was afraid she might be sick. She reached over and touched Shaw's hand. Shaw flinched. Shaw looked down at Kate's hand covering hers. She blinked a few times as if she were fighting back tears.

"Will you excuse me a minute?"

"The bathroom is down the hall on the right." Kate anticipated the question before Shaw asked it.

"Thanks."

Kate finished the small serving of dessert before Shaw returned.

Shaw sat back down and looked at the sagging dollop of whipped cream.

"Don't feel like you have to eat the rest of it." Kate wanted to reach for Shaw again. She fought the urge to comfort her, to help in some way, but she wasn't sure what Shaw wanted or needed.

"It was really good. Everything was really good, I just…" The words trailed off.

"Don't worry about it." Kate started to clear the table.

"No, I'll do that." Shaw stood up to help. "Why don't you get your mother settled and I'll clean up."

"Are you sure?"

"Yeah, I need something to do." Shaw had a plate in each hand. She smiled weakly at Kate.

It took about a half hour to get her mother situated in bed watching TV. She propped her up with pillows and made sure she was comfortable before going back to check on Shaw in the kitchen. Sounds of running water and clanging dishware had stopped. It was dark outside. Shaw was sitting on the sofa. Kate was about to turn on a lamp, but Shaw hadn't stirred. She seemed lost in another world, and Kate decided she preferred the ambient light from the kitchen instead.

The sofa cushions were comfortably broken in so that when Kate sat down she rolled toward the middle, her leg coming to rest against Shaw's.

"Sorry." Kate put her hand on Shaw's thigh to right herself.

Shaw had been staring at the black rectangle of nighttime through the living room window. She'd let her mind wander until Kate touched her. Tingling heat radiated from Kate's hand on her leg. She wanted Kate to keep it there so she covered it with hers. The gesture seemed to surprise Kate. She cleared her throat and settled back, but she left her hand where it was.

"Is your mother okay?"

"Yes, she'll be asleep in fifteen minutes. I'll go in later and turn the TV off. She likes to fall asleep to the sound of it."

"Thanks for dinner."

"You're welcome." Kate shifted beside her. The sofa was like a broken-in mattress. No matter how they attempted to reposition, they rolled against each other in the center of it. "Sorry, maybe I should move to the chair."

"Don't." Shaw stopped her. "I like having you close."

"Do you want to talk?"

Shaw shook her head. She wanted to do a lot of things. But right now talking wasn't one of them. She didn't want to think about Charlie, or her mother, or what might have been. At this point everything was still a mystery. Brief glimpses from Miss Edith's memory. Who was to say those memories were even accurate.

"Are you sure?"

"Yeah, thank you." She traced the contour of Kate's cheek with her fingertip as if she were some finely sculpted figure.

Shaw angled toward Kate. She wanted to kiss her, but she stopped short of making contact. Kate's lips were parted as if about to whisper something. Shaw hesitated, but when Kate didn't move she titled her head and kissed Kate, the softest caress of a kiss. She held her breath as she pulled away. They regarded each other in the low light as if they'd both been taken by surprise by the fleeting contact.

"Shaw, I…"

"It's okay. I shouldn't have done that. I'm sorry." The expression on Kate's face told her the kiss had been a mistake. She turned to stand up, but Kate reached for her.

Kate cradled Shaw's face in her hands and kissed her. Soft, lingering, tasting of strawberries, this kiss lasted longer than the first. Shaw felt this kiss like teasing tentacles all up and down her spine. Kate was an excellent kisser. That just made Shaw want more. She angled closer to Kate.

She felt Kate's fingers in the short hair at the back of her head. She could happily drown in this kiss. She was lying partially on top of Kate now and they were still kissing. Kate broke the kiss, breathing hard.

"Should I apologize for doing that?" Kate caressed Shaw's face.

"No, definitely not."

She let her hand drift over Kate's ribs to the soft curve of her hip. She wedged her body against Kate's so that they were in full contact. She pressed her lips to Kate's and Kate opened up to her, deepening the kiss. Shaw instinctively slid her thigh between Kate's legs. Kate moaned softly.

Shaw traced the contour of Kate's body with the palm of her hand, sliding it slowly over the outside curve of her breast. She paused, taking care to massage the sharp point of Kate's nipple through the fabric of the blouse.

She felt Kate's fingers at the hem of her T-shirt and then her nails lightly scraping up her back. Shaw's face was on fire; her heart pounded loudly in her ears.

"Kate, are you still up?" Miss Edith was standing at the back of the couch but didn't see them because of the low light.

Kate lurched, shoving Shaw so hard that she rolled off the sofa with a thump.

"Kate?"

"Hi, Momma, I was just lounging on the couch." Kate stood, smoothed her hair down, and straightened her shirt. Shaw was fairly sure that Miss Edith still couldn't see her. Especially now that she was on the floor halfway under the coffee table.

"I think I forgot to take my medicine. I woke up and just now thought of it. I must have dozed off watching TV."

Kate rounded the couch and gently ushered Miss Edith back to her bedroom. "You took your medicine already. I gave it to you right before you got into bed."

"Oh, okay. I'm sure you know better than me."

Their voices faded as they disappeared into the bedroom. Shaw pressed the palms of her hands to her face. What the hell was she doing? Almost getting caught by Kate's mother made her feel as if she was back in high school, trying to sneak a kiss from some girl she was totally crushed out on.

She got to her feet just as Kate came back to the living room.

"I'm so sorry." Kate kept her voice low.

"Don't worry about it. I should go." Shaw was having second thoughts about everything. She was all wrought up inside, and she worried that she was using Kate as some emotional distraction from whatever was going on in her own life, the reason she'd come back to Cooper's Creek. She hadn't come back looking for romance, she'd come back to take a break, to find herself.

For a minute, she thought Kate might ask her to stay. She had an expression on her face that Shaw couldn't quite decipher. But she didn't.

"I'll walk you out." Kate slipped on her shoes.

They stood by the Jeep, and Shaw was unsure what to do. Should she kiss Kate good night? It was like Kate gave off signals that she didn't want anything from Shaw, but then they'd get close and things would simply happen.

"Thank you again for dinner." Shaw wasn't sure what to do with her hands so she shoved them into her pockets.

"Shaw, I'm really sorry I reacted like that. It was silly. I'm not used to being in someone else's house, especially not my parents' house. But I'm an adult and I shouldn't have reacted that way."

"It's okay, really. I'm not fond of the idea of your mother catching us making out either."

Kate put her hands on Shaw's arms. They were soft and warm, and she caressed Shaw's forearms lightly as she leaned against Shaw and kissed her. It was brief but one of the sweetest kisses Shaw had experienced in a long time.

"Have a good night, Shaw."

Kate turned and walked back toward the house, leaving Shaw leaning against the driver's side door wanting nothing more than to follow her inside.

Shaw drove back through the woods from Kate's place to hers. It was dark, and as she neared the creek she captured two deer in her headlights, a doe and her spotted fawn. They froze, staring into the light with saucer sized black eyes, then the doe twitched her ears and the two of them sprang into the grass at the shoulder and disappeared into the woods. She heard them springing through the dry underbrush when she could no longer see them.

She cut the engine and killed the lights, allowing the darkness to swallow her up. It was midnight dark even though it couldn't have been much past nine o'clock. There was no moon and no glimmer of house lights visible through the trees. Kate's place was up the densely wooded hill, completely hidden from view. That's assuming lights were still on.

Night sounds passed through the open cockpit of the Jeep. Tree frogs, cicadas, and one distant call of an owl. She leaned her forehead against her arm across the steering wheel and closed her eyes. She was never this alone in San Francisco and yet she felt lonelier there than here, in the dark woods, by herself; she felt peaceful and grounded.

Closing her eyes allowed her to call up the sensation of her body pressed against Kate's on the sofa. Warmth spider-webbed through her entire body. Kate had kissed her. Kate had kissed her like she meant it, not like some casual, friendly kiss. At least that's the way it felt to Shaw, and she hoped she was still able to tell the difference.

But what did that matter?

Her life was in San Francisco and Kate's life was here. Plus, Kate had big responsibilities right now caring for her mother. Did Shaw want to get in the middle of that sort of family stress? No, absolutely not. It had taken her years to wrest control of her own life away from her mother's chaotic reach. Freedom came with independence. This was exactly why she didn't have a girlfriend in San Francisco. She didn't want to be tied down or obligated to anyone again, ever.

She'd gone to Kate's for dinner with the intention of talking with Miss Edith about Charlie, not to start something with Kate. But it was almost as if she couldn't help herself when Kate was around. She compulsively flirted, and the minute she'd gotten the chance she'd kissed her. What a selfish ass.

Shaw knew what sort of woman Kate was. It was obvious. Kate was not a woman wired for casual sex. Shaw could read the signs, and she'd blown right past all of them because she apparently had no control over her own libido. This was Kate Elkins. This was Miriam's little sister. She'd known Kate since she was eight and Kate was two. Kate was not a woman she had any business fooling around with. She needed to get her head out of her ass and deal with her own stuff right now.

She slumped back in the seat and sat listening to the sound of running water. She couldn't see the stream just ahead in the darkness, but she could hear it. The water was still running a little high and fast from all the recent rain.

Then inspiration struck. Shaw needed a project, and she knew just the project that needed to be tackled. She'd call Jimmy first thing in the morning. The soothing night sounds rippled through the air, and she inhaled the scent of damp earth. After a few more moments of communing with the dark, Shaw cranked the Jeep and lumbered up the rough trail through the woods to her grandparents' place.

CHAPTER FIFTEEN

Morning couldn't come soon enough. Shaw's mind refused to be still for most of the night. She'd tossed and turned and hardly gotten any sleep. She could blame stress or whatever crisis she was going through, but the truth was she couldn't stop thinking about Kate. Every time Shaw closed her eyes she easily conjured the electric sense phenomenon of kissing Kate, of touching Kate, of holding Kate. Torture, that's what it was, torture.

When Kate walked back into the house she regretted that she hadn't followed her. Should she have followed? Or had Kate given her a clear message that the night was over? Now she wasn't sure.

The porch felt cool under her bare feet as she leaned against the doorframe sipping her coffee. Early morning mist hovered along the ground making it look as if the mountain ridge had become separated from the Earth, as if it were floating. She'd pulled on a flannel shirt over her T-shirt. It was cool now, but probably by late morning the temperature would warm.

After toast and a second cup of coffee, Shaw pulled on boots and struck out across the yard. She carried the vintage porcelain basin under one arm. The lush dew-laden grass soaked the cuff of her jeans by the time she'd reached her grandfather's shop. The structure was a simple square cinderblock building with a retractable door at the front. The correct key eluded her, and she had to try several on the ring she'd brought from the house before the door at the side of the large bay door opened. The air inside was stale. She left the door open behind her and heaved the garage door up. It screeched loudly in complaint. Dust particles danced through the light that streamed across the concrete floor that was oil-stained in spots.

This was the shop where her grandfather had done side work as a mechanic and bodywork on cars. All his tools were mostly where he'd left them, on the long rough-hewn wooden workbench across the back wall of the garage, some hanging on hooks, some in open tool cases. Shaw leaned across the bench and cranked the two windows at the back of the shop open. Jimmy had a key, but it didn't look as if he used it much.

Under a canvas tarp in the corner, she found what she was looking for, a welding gun and a tank of CO_2 and argon gas. She opened the main valve to make sure there was still gas. The gauge read a little over 2000 PSI. That was great news because it meant the tank was almost full. She threw off the tarp and rolled the tank out away from the workbench toward the large bay door. She wanted plenty of fresh air while she was working.

Along the base of the wall, past a rolling work surface with a heavy-duty mounted bench vise clamp, Shaw found what she was looking for. She rolled the heavy work surface aside and knelt to examine a random assortment of steel rods and pieces. They were dusted with orange from rust, but she didn't mind. The coloring added character. The design she had in mind was shabby chic anyway.

A dusty legal pad and square carpenter's pencil were at the far end of the workbench. She tore off the top sheet, then measured the basin she'd brought with her from the house and started to sketch a frame for it on the legal pad.

Kate was watching her mother fuss over her flowerbed when a car approaching called her attention to the driveway. Miriam's aging green Ford Explorer crested the rise. Kate had hoped Shaw might surprise her with a visit, but that hadn't happened. There'd been no phone calls either. Almost twenty-four hours had passed since they'd kissed on the couch. Twenty-four hours that felt like two weeks. She supposed that both of them were waiting to see who would make the next move. Or trying to figure out if they should make a next move. It seemed neither of them had settled on an answer to those questions.

"Hey, Sis." Miriam waved as she climbed out of the dusty green SUV. She looked more like their father, where Kate took after their mother. Miriam had more rounded features, brown hair, and a little extra baby weight. She always complained about the fact that she needed to lose twenty pounds, but Kate thought her sister was beautiful. She managed two kids, a husband, and a part-time job at a florist shop in town and somehow always looked like she was completely together and on top of things.

"How are the girls?" Kate shielded her eyes from the sun.

"They're fine. Feeling much better after eating their body weight in Jell-O and Popsicles." Miriam hugged Kate.

Teaching first grade awarded Kate the immune system of an armored tank. Almost nothing took her down. She was practically immune to the common cold. But if one kid in her class got sick it seemed to travel through the whole group.

"I'm so glad they're better."

"And how are things here? I thought you might need a day off. Sorry I didn't call first, but I wasn't sure until the last minute that Greg would be home to stay with the girls."

"Don't worry about that. Surprise visits are great anytime."

"That's not what I heard." Miriam quirked the side of her mouth up playfully.

"What?"

"Well, someone told me Shaw is staying at her grandparents' place, and rumor has it you two have at the very least exchanged phone numbers…maybe more."

"I assume these rumors came from Greg?"

"He's a very reliable source. He hardly notices anything and he said you were acting all jumpy when Shaw stopped by. I'm no mathematician, but I can put two and two together."

"I was *not* jumpy."

Her mother had waved when Miriam first pulled up and finally left her weeding to join them on the porch.

"What are you girls talking about over here?"

"Kate's new girl—"

"Nothing, Momma." Kate cut Miriam off. "There's iced tea in the house. Would you like some?"

"No, I'm going to stay with these weeds a bit longer, until I give out. It's nice to be in the sun a little. You girls go ahead without me."

Her mother seemed completely fit today, no stumbles, no dizziness, and no memory lapses. It had been a good day.

Kate poured iced tea for them and they settled at the counter. Miriam had the air of someone about to hatch some devious plan.

"So, have you kissed yet?"

Kate coughed, sputtering in her tea.

"I'll take that as a yes." Miriam sipped her tea. She looked as satisfied as the Cheshire Cat, a grin spreading slowly across her face.

"We kissed, but we probably shouldn't have. And then Momma walked in and almost caught us making out on the couch. I shoved Shaw on the floor. It was completely embarrassing."

Miriam tried not to laugh but failed.

"Go ahead and laugh. It was truly awful."

"I'm sorry. I don't mean to laugh, but you've got to admit the whole situation is pretty comical." Miriam patted her hand. "Here you are, a stone's throw from the biggest unrequited crush of your life, and the minute you finally get to kiss her Momma walks in and busts it up. It's like a scene right out of some romantic comedy."

"What do you mean?"

"I mean, the scene you described sounded like something from a classic romantic comedy."

"Not that part, what you said before that."

"Oh, about how Shaw is the biggest unrequited crush of your life?"

"Yes, that part. It's not true." Kate hoped she was giving Miriam her best *I'm serious* look.

"Please. It was obvious to everyone but you."

Kate's mouth was open, a clever retort on the tip of her tongue… maybe. At least she'd hoped, but nothing came to her. Miriam had a teasing expression on her face as she took a long swig of her iced tea.

"Do you think Shaw had any idea?" Kate would be so embarrassed if she thought there was any way Shaw noticed.

Miriam shrugged. "Probably not. It's just that I know you, so it was plain as day to me. The way you'd watch her every move when she was around. How you followed her like a little lost kitten. The way you'd sit and stare at her, as if you wanted to commit every physical detail to memory."

"At the time I think I just thought she was interesting, but I suppose I did sort of have a crush on her."

"Sort of?"

"Okay, maybe I had a big crush on her."

"So what happens now?"

"What do you mean?"

"Well, you two finally kissed, you finally crossed that line, now what?"

Kate wondered the same thing. Her stomach sank a little. She rested her elbows on the counter and her chin in her hand. What was going to happen? Probably nothing.

"I don't know what happens now." Kate tried to sound nonchalant about it, when actually she was anything but.

"Oh, Sis, don't overthink this. You always overthink things to the point that nothing spontaneous can possibly happen."

"I do not."

"Yes, you do." Miriam leaned forward and reached across the counter to capture Kate's hand. "You should go over there right now. Just drop in and see what she's up to."

"Right now?"

"Yes, right now. I'm here and I can stay and visit with Momma for a while. Walk over to Shaw's place and see if she's home." Miriam rousted Kate from her chair and nudged her toward the door. "Don't wait until she's gone back to California. You'll regret it if you don't find out once and for all if there's any substance behind this crush of yours."

"I can't just show up over there." Kate skidded flatfooted across the threshold as if she was trying to apply the brakes, but Miriam kept playfully shoving her until she was standing on the porch.

"Yes, you can. Go. And don't come back for at least an hour, maybe two." Miriam blocked the door with her hands on her hips.

Kate ran her fingers through her hair as she cut through the woods toward Shaw's house. What was she even wearing? Khaki shorts and her favorite T-shirt from a girls' weekend in Pensacola. It had been washed so many times that the fabric was super soft and had shrunk a little so that the fit was on the snug size. Hopefully, that would work in her favor. Miriam hadn't even given her a chance to look in the mirror before she'd hustled her out the door.

There was a steep path that followed the edge of a spring feeding into the creek. It was a quicker route going downhill, although a little too steep for the return trip. It joined the main dirt road where it crossed the culvert over the creek.

Kate slowed her pace and inspected the muddy bank for the turtle. She thought of the first morning they'd crossed the flooded stream together in Shaw's Jeep and how they'd seen the old snapping turtle. After all the times she'd looked for him and he'd been missing, it had to be some sort of good omen that he'd shown himself the one time she'd been with Shaw.

As she climbed the uphill path toward the Daily place, Kate wracked her brain for an excuse to make an unannounced visit. She'd forgotten to give Shaw cash for the prescription for her mother. That was an excellent reason to walk over. But when she checked her pockets she realized she had no cash. Okay, that excuse wouldn't work. She took a few deep breaths as she crested the hill at the side of the house. She'd just have to say hello without an excuse to explain her visit.

The front door was open. Kate knocked but heard nothing.

"Hello?" She stepped into the kitchen but didn't see Shaw.

She stood on the porch for a minute and then noticed the old shop door was open. She headed in that direction. Maybe Jimmy was working on something and would know where Shaw was.

Kate stopped dead in her tracks when she reached the bay door. Shaw was wearing a welding mask and heavy gloves and working on a curved piece of steel held firm by a vise grip. Mesmerized, Kate watched as Shaw heated the metal and then hammered it into an arc. The opening of her shirt showed a bit of skin, glistening with a light sheen of perspiration. Somehow, Shaw noticed Kate and turned the welding gun off. She flipped up the dark mask and smiled. Kate had to lean against the wall to keep from wilting. This was like some surreal *Flashdance* moment except instead of sexy Jennifer Beals, Shaw was a true-life hot butch, complete with boots and power tools. Shaw tossed the gloves on the workbench and sauntered over in Kate's direction. Meanwhile, Kate focused on breathing.

"Hi, I hope you weren't standing there for long. I can't see very well with the mask on." Shaw rolled her sleeves up, exposing well-defined forearms.

Kate smiled, cleared her throat, looked away, and then turned back and smiled again. She crossed her arms to offer a buffer of safety between herself and butch dream girl of the year.

"Are you all right?" Shaw had a look of concern on her face. She dropped the mask to the floor. "Do you need to sit down?"

"I'm fine, sorry. I must have walked up the hill too fast. I just needed to catch my breath." She waved Shaw off. Good Lord, if Shaw touched her right now she might actually burst into flames.

"Let's go to the house and I'll get you something to drink."

Kate nodded, too embarrassed by her reaction just now to speak. She sat in one of the chairs on the porch and fanned herself. *Get a grip!*

After a moment, Shaw returned with two glasses of ice water.

"I'm sorry I interrupted you."

"Are you kidding? I'm happy to see you. Besides, I needed to take a break anyway. I was getting overheated under all that safety gear."

The mention of safety gear made Kate giggle.

"What's funny?"

Kate shook her head.

"No, really, what's funny?"

"You said safety gear and, well, my mind went somewhere else." Kate felt her cheeks flame, and she knew there was no way to hide the fact that she was probably blushing.

"Oh, really?" A mischievous grin spread slowly across Shaw's face.

"Can we change the subject?"

"Absolutely not." Shaw angled toward Kate, smiling. "What sort of activity were you thinking we might need safety gear for?"

"More like a safe word." Kate mumbled as she took a sip of water, glancing sideways at Shaw.

"A safe word?" Shaw leaned back in her chair. She took a drink and gave Kate a smoldering look over the top of the glass. "Maybe I should take a shower then."

Oh no, Kate had really started something now. She hadn't meant to flirt, but as God was her witness, she couldn't help herself. A woman could only stand so much temptation, and Shaw was unadulterated temptation wrapped in faded jeans and flannel.

"Let me get cleaned up. I'll be quick."

Kate nodded, afraid to speak because she clearly couldn't trust herself not to shamelessly flirt. A few seconds later, Shaw leaned through the open door.

"Should I invite you to join me?" The timbre of her voice was low and throaty.

Kate stared at her.

"I mean, I just thought if we were to the point of needing a safe word that taking a shower together was the next logical step." She had to be joking.

"I don't think logic has anything to do with this." Kate shooed her inside. "Go take a shower before I take you up on that offer."

Kate waited until she heard the shower running before she got out of her chair to take her empty glass to the kitchen. She wandered casually around the living room looking at photos of Shaw's grandparents and younger iterations of Shaw. One of the photos was of Miriam and Shaw together, leaning against each other arm-in-arm.

The cell phone on the coffee table buzzed, and Kate couldn't help but notice there were several text messages on the screen from someone named Raisa. She was probably some gorgeous blond woman on the West Coast who was anxiously waiting for Shaw to return. She sighed and stared out the window.

Shaw snuck up behind Kate, and Shaw's lips were dangerously close to her ear. Shaw smelled like soap and vanilla. Kate must have been lost in thought because she didn't hear the shower turn off. She leaned back against Shaw's chest. Shaw gently spun her around. Shaw had changed into a clean white T-shirt and linen cargo shorts that hung loose on her slender frame.

"Would it be all right if I kissed you?" Shaw's lashes were long and dark, her skin warm from the shower.

Kate didn't answer; she simply tilted her head up and kissed Shaw deeply; she draped her arms around Shaw's neck, pressing her body into Shaw's.

Shaw swept her palms slowly up Kate's back and drew her close. The soft crush of Kate's breasts against her chest and Kate's mouth against hers caused her stomach to drop away. She filled her fingers with Kate's hair and cradled her neck. Their bodies fit together so tightly that no space existed between them, and Shaw was having a hard time distinguishing where her body ended and Kate's began.

She reached out, placing her hand on the wall, then she eased Kate backward and pinned her.

Kate broke the kiss, pushing against Shaw with the palms of her hands. Shaw felt flushed. She was breathing hard as she studied Kate's face.

"What's our safe word?" Kate ran the tip of her tongue over her glistening lips.

"Do we need one?"

"Yes." Kate seemed as breathless as she was.

"Um, I don't know…I can't think right now…"

Kate laughed. "Okay, how about *Flashdance*?"

"*Flashdance*? How the heck did you think of that just now…oh, wait, the welding…"

"Shut up."

"Shutting up now," she whispered, smiling against Kate's velvet soft lips.

Kate's palms drifted down Shaw's chest coming to rest over her breasts, which at the moment were acutely sensitive to Kate's touch. She closed her eyes and groaned involuntarily as Kate caressed her nipples through her T-shirt. Kate feathered kisses over her eyelids and her forehead before she returned to her mouth.

Shaw braced her arm on the wall again. She was feeling seriously weak in the knees as Kate massaged her breasts. She managed to slip her other hand up inside Kate's form-fitting shirt. She trailed her fingers up Kate's back and then let them slide down to Kate's ass.

Her cell phone rang. It caused both of them to jump as if an alarm had sounded.

"I'm sorry. I meant to turn that off."

Kate felt as if she'd gotten caught up in some drug-induced fog. She settled her hands on Shaw's hips, safely away from other sensitive areas. If Shaw's cell phone hadn't rung would she have stopped? She swept her fingers through her hair. She wasn't sure.

"Maybe you should get that. It buzzed while you were in the shower." Kate reminded herself that someone named Raisa had something urgent and likely personal to speak with Shaw about.

Shaw released Kate and reached for the phone. She made a deliberate show of turning it off.

"There's nothing more important to me than what's happening right now."

"Are you sure?" Kate pulled the hem of her T-shirt down and moved away from Shaw. "I know you have a life in California that I know nothing about. A life that you're going to return to." Was Kate talking to Shaw or herself?

"Kate." Shaw caught her wrist.

She turned to face Shaw, and something on the mantel caught her eye. A brushed silver urn that appeared oddly out of place in the rustic interior. How had she missed it before? She looked at Shaw and then back at the urn.

"Shaw, what is that?"

"My mother's ashes." Shaw dropped Kate's hand. She sighed.

"Your mother died six months ago."

"Yeah."

"Oh." Kate was at a bit of a loss.

"I'm not sure what to do with them, so I just brought them along." Shaw seemed suddenly sad. "I should…I dunno…maybe see about finding a place for them in a cemetery somewhere."

"Did you have a service for her in California?"

"No." Shaw swept her fingers through her still damp hair. "I'm sure she doesn't care one way or the other."

"I've always been of the opinion that funerals are for the living, not the dead." Kate worried that Shaw was going through something bigger than she'd been aware of. Was this why Shaw had come home to North Carolina? Kate reached for her, and at first Shaw brushed her off, but after Kate refused to relent she allowed herself to be drawn into a hug. "You need your mother's funeral more than she does. So that you know that people care for you."

"No one even knows me here anymore."

Kate held Shaw at arm's length and searched her face. "That's not true. I know you. Miriam knows you. Jimmy knows you. Even my mother knows you, although she thinks your name is Charlie."

Shaw smiled. Kate had successfully lightened the mood in the room.

"I'll speak to Reverend Gilreath about this, okay?"

Shaw nodded.

The spell between them had been broken again. It was just as well. Kate wasn't emotionally prepared for things to go further than they already had, and she wasn't sure she could be trusted to stop things once they started in earnest. She seemed to have very little self-control where Shaw was concerned.

Talking about her mother had definitely darkened Shaw's mood.

"What can I do to make you feel better?" Kate reached for Shaw's hand.

"You mean, besides taking me to bed?" Shaw smiled playfully.

"Yes, besides that." Kate wasn't ready for that step just yet.

"Want to go for a drive?"

"Sure. Oh, wait, I should call Miriam to make sure she's okay staying at the house for a while. Do you mind if I borrow your phone?"

Shaw nodded and handed Kate the phone after she unlocked the screen.

"Hello?"

"Miriam, it's Kate. I'm calling from Shaw's phone."

"I guess she was happy you stopped by to say hello then," Miriam teased her.

"Yeah…Listen, are you all right staying over there if I go for a drive?"

"Of course. Take your time."

"Great, thanks." She was about to end the call when she heard Miriam say something.

"Hey, Kate…"

"Yes?"

"Have some fun."

Typical big sister, always giving advice.

"I will. Thanks." Kate handed the phone to Shaw after she clicked off. "Maybe you should save that number in your contacts. You know, in case of emergencies."

"Touché." Shaw grinned.

CHAPTER SIXTEEN

Shaw glanced at Kate in the passenger seat. Kate had twisted her hair and was holding it with her hand. Wisps swirled around her face in the open air Jeep.

"This might help with the wind." Shaw offered her baseball cap to Kate. The wind didn't bother Shaw. In fact, getting windblown made her short hair seem as if it had body.

"Thanks." Kate pulled her hair into a ponytail through the opening at the back of Shaw's cap. She had to adjust it a little to fit.

Shaw decided Kate looked adorable wearing her hat. Hell, Kate just plain looked adorable pretty much every time Shaw had seen her. Kate had an effortless natural beauty.

"My hat looks good on you."

"Does it?"

"Yeah, it does." It was hard to believe that less than fifteen minutes ago they'd been wrapped in each other's arms kissing. And possibly about to do even more than that if her stupid cell phone hadn't rung and ruined the mood. Maybe that was a good thing. She didn't want to get carried away until she was absolutely sure that's what Kate wanted.

Shaw returned her focus to the road. The path her thoughts had taken surprised her. She was genuinely more interested in what Kate wanted than what she wanted. This was virgin territory. Usually if she knew a woman was attracted to her she'd just go for it. It wasn't her job to promise anything more than she was willing to offer in that moment. Unless she said otherwise, which up to this point, she hadn't. Her priority had always been autonomy; the freedom to leave or stay was her choice and no one else's. It was the other person's responsibility to take care of themselves.

But that approach seemed callous where Kate was concerned. For some reason she felt responsible for Kate's happiness. Maybe it was because she'd known her since they were kids. Maybe it was because of Miriam. Maybe it was because what Jimmy had said was true, that Kate was special. She felt protective and that was a new sensation.

Shaw mulled that over. She tried that emotion on for size. She moved around in it and decided she liked the fit.

"So, where are we going?" Kate was watching her and she was very glad that Kate had no idea what she'd been thinking just now.

"I wanted to see Addie Miller again. I was thinking she might be more receptive if you were with me."

"What makes you think that?"

"Just a gut feeling I have." Shaw was pretty sure Kate had the ability to charm paint right off the wall. That theory was about to be tested.

"Hmm, I'm flattered...I think."

"You should be."

After another ten minutes, they turned onto the dirt road that lead to the Miller place. Once they'd parked Kate removed the hat and ran her fingers through her hair. The breeze captured it and it swirled around her face. Damn, Kate was beautiful. For an instant, Shaw almost forgot why they'd come. But the familiar bang of the screen door jolted her from her trance.

"Are you lost?" Addie stood on the porch with her arms crossed in a defiant pose.

"Hi, Miss Addie, I'm Kate Elkins. Maybe you know my momma, Edith?" Kate was the embodiment of Southern diplomatic perfection as she put her hands in her back pockets and slowly walked toward the porch. She'd exaggerated her usual sweet melodic drawl and it seemed to be working. Apparently, even the surly Addie Miller wasn't immune to Kate's charms.

"Yeah, I know your momma. How is she?" Addie's demeanor seemed to soften as Kate approached the porch. Shaw hung back, giving Kate room to work her magic.

"She's had a stroke, but she's better now. She just has a hard time sometimes remembering things."

"I'm sorry to hear that. Miss Edith is a fine woman."

"Thank you. I think so. I'm staying with her for a little while."

"That's good of you." Addie looked around Kate at Shaw. "You can come on up here. I ain't gonna bite."

Shaw wasn't so sure about that, but she approached the porch anyway.

"Can I offer you some iced tea?"

"Thank you, I'd love some." Kate smiled.

Addie nodded and disappeared into the house. Shaw joined Kate on the porch, but she certainly wasn't going to take a seat until she was invited to do so. She'd been right about Kate. She was pretty sure that if she'd come by herself she'd have never gotten this close.

"Just relax," Kate whispered.

"Easy for you to say."

Addie pushed through the door carrying a pitcher and three glasses. Shaw held the door open for her.

"Ya'll take a seat." Addie tipped her head in the direction of some rockers at the far end of the long front porch.

"Here, let me help you." Kate took the glasses from Addie and followed her to the chairs.

Addie poured tea for each of them, waited for them to sit, and then took a seat herself. Shaw sampled the tea. It was sweet and nicely chilled.

"I suppose you want to hear more about Charlie." Addie's tone was matter-of-fact as if she was giving a news report. This surprised Shaw since the last time she'd seen her she was ready to take Shaw's head off with a shotgun just for asking.

"If you don't mind talking with us about it." Kate took a sip of tea. "Momma has been remembering things from a long time ago. I think a stroke sometimes causes that."

Addie nodded as if she knew exactly what Kate was talking about.

"Momma has been talking about Charlie lately, and I was hoping you could tell us something about him. That might help me understand what memory my mother is having. I think Charlie must have been friends with Shaw's mother, Iris, too."

At the mention of Iris's name, Addie frowned and looked in Shaw's direction. She tried to make herself as small as possible, but there was no escaping Addie's glare.

"Your momma, Miss Edith, she was always good to me and Charlie when we were all a lot younger. Your daddy too. He was a good man. I was sorry to hear of his passing. Not enough kind folks in the world these days."

"I agree with you about that." Kate rocked back and forth in her chair.

Shaw couldn't believe the change in Addie. It was almost as if she wanted to talk, needed to talk. Shaw sat quietly and listened. She was afraid to speak for fear of sidetracking Addie into wrath like before.

"I teach first grade now and it's hard to instruct children about how to become good adults when right now it seems that the worst traits receive all the rewards. Everything that currently makes the world run and the men in charge of it directly contradicts what we teach children about what's morally right. Empathy, sharing, forgiveness, charity are all traits seen as weakness by those in power."

"Girl, you should find yourself a pulpit. You're speaking the truth."

Kate laughed. "Sorry, I do tend to get up on my soapbox from time to time."

"Ain't nothin' wrong with that." Addie clearly approved of Kate's opinion.

Shaw was a little bit in awe of Kate. Her students must all fall in love with her and hang on her every word. Shaw couldn't imagine what it would be like to have Kate give you your start in life. She could barely remember first grade, except that she'd gone to two different schools in two different states that year.

"I hope we're not keeping you from something." Kate was probably trying to offer Addie an out in case she didn't want to talk further. Shaw hoped Addie wouldn't take it.

"No, I was just doing some sewing. It'll keep." Addie took a swig of tea and studied Shaw.

She tried to meet Addie's scrutiny with good eye contact, but without any sort of challenge. Staying within Addie's good graces was like walking a tightrope when you had poor balance.

"Charlie got into some trouble with the sheriff. That's how it started." Addie was facing Shaw, but her eyes seemed unfocused. "Him and the Crawford boys set off some fireworks near those cabins at the lake and one of them cabins burned down. That was willful destruction of federal property, at least that's what them deputies with the sheriff's office said when they hauled all of 'em off to the county lockup." Addie took another sip of tea. "Willful destruction, my ass. They were just stupid teenagers. It was an accident."

"How long did they have to stay in jail?" Kate prompted Addie for more. Shaw was on the edge of her seat but was afraid to chime in with her own questions.

"The Crawford boys got out the same night. Their daddy paid bail for them. My daddy thought children should suffer the consequences of their actions. He left Charlie sittin' down there for a week until they went before the judge. I don't know exactly what happened. I was there, but I was younger and I didn't understand all the legal talk, but in the end, the Crawford boys got off with community service under their father's supervision. Charlie was eighteen at the time so he was given a choice. Daddy wasn't willing to help him none, so his choice was that he could do jail time for some months or join the army."

"Why wouldn't your father help him, if you don't mind me asking?" There was no judgment in the question. Kate seemed to genuinely care about the answer.

"Daddy thought Charlie was soft and he believed either jail or the army would toughen him up. See, Charlie liked to create things. He was very artistic, and my daddy never understood that."

Nausea washed over Shaw. She lurched from her chair and stumbled down the uneven porch steps. She strode to the edge of yard and bent over with her hands on her knees. Luckily, she didn't throw up, although she'd been sure she was going to seconds earlier.

Footsteps approached. Shaw figured Kate had come to her aid. But it wasn't Kate that stood beside her. Duct tape on the toes of her shoes gave Addie away. Shaw gave her a sideways glance ready at a moment's notice to move out of her way should she reach for her. Addie regarded her with an emotionless expression, her arms crossed in front of her.

"You're like him aren't you?"

"What do you mean?" Shaw straightened and took a step away from Addie. She took a deep breath and tried by force of will to get her stomach to settle.

"You like to create things the same as Charlie."

"Yes, I do. Or I used to." She glanced back at Kate still seated on the porch.

"Hmm, you look like him too."

"Do I?"

"Yeah." Addie studied Shaw then turned to walk back toward the house. She took a few steps then turned. "You tell Iris there's nothing here for her."

"My mother is dead."

That news seemed to surprise Addie. She hesitated. Then, without another word, she walked up onto the porch. She said something to Kate that Shaw couldn't hear and then went inside. Kate waited a few seconds and then joined her at the edge of the yard.

"Are you okay?" Kate touched Shaw's arm.

"I'm fine." But she didn't feel fine and she was sure Kate could tell that she wasn't.

"Let's get out of here."

Shaw nodded. She was shaken and feeling off balance.

"Why don't you let me drive? We can go into Hendersonville and get some lunch." Kate must have sensed she wasn't feeling herself.

"That sounds good. Thank you." Shaw handed Kate the keys and climbed into the passenger seat. As they pulled away, she glanced back at the house. Addie was standing at the front window watching them.

Shaw was quiet the entire half-hour drive into Hendersonville. Every other time Kate looked over Shaw's eyes were closed and she kept clenching her jaw muscle. It was as if she were carrying on some sort of internal argument.

They reached the edge of downtown and Kate considered options for lunch spots.

"Does pizza sound okay?"

"Sure. Whatever you like will work for me." Shaw gave Kate a weak smile.

West First Pizza was a bright, inviting space half a block off Main. It had a warm contemporary atmosphere, with metalwork all around a raised counter with tall stools. Kate angled toward a corner table at the back. She looked over her shoulder to make sure Shaw was following.

"Are you sure you're okay?"

"I'm fine. You don't need to worry about me."

But Kate was worried about Shaw, and at this moment she looked everything but fine.

A waitress interrupted them with two glasses of water and Kate ordered food for them.

"I'm sorry. I didn't mean for that to sound the way it did." Shaw leaned forward and covered her face with her hands. Then she briskly ran her fingers through her hair a couple of times before she settled back in her chair.

"It's all right."

"You know, I always wanted to know my father."

Kate sat quietly allowing Shaw to continue.

"As a kid I imagined that he was possibly a pilot. That he traveled a lot and that's why he couldn't have a family." Shaw took a long draw of her water. "And now it turns out he was here all along. He was right here and I never got to meet him."

Shaw was looking down as she pulled at the frayed edge of her napkin.

"He wasn't actually here, though was he?"

"You know what I mean." Shaw's words were edged with frustration.

"I know, I'm sorry." Kate wasn't sure what she could possibly say that would offer Shaw some comfort. "What do you need, Shaw?"

Shaw met her gaze with penetrating intensity. It was as if Shaw had reached across the table and touched her. The look Shaw gave her pinned her to her chair. Her breath caught in her throat.

"I don't know what I need."

Kate had no idea what that felt like. She knew what she needed. What she didn't know was how to get it.

"It's like his absence was a physical presence in our lives and I never understood why."

Kate reached for Shaw's hand just as a young woman delivered their pizza. She withdrew her hand as the waitress settled the pie in the center of the table. Kate served them each a slice.

"What did Addie say to you when you were standing in front of the house?" Kate had been curious but didn't want to ask while they were in the car. The wind noise made it hard to talk about anything serious.

"She asked me if I like to create things like Charlie. She said I looked like him. And then she said for me to tell my mother that there was nothing there for her." Shaw leaned back in her chair. "I told her my mother was dead."

"You do like to create things, don't you?"

"I used to."

"Wasn't that what you were doing earlier today when I stopped by?" An image of Shaw in welding gear flashed through Kate's mind and her body instantly warmed.

"I majored in art, but my life ended up taking a different path. It's hard to make a decent living doing sculpture and I had student loans to pay off. I was luckier than most because I did get grant money, you know, because at the time I was living on my own, but when I got the chance to work with Raisa at Red Rock I took it."

So that was who Raisa was. They worked together. One question answered. Kate relaxed a little. She loved that she was finally getting a glimpse into Shaw's world and she wanted her to keep talking.

"You must like what you do though. You get to travel. I would love to travel more."

"I used to like what I do. I've been feeling burned out, or restless, or something…I don't really know what's going on with me." Shaw fidgeted in her chair and glanced toward the door. "Should we be getting you back to your mother's place?"

"Oh, I guess so. Silly me, I lost track of time." Kate looked down, folded her napkin, and set it on the table.

Shaw heard a twinge of something in Kate's voice and felt like a jerk. She'd obviously made Kate feel as if she was restless with her, which wasn't the case at all, but at the moment Shaw felt like crawling out of her own skin. She needed to be alone to sort through everything she'd heard from Addie, and she knew she was terrible company right now. There was no reason to drag Kate down with her. She reached across the table for Kate's hand.

"Hey, this is all my stuff. This has nothing to do with you." Kate nodded, but Shaw felt like she hadn't made Kate feel any better.

Kate searched the area around her chair as if she'd lost something. "Oh, no, I just realized I left my purse at home. I don't have any cash. I'm sorry, I didn't even think of it when I drove us here for lunch."

"Don't worry about it. I've got this. After how you just handled Addie for me I owe you at least a month's worth of lunches. If you ever decided to have a second career I think it should be in diplomacy." That made Kate smile. Shaw was relieved that she'd brought the sparkle back to Kate's eyes. "Seriously, thank you. Addie would never have talked to me the way she did if you hadn't been there."

"Any time, Shaw. I was happy to be there with you."

Shaw got the check and they were standing on the sidewalk near the Jeep when someone called Kate's name. A blond woman with a child in tow waved from a half a block away. The woman hugged Kate with one arm while holding the child's hand with the other.

"Emily, this is Shaw. Shaw, this is Emily."

"Nice to meet you." Shaw extended her hand.

"Emily and I teach together."

"Pleasure to meet you, Shaw. Did y'all just eat at the pizza place?"

"We did. It was good," said Kate.

"Dillon and I were on our way to the market when I saw you." Dillon looked to be about five or six. He stood in front of his mother as she absently swept her fingers through his tousled blond hair.

"Are you enjoying summer so far, Dillon?" Kate bent down a little to speak to him directly. He nodded but didn't say anything.

"Well, we'll let y'all get going. Nice to meet you, Shaw."

"You too." Shaw started to walk away, but she caught Emily out of the corner of her eye as she mouthed the words *call me* to Kate.

"Stop by the house and say hello to Momma sometime." Kate waved as she climbed into the Jeep.

"We will." Emily waved back.

Shaw cranked the car and turned on Main heading back toward Cooper's Creek.

"Emily seemed nice."

"Yeah, she's probably my closest friend." Kate put on Shaw's hat again to tame her hair in the wind. "We don't get as much time together now that she has kids, but we've managed to stay close." There was a wistful air in Kate's manner. As if she wanted to add something to that statement.

"Were you going to say something else?"

"Just that, well, I really want to have kids. But it doesn't look like that's going to happen anytime soon."

"Really? You want kids?"

"You don't?"

"I suppose I never really considered it." That was the truth. She'd never felt the biological imperative to have kids, and since she hadn't been in a relationship serious enough to reach that point, the subject simply never came up. She certainly wouldn't have considered having a child by herself.

"You never imagined yourself with a family?"

Kate was giving her a look that suggested she should have imagined it, but she honestly hadn't.

"I think it would have been hard for me to visualize something that I didn't experience myself. You know what I mean?"

Kate nodded, but she looked away as if she were upset. Shaw wasn't sure what she'd said that could possibly have been hurtful.

"I think it's great when other people have kids. I'm not against children or procreation in general." Hmm, that didn't sound right, and the expression on Kate's face seemed to darken further. Shaw was digging a hole that she didn't know how to climb out of.

Miriam greeted them from the porch when they arrived at the house.

"Shaw Daily, I haven't seen you in years, but I'd recognize you anywhere."

Miriam hugged Shaw before she even got on the porch. It wasn't one of those straight girl A-frame sorority hugs either. Miriam gave Shaw full body contact and held on to her for several seconds longer than was necessary. Miriam looked a little older and carried a few more pounds than the last time Shaw had seen her, but she looked terrific, and happy.

"Miriam, it's great to see you."

She stood awkwardly upon her release from Miriam's embrace. Kate's mood still seemed oddly downcast. Shaw was sure it was her fault, but for the life of her she couldn't figure out what she'd said. Maybe now that they were back at the house Kate was worried about her mother.

"Did you two have a nice drive?" Miriam stood with her hands on her hips and looked from Shaw to Kate and then back to Shaw.

"Yes, it was nice." Kate was clearly giving a one-star rating to their afternoon out. That was disappointing.

"Well, I'll let you get on with the rest of your day." Shaw wasn't going to stand around if Kate was ready for her to leave, which plainly she was. "Thanks again for riding over to Addie's with me, Kate."

"Sure." Kate crossed her arms in front of her chest. "Thanks for lunch."

"Good to see you, Miriam." Shaw gave them both a thin smile and climbed back into the Jeep. She waved as she did a three-point turn to head back down the long drive.

Kate watched the taillights disappear beyond the crest of the hill. The afternoon had started off with such promise only to go down in flames on the drive home.

"What was that about?"

Kate realized Miriam was looking at her.

"What do you mean?"

"You were out for the afternoon with your big crush and just now you acted as if she couldn't leave fast enough for your liking."

"It'll never work with us, Miriam. We're too different." Kate felt sick to her stomach. She turned and went into the house to look for a drink to settle her stomach. She popped the top on a bottled 7 Up and took a long drink. Then she slumped onto a stool near the island bar in the kitchen.

"You know that after one afternoon out?" Miriam leaned against the counter across from her.

"She doesn't want kids. She doesn't want a family. She's never even thought about it in the abstract."

"Kate." Miriam gave her a stern look.

"What?"

"Don't you think you're making an awful big leap here?"

"How so?"

"Did she say she never wanted to have kids?"

"No, but she did say she'd never thought about it."

Miriam glared at her in her usual *I know better than you* big sisterly way.

"I know what you're going to say, Miriam. And I'm *not* overthinking this. Some things are core values that can't be overlooked. This is one of them. I want a family."

"I just don't want you to make an irrevocable decision before you even give this a chance. You two haven't even had a real date. Now you've had one hypothetical discussion about having children and you've decided a relationship will never work. Shaw probably has no idea what you were even talking about."

"Not to mention that Shaw lives in California and I live here. And I have Momma to think of."

"Don't hide behind geography or Momma. If you wanted to be with Shaw we would figure out a way to make it work."

"How?" Kate felt a knot rising in her throat and swallowed it down. She didn't want to cry in front of Miriam. She didn't want to let on how invested she already was in whether things could work out with Shaw or not. "You have Greg and the kids. You can't be here. And I want Momma to be able to stay at home."

"What are you girls going on about out here?" Her mother shuffled into the room from the back of the house. Her hip must have been bothering her today because she was using her walker, which she rarely did.

"Nothing, Momma." Kate took another sip of her soda.

"We're just solving all the world's problems."

"I'm glad someone is." Her mother moved slowly to the living room, and Miriam helped her sink into her favorite floral print recliner.

"Well, I need to get back to the house. I'm sure the girls have run Greg ragged while I've been gone. I'll see ya later, Momma." Miriam kissed her mother on the cheek.

"Bye, sweetie, you hug those girls for me."

"I will, Momma." Miriam put her arm around Kate's shoulders and squeezed. "Think about what I said, Sis." Miriam pressed a kiss into her hair.

Kate nodded to Miriam as she left. Tears gathered at the edge of her lashes. Maybe a good cry would make her feel better.

"Momma, I'm gonna go lie down in my room for a minute." She tried to keep her voice steady until she could get to the privacy of her own room.

Kate lay on her side on the bed. She hugged a pillow to her chest, pulled her knees up, and cried. The down pillow absorbed her sobs. She didn't want her mother to hear her. Why was she so stubborn? Why did she cling to this idea she had for her life when everything seemed to conspire against it? Maybe she was never meant to have a family or children. Even if that were true she didn't think it was within her power to let the dream go. She rolled onto her back and looked up at the ceiling. She sighed and squeezed her eyes shut. One last tear slid down her cheek and was lost on her pillow.

Chapter Seventeen

Restless and in need of something constructive to do with her hands, Shaw returned to the shop to finish her project she'd started before Kate had arrived. The sun was almost gone by the time she finished. She'd constructed a steel podium for the old porcelain basin. She carried the metal stand to the house and set it down in the grass several yards from the porch. Then she carefully fit the basin onto the steel supports. She trotted into the house for a pitcher of water and filled the basin.

She stepped back a few feet to admire her handiwork, a shabby chic birdbath. The water in the basin caught the red orange of the setting sun. Shaw tapped the surface of the water and watched bands of orange ripple out from the center.

There were still two beers left in the fridge when she checked. She returned to the porch with one of them. She leaned the chair back against the wall and propped her booted foot up on the railing. She'd changed out of her shorts before heading to the shop even though the air temp was still warm. Welding required long sleeves, long pants, and boots. Natural fabrics were the best. In case of sparks, natural fibers didn't melt to your skin. That was always a bonus.

She sipped the beer and tried to decide if she was hungry since she hadn't eaten since lunch. Thinking of lunch made her think of Kate. What had she said to upset Kate? Was it the kid thing? That was the last thing they'd talked about before she dropped Kate off. Shaw tried to remember exactly what she'd said. Nothing stood out to her, but something had definitely altered Kate's mood.

Maybe she should give Kate a call and apologize. But how could she apologize when she wasn't even sure what she'd done? Forget it. She needed another shower before she could even think about food.

Under the stream of hot water, Shaw examined old wounds. Not the internal ones, those were much deeper. The burns she'd gotten in her college years when she was just learning to use the torch. They weren't bad and they didn't even show when she wore long sleeved shirts. If anyone noticed them they might just think they were birthmarks. Small, raised red marks on the inside of her left wrist.

She traced the raised marks with her thumb. She closed her eyes and let the water rain down on her. After she'd toweled off, she pulled on sweats and a T-shirt and stretched out on the sofa facing the living room window. The ridgeline was nothing more than a pink thread zigzagging across the near dark sky. She folded her arm behind her head and waited for the house to darken as she watched the pink line fade to gray and then disappear.

She was suspended in warmth and darkness. Floating. The muscles in Shaw's arms and shoulders relaxed. Then space opened up. Everything dropped away. She was in a free fall. Shaw lurched, flailed her arms, and banged her arm on the edge of the coffee table.

Her phone vibrated across the table surface.

The dream again. Her heart thundered in her chest as if she'd just sprinted a mile. She rubbed sleep from her eyes and reached for her phone. She checked the incoming call. It was Kate.

"Hello?"

"Uh-oh, you sound sleepy. I hope I didn't wake you up." Kate sounded normal, not like before.

"I dozed off on the couch, but I wasn't really asleep." Shaw hesitated. "I um, I thought about giving you a call earlier."

"You did?"

"Yeah, I felt like maybe I upset you."

"You didn't. I think I was just tired."

Shaw wasn't convinced.

"Well, I'm glad you called. You sound better now."

"I am. I'm sorry about earlier. It wasn't your fault."

Hmm, so there was more to the story than Kate was willing to give her.

"I'm glad. I would never want to hurt you, Kate."

There was silence on the other end.

"Kate?"

"Yes, sorry, I'm here." Kate cleared her throat. "Listen, I know we didn't really get a chance to talk about this earlier, but I called Reverend Gilreath about a service for your mother sometime this weekend or next week." Kate paused. "Because I assumed you'd need to get back to California soon."

Shaw was speechless.

"I suggested to him that a simple, small graveside service would be best and that we wouldn't have a wake or food at the church or anything."

"Food?"

"Yes, normally when there's a funeral all the church ladies bring food to the fellowship hall for the family, for after the service. But I thought that might be more attention than you'd want. You might still have to receive a few casseroles at your house once they get wind of what's going on. They'll want to feed you whether you want them to or not. You know, it's in our nature."

"Oh, right."

Kate's sense of humor was back. Shaw suddenly remembered the dish in her fridge that Jimmy's wife had sent over, and her stomach growled.

"Is it okay that I did this for you?" Kate sounded unsure.

"Yes, thank you. It's probably the right thing to do." Shaw wasn't sure she was ready for a funeral and would likely never have gotten around to calling the pastor herself. But it did feel a little weird, and a little personal that Kate had called on her behalf.

"If you've got a pen I'll give you the pastor's number, or you could drive over to the church. He said he'd be in the parsonage most all day tomorrow working on his sermon for Sunday."

"I'll go see him then. It might be simpler to talk in person." Shaw wanted to meet him and see the church. She'd attended vacation Bible school at that church as a child, but unless Reverend Gilreath was a hundred years old, then she'd never met him. He couldn't possibly be the same pastor that she'd met in her childhood.

"Shaw, I found out something else."

"What?"

"There's a plot available next to Charlie Miller."

Shaw sank back against the cushions, the wind completely knocked out of her as if she'd just been punched hard in the gut. She hadn't even thought of where Charlie was buried or had any notion that she could actually go visit his grave.

"I have to give that some thought." Shaw figured there was also a family plot near where her grandparents were buried. Would that be a better choice? She wasn't sure.

"I'd be happy to go with you to see the site if you want me to."

"Thanks, but I should probably give it some thought first." If she did go visit the grave, Shaw thought maybe that was something she should do alone, at least the first time.

"Of course. Just let me know if you change your mind." Kate was quiet on the other end of the phone for a few seconds. "Okay then, I'll let you go."

"Kate?"

"Yes?"

"Thank you." That seemed inadequate, but Shaw didn't know what else to say.

"You're welcome, Shaw."

❖

Kate walked through the house switching off lights.

"Momma, where are you?"

"I'm in here."

Kate found her mother standing in the bathroom with one hand on her walker and one hand on the sink.

"What are you doing? Do you want me to help you with your nightgown?"

"No, I've got it on. I'm just standing here trying to remember if I brushed my teeth."

"Well, you could always brush them again just to be safe."

"I suppose that's true." Her mother applied toothpaste and brushed her teeth.

Then Kate helped her into bed. She climbed up on the other side and crossed her legs, facing her mother.

"Momma, how did you know Daddy was the one?"

"Oh, now, you just know don't you? When you meet the one you know it."

"Yeah, everyone says that, but how exactly?"

"Well, let me see…with me and your daddy it didn't happen all at once. I think he liked me before I liked him. He got my cousin Milton to introduce us at a square dance up at the lake." Her mother adjusted her pillow. "I hadn't noticed your daddy before that, but once I did I couldn't take my eyes off him. We danced and talked and then he asked to walk me home. And that was that."

"You just knew."

"When he talked the sound of his voice made me feel peaceful and excited at the same time. And when he finally held my hand, well then I knew for sure that he was the one for me."

"Do you miss him?"

"Every day." Her mother's eyes glistened. "But he went on before me and maybe that's how it had to happen."

Her mother looked tired so Kate kissed her cheek and climbed off the bed. "I'll let you get to sleep, Momma."

"Okay, then. You sleep well, sweetheart."

"Good night."

Kate switched off the kitchen light on the way to her room on the other side of the house. She wondered what Shaw was doing right now. She might be in the shop working on another project, or possibly sleeping, or talking to friends on the West Coast. It would still be early over there. She pulled on a cotton camisole and then shimmied out of her shorts and climbed under the covers.

She'd asked her mother how she'd know she was in love. It all seemed so vague and non-specific. *You just know.* Everyone said that and what did that even mean?

Kate hoped she hadn't made Shaw uncomfortable calling the pastor on her behalf. She'd tried to get Shaw to give her an idea about when she was leaving. Suggesting a timeframe for the funeral didn't reward her with any sort of conclusive answer from Shaw. So she still had no idea how long Shaw was planning to stay. Maybe she should try the direct method and simply come right out and ask her. Kate laughed at herself.

Why was Shaw occupying almost every waking thought she had? And some nighttime thoughts as well.

Did she just know and was afraid to admit it to herself?

Is that why she'd gotten so upset about the discussion of kids?

Kate rolled over and pulled the covers with her. Her mind was spinning, running through all the conversations she'd had with Shaw throughout the day. She was going to have a hard time falling asleep. She reached for her laptop and sat up.

She'd heard back from *Blue Ridge Getaways*. They wanted eight hundred words highlighting some scenic day hikes in the area. Jump Off Rock was the spot she had in mind. It was a granite outcropping that offered a spectacular scenic view of the mountains year-round. If she was going to make the deadline she'd need to go hike the trail in the next couple of days. There were three different trails, and Kate had done two of them, but she should revisit the path to make sure conditions hadn't changed drastically since the last time she was there.

Maybe Shaw would like to go for a day hike. It would do Shaw some good to get out into the trees. Kate found the woods nurturing, soothing even. She wanted to share that with Shaw. Maybe some outdoor time would help Shaw sort out whatever was troubling her.

Kate closed her laptop and sank under the covers again. She had a plan. She hoped that would help her settle into sleep.

CHAPTER EIGHTEEN

S haw woke up to rain the next morning. By ten o'clock, she had cabin fever and decided to drive over to the general store. Her cap and jacket were good and wet just from crossing the road. With no doors, the wind drove rain sideways into the open cockpit.

She'd wanted another cup of coffee but didn't feel like drinking it alone in her kitchen. She probably could have asked Kate to come over, but she'd decided to go see if she could catch the pastor at the church while it was too wet to do anything outside.

Jimmy was supposed to stop by later to discuss a project, but that wouldn't be until well after lunch.

"Edwina, can I use one of these mugs or was I supposed to bring my own?" Edwina was at the register on the other side of the store.

Shaw studied a rack attached to the wall with an assortment of well-worn coffee mugs of various sizes, colors, and designs. Directly over the coffee cup rack was a bobcat, one of several deceased animals victimized by taxidermy on display in the general store. None of the others were quite as threatening. And for a moment, Shaw wondered if Edwina had shot them all herself. She appeared to be capable of such a thing. There was a barn owl and two deer. This particular bobcat was mounted on the wall right above the coffee pot scowling down as if he were about to attack the next person who dared reach for caffeine.

Shaw couldn't help wondering if the glassy-eyed feline encouraged caffeine addiction or discouraged it.

"You can pick whichever one you want, just make sure you return it. That's how it works."

"Okay." Shaw reached for a mug featuring a frazzled housewife that read *I child-proofed my house but they still got in*, because the quote made her smile, but at the last minute changed her mind and selected one that featured Bigfoot. A cup of coffee was fifty cents, with one free refill. She expected it to be worth a quarter, but she was pleasantly surprised.

This was a good cup of coffee. She took a few sips and then topped it off again.

There were faded photos of locals framed and hanging at the back of the store near the wood stove. Shaw sipped her coffee and leaned in to study the details of each shot. One of the older photos dated back to at least the forties. It featured four men holding rifles and jugs of moonshine.

"What are you up to over on the hill?" Edwina yelled from the front of the store.

"Nothing much." Shaw strolled to the counter and handed a dollar to Edwina. "I made a birdbath."

"Do tell."

Shaw nodded. Edwina didn't seem very impressed.

"Where are you off to in such a hurry?"

Edwina clearly had a gift for sarcasm.

"I'm going up to the church to talk to the pastor."

"You gonna get you some religion?"

"I doubt it."

"Good on ya. Nothin' good ever comes of it no how." The TV was on near Edwina's elbow. She was half watching some talk show and half talking to Shaw. She handed Shaw her change without looking at her.

There were all sorts of odds and ends stacked near the counter. Bottle openers shaped like cowboy boots, air fresheners with prancing white-tailed deer, cigarette lighters featuring different NASCAR drivers, and small Confederate flags wrapped in plastic. Shaw picked up one of the flags and flipped it over. She couldn't help smiling.

"Edwina, these flags are made in China."

"Yeah, ironic isn't it."

"Why do you even carry these? I thought we were past all that."

"We are, but rednecks and tourists love them things so I always keep a few around." Edwina reached for some chips. Edwina clearly valued commerce over politics. "You want to hear a good story, ask the pastor about the ruckus he caused trying to deflag the pickup trucks of some local good ole boys."

"I'll try and remember to ask." Shaw finished her coffee. "What should I do with this?" She held the empty mug up in front of Edwina.

"Set it in the tray there and I'll wash it with the others later."

"Have a good day then."

"You do the same." Edwina only glanced briefly from her show to acknowledge that Shaw was leaving.

The church was two miles from the intersection in front of the general store. There was only one car in the small parking lot next to the church when she arrived. She assumed that belonged to the pastor. The church was a simple red brick building with a white steeple at the front. The entryway was no larger than a coat closet that you passed through as you headed into the narrow sanctuary lined on either side of a carpeted aisle with straight-backed wooden pews. No one was inside so Shaw backtracked and took the stairs down to the fellowship hall, which was one large room on the floor beneath the sanctuary. The fellowship hall was partially underground as it was sunk into the hillside next to the cemetery.

"Hello?" Shaw saw movement in one of the small Sunday school rooms off the main room.

"Hello. Can I help you with something?" A man, probably in his sixties, peeked out at her from the smaller room. He had thinning gray hair and the girth of a man who ate at a lot of church dinners. He looked well fed and had a jovial air about him. He was dressed in dark dress pants and a white oxford shirt.

"Are you Reverend Gilreath?"

"I am."

"I'm Shaw Daily. I think Kate Elkins spoke to you over the phone about arranging a small service for my mother." He extended his hand to her and she took it. She was just a wee bit curious how she'd be received by a Baptist minister, looking the way she did, straight out of San Francisco and gay to boot. But he didn't seem fazed at all. Or if he was, he did an amazing job of covering it up.

"Yes, yes, Kate did call me. I'm so sorry to hear of your loss. I didn't really know your mother, but I understand from Kate that she grew up here. Her parents, your grandparents, are buried in the cemetery here I believe."

"That's right. I actually haven't been here since their funeral, but I don't think you were the minister here back then."

"No, I've only been here for the past three years or so. I should be retired by now, but I took on this congregation because they needed someone. It's small, and well, I wasn't quite ready to be retired. But I also can't really keep up with a larger congregation any longer. So, here we are."

Here we are. Shaw hadn't really expected to be here, but here she was.

"Now, what did you have in mind? Why don't we sit down and discuss some details?" He motioned toward a table with folding chairs set around it.

Shaw was wishing now that she'd taken Kate up on the offer to come with her. Because the truth was she didn't have anything in mind.

"My mother was cremated and I brought the urn with me from California. I suppose something simple would be appropriate. I'll be honest with you, I don't really have any idea what that would be."

"Was your mother a religious person?"

"Not particularly. I mean, she grew up attending this church, but I don't remember going to church much with her."

"Why don't we pick a day and time and then I can suggest something for the service itself."

"That sounds good, thank you."

A half hour later, they'd settled on Tuesday of the following week. Shaw still hadn't decided when she'd travel back to the West Coast, but she knew it wouldn't be before Tuesday. He'd asked about the burial location, but Shaw didn't have an answer for him. She wanted a chance to look for Charlie's grave and see where it was in relation to where her grandparents were buried. Apparently, there was a plot for Shaw and her mother that had been set aside by her grandparents. She'd never even known about it.

The rain had mostly stopped when she walked up to the cemetery. A fine mist hung in the air and made the trees and hillsides look smoky gray. Her hat and denim jacket were damp. She adjusted her hat low over her eyes as she searched the headstones. It took her a little while to locate Charles Shaw Miller. The headstone was weathered but readable. It was next to an ancient gnarled dogwood. For some reason, he wasn't buried next to his parents. And he wasn't near Shaw's grandparents either.

"Pappa wanted him over here by himself." Shaw hadn't seen Addie walk up. She didn't know she was there until she spoke. "Sad isn't it? Now it don't even matter. They're all gone. You and me is all that's left."

Shaw looked at her in shocked silence. She'd said *you and me* as if she meant to infer Shaw was family.

"The world is full of words and most of them don't mean much." Addie had been staring at Charlie's grave and now she turned to look at Shaw. And for the first time with Addie, she felt as if she were truly being seen.

"What happened back then?" Shaw wanted so badly to know the truth.

"Your momma was a wild one. No one could keep Iris in check. She was with them boys the night that fire was set." Addie paused as if the story was hard to tell and she felt burdened with the telling of it. "Iris was the one that set the fire."

Shaw waited for more.

"Charlie knew she was pregnant and he didn't want her to get in any trouble. She was gonna be in enough trouble once her daddy found out that they'd been fooling around. So he told the sheriff that he was the one who'd set the fire that night."

"Charlie took the blame for my mother?"

"Iris was pregnant with you. He was trying to protect his girl and his unborn baby. He was doing what any good father would do." Addie's gaze bore into Shaw making it hard to breathe.

Tears came and Shaw was helpless to stop them. She swiped at them with the sleeve of her jacket. "Why didn't anyone ever tell me the truth?"

"Hard to say."

"It was cruel not to tell me." Anger swirled around with grief in Shaw's chest.

"If your grandfather had known Iris was pregnant he probably would have forced them to marry, although he had no love for Charlie. I think he thought our family was low class, white trash, not good enough. That fight goes way back, before my time. My daddy and your granddaddy was never at peace with each other."

Shaw had rebelled against her mother, whom it turned out had rebelled against her parents, all because of something that happened a long time ago between two stubborn old men. After all this time she was finally discovering what had been at the root of her mother's insurmountable sadness. Even as a child she'd always had a sense that was what it was, not anger, but sadness—deep, dark, bottomless grief. She just didn't know until now what her mother was mourning.

Her mother had known Charlie had taken responsibility for her careless crime and then he'd been killed during his term of service. Shaw couldn't imagine how that must have felt, but now some of her mother's behavior made perfect sense. The endless searching. Searching but never finding that one thing that could fill the hole left by Charlie. And by her guilt because of what Charlie had done for her.

Shaw's one remaining question was why her mother never shared the truth with her.

"I wish she'd told me. Why didn't she?" The rain had started again, but neither of them made a move to head for the cover of the church building.

"You might have to forgive her without knowing the answer. I'm guessing she couldn't stand to be here in Cooper's Creek without Charlie, but she wanted you to know your grandparents. On some level she must have wanted you to know the place you come from."

"Why are you being so nice to me?" Shaw wasn't sure she should embrace this new version of Addie. She felt drawn to her but didn't yet trust her.

"You're the only kin I've got left." Addie looked solemn. "You're a lot like Charlie, but I think you might also be a little bit like me."

Addie offered Shaw a thin smile, and for the first time, Shaw really looked at her. Men's trousers, a flannel shirt one size too large, short hair, and what had probably once been a lean athletic frame. Why hadn't she seen it before?

"I never liked boys that way either." Addie bent down and pulled a leafy weed away from Charlie's headstone. "You should bring your friend out to the house. I've got something I want to show you."

Shaw watched in stunned silence as Addie turned toward the parking lot. She'd only gone a few feet when she looked back. "You should bury Iris next to Charlie. It's the right thing to do. They've been apart long enough."

"Addie?"

"Yeah?"

"Thank you."

"Just remember, Shaw, forgiveness is for the one who offers it."

She watched Addie stride to an old beat up seventies era Ford truck and drive away. She turned back to the grassy spot next to Charlie's grave. The rain was soft as a feather, misting all around, making the green grass even greener.

Shaw took a deep breath and closed her eyes. She realized she felt sorrowful empathy for her mother finally. And forgiveness was the next step. She let out a long sigh, and with the exhaled breath, years of holding herself in. Standing in the rain by her father's grave, she forgave her mother.

She let go of it.

And it dropped away.

She was above it, looking down.

She felt set free, as light as air. But letting go of it meant she didn't know who she was any more. The absence had been filled and so many questions answered. Time seemed suddenly expansive and intimate in the same instant.

There was still time to make things right.

Chapter Nineteen

Kate was at the sink doing dishes. Movement caught her eye. She looked up to see the shadowy outline of a figure standing in the rain. She squinted and wiped the steam from the hot dishwater off the window. Shaw was standing in the front yard. What in the world was she doing?

She dried her hands and went outside. There was an umbrella by the door. She grabbed it and walked over to where Shaw was standing.

"Shaw, what are you doing?"

"I wanted to see you."

"You scared me. Why didn't you come to the house? You're just standing here in the rain." There was something odd about Shaw. When Kate had joined her just now, she'd been smiling and looking up directly into the falling rain with her eyes shut. Her clothing was soaking wet. "Please come in." She looped her arm through Shaw's and tugged her through the door.

"Where's your mom?"

"In her room watching TV." It was late afternoon, just past dinnertime, although her mother had mentioned she wasn't hungry, Kate had made her some soup anyway and she'd gone to lie down and watch a show right after.

The laundry room was just off the kitchen. Kate led Shaw in and helped her out of her denim jacket, darkened and heavy from the rain.

"Shaw, how long have you been out in this weather? You're soaked through."

"A while." Shaw just kept smiling at her.

"Are you drunk?"

"Nope." Shaw's limbs were limp as a rag doll's as Kate pulled her arms free from her jacket. The saturated T-shirt was next.

"Are you sure about that?"

"Okay, maybe I have a teeny weeny little buzz." Shaw held her index finger and thumb about a quarter inch apart. "Jimmy stopped by and brought some of my favorite bourbon."

"And then you drove over here?"

"I could have walked but it was raining."

"So you drove over here and stood in the rain." Kate bit her bottom lip to keep from laughing. Shaw was tipsy and adorable and affectionate. She kept trying to kiss Kate.

Shaw wasn't wearing anything under her shirt, and Kate tried not to stare at the well-defined torso and small breasts that greeted her view. The dryer had shut off moments earlier, and the towels inside were still warm. She pulled one free from the wad of clean laundry and wrapped it around Shaw's shoulders because she'd started to shiver.

Kate held Shaw's face in her hands.

"You feel hot. Are you getting a fever?"

"I don't think so, but I do feel cold all of a sudden."

"Take these off too, they're soaking." Kate tugged at the waist of her jeans. They were button fly, and after she freed the third button, they slid down from their own waterlogged weight. Shaw kicked her shoes off and stepped out of her jeans that were in a heap around her ankles. She was wearing boys Y-front briefs now and nothing else, except the towel around her shoulders. "Come lie down for a minute and warm up." She briskly rubbed Shaw's arms through the towel.

"Hey…" Shaw caught Kate around the waist and drew her inside the towel against her bare chest. Kate instinctively resisted because she worried that Shaw was under the influence. "Hey, don't fight me." Shaw coaxed her as she held Kate firmly.

"Shaw, I don't want—"

Her words were swallowed up by Shaw's kiss, passionate, possessive, open, searching, and tasting slightly of bourbon. Shaw's lips were hot and swollen against her forehead now. Breathless, she relaxed into Shaw as they leaned against the front of the dryer in the tiny space.

She freed herself, took Shaw's hand, and pulled her toward her bedroom and shut the door.

"Get under the covers and warm up." Shaw did as she was told. Kate sat on the bed next to her and stroked her forehead. "What's gotten into you?"

"Everything." Shaw grinned, her eyes were heavy lidded and her hair was damp despite the cap she'd been wearing.

"What were you doing standing in the rain just now?"

"Feeling things." Shaw brought Kate's fingers to her lips and kissed them. "Lie down with me. We don't have to do anything but cuddle."

"You warm up and I'll come join you in a minute." Something had shifted with Shaw, something more than a few shots of bourbon, and Kate didn't trust herself to get into bed just now. Shaw suddenly seemed so unguarded and open that it scared Kate.

"Promise."

"I promise." She leaned over and kissed Shaw's cheek. Then she went back to the laundry room and threw Shaw's wet things in the dryer. She braced her arms against the dryer and took several deep breaths. What the hell just happened? She'd instinctively helped Shaw out of her clothes and then tucked her into her bed. Kate's subconscious clearly had issues with firm boundaries.

She finished the dishes and went to her mother's room. Her mother was asleep so she turned the TV off, then the living room light. It was probably only eight o'clock, but the storm had darkened the sky so that it seemed later. She peeked in her room. Shaw didn't stir. She was asleep. That was probably for the best. Whatever Shaw had been up to she'd apparently exhausted herself.

Kate undressed quietly and slipped into a cotton T-shirt before she got into bed. She was careful not to wake Shaw. For several minutes, she propped up on her elbow and watched Shaw sleep. Kate brushed a clump of errant dark hair off Shaw's forehead lightly with her fingertips. Then she snuggled close to Shaw, resting her cheek on Shaw's shoulder.

In the last half hour, the storm had strengthened. Wind whistled around the eaves of the house and rain pelted the window. Beside her, Shaw's breathing was slow and the warmth of her body made Kate relax.

❖

Shaw brushed her fingers across her stomach and realized Kate's hand rested there. She blinked several times trying to get her brain to wake up. It took several seconds for her to reconstruct the events that led her into Kate's bed. And where were her clothes? Oh yeah, the laundry room. Kate was snuggled tightly against her, and every nerve receptor in Shaw's body was buzzing from the warm, soft skin on skin contact. Kate's palm rested on Shaw's stomach, and her thigh was partially covered by Kate's.

Shaw was surprised her head wasn't pounding from the bourbon. That would no doubt come with the sunrise. At the moment, she still had the pleasant remnants of a relaxing buzz.

She covered Kate's hand with hers and thought of guiding Kate's fingers to places farther south. Maybe she should wake Kate up. But she was sleeping so adorably on Shaw's shoulder that she fought the urge and instead rotated her head just enough to press her lips against Kate's hair. Kate moaned softly and stroked Shaw's stomach with her hand. *No, don't do that.* If Kate started moving around, Shaw knew her libido would kick into high gear. It was already idling pretty fast. She tried to redirect her thoughts, but that was impossible. Maybe she should try to roll over, away from Kate. She could sneak out and go back to her house, but she wasn't sure where her clothes were.

Kate's hand slid up to the center of her chest and then drifted over her extremely sensitive nipple. Kate stirred, shifted her leg, tilted her chin up, and kissed Shaw. She wasn't sure if Kate was dreaming. Even so, she kissed her back.

"Kate, are you awake?" she whispered.

Kate's response was more of a moan than a conclusive answer. Shaw wasn't sure what to do. She knew what she wanted to do, but she wasn't sure that was the right thing to do. Kate's fingers teased at the waist of her briefs and then slipped inside. The light touch of Kate's fingertips at the lowest part of her stomach tipped Shaw over the edge. She squeezed her eyes shut and clenched her fist. Was Kate going to make love to her in her sleep? This must be some kind of dream she was having.

When she opened her eyes she realized Kate was no longer asleep. Her lids were heavy, but they were open. Kate withdrew her fingers from their downward journey as if she'd suddenly realized what she was doing. She pinned Shaw to the bed with the most sizzling gaze, which she only broke long enough to pull her T-shirt over her head. Now there was more skin in contact with skin. Kate was partially on top of Shaw, her breasts pressing against Shaw's.

She rolled Kate onto her back. She hovered above her and then slowly, tenderly began to kiss her. She explored the sensitive skin near the base of Kate's ear and then down her neck until she reached her collarbone. When Kate didn't stop her, she took Kate's breast into her mouth and circled Kate's nipple with her tongue. Her nipple came to a hard point and Kate arched against Shaw's mouth.

She slid her hand up the inside of Kate's thigh until her fingers made contact with the damp fabric of her underwear. Kate was so wet. Shaw wanted to pull the fabric aside and touch her, but she knew if she went that far there would be no turning back. Shaw's body was already telling her that she might be at that point.

"Kate." Shaw whispered her name. "I want to make love to you."

Kate's mouth was on hers. She kissed Shaw deeply. Shaw didn't usually wait for permission, but this time she wanted it. She knew she still had enough alcohol in her system that she might not be making good choices and that her defenses, already weakened by her attraction to Kate, might be at an all-time low.

Kate opened her legs for Shaw, and the desire to touch her, fuck her, grew even more powerful.

"Kate, talk to me. I'm on fire here."

"Don't ask me."

"What?"

"Don't ask me what I want right now. Because my head will say no, and the rest of me wants you desperately."

Shaw knew they were reaching some critical point of no return. And now she had doubts.

"Kate, I'm afraid you'll regret this in the morning." Which would make life unbearable for Shaw. The last thing she could handle would be to see disappointment or regret in Kate's eyes. She'd be undone by it.

"Shaw, touch me." Kate pushed her underwear down and off somewhere under the covers. They were about to cross some primal threshold, and Kate was asking Shaw to take the first step.

Her fingertips came into light contact with Kate's arousal. That was it. The last barrier gone between them except Shaw's underwear, which Kate helped remove. She covered Kate with her body and began to caress with her fingers. She felt the sting of Kate's fingernails pressed into her back as she thrust, slowly at first, teasing, stroking, and then thrusting again.

Kate felt as if she was caught up in some fevered dream. Except this was no dream. Shaw was thrusting inside her, sliding her slick center against Kate's thigh, and Kate sensed her climax building swiftly. Shaw's touch was nuanced yet strong as if they'd made love a thousand times and Shaw knew precisely how she wanted to be touched, how she needed to be touched.

She clung to Shaw, rising to meet each thrust. Their movement more frantic now, her need for release more demanding. "Yes, Shaw, I'm going to come, oh God." She pressed her open mouth against Shaw's shoulder. Words were gone. Thought was gone. There was only her desire for more, deeper. "Don't stop."

Her head was back as she gasped through her release and then plummeted over the edge.

She stayed Shaw's forearm with her hand and kissed her deeply.

"Stay there." She didn't want Shaw to pull out as she slipped her hand between them and stroked Shaw. She was close. Kate could sense it.

"Is this okay?" She searched Shaw's face as she sought entrance. When Shaw nodded, she slid inside.

Shaw was so close. She came fast and hard, riding Kate's hand pressed against her thigh. Shaw tightened and she felt Shaw's pounding heart through the tips of her fingers. They were still joined when Shaw collapsed on top of her breathing hard.

Sleep came for her, tangled as she was in the warmth of Shaw's embrace.

CHAPTER TWENTY

Shaw slowly fought her way out of sleep and just as slowly realized where she was. Her head was foggy. She blinked several times to try to get her eyes to sharpen their focus. Pink light filtered around the drapes. The sun was up, but it hadn't been for long. Beside her, Kate stirred.

And then Shaw became fully aware. Oh shit, she was naked in bed with Kate and Kate's elderly mother was somewhere in the house. She'd have launched out of bed except that Kate was still dozing on her shoulder.

"Kate." Shaw stroked Kate's face, sweeping her hair back. "Kate, are you awake?"

"Hmm." Kate stretched, sliding her hand across Shaw's midsection.

That wasn't helping. The warmth of Kate's body pressed against hers was enticing her to linger when every bit of gray matter in her head was sounding an alarm that she should get up and get dressed. She tried to gently extricate her shoulder and arm from beneath Kate. That did it. Kate blinked a few times and then squinted at her in the low, early morning light. Realization seemed to dawn and Kate regarded her with wide eyes.

"We fell asleep. What time is it?" Kate glanced over her shoulder for the clock on the nightstand. The back of her hair was all adorably mussed from their night together. "It's six o'clock. Maybe Momma's not awake yet."

They both stilled and listened for any sound that might be coming from another part of the house.

"I don't hear anything. Maybe you should help me find clothes before we do hear something." Shaw was normally inclined to offer a more romantic morning after, but that was usually when someone wasn't living at home with their parents.

"I promise not to throw you out of bed if she knocks on the door."

"Even still, I'd rather not greet your mother at the breakfast table in my birthday suit." Shaw felt around under the covers at the foot of the bed for her underwear and pulled them on. Kate did the same.

There was enough light in the room for Shaw to see Kate as she stepped from the bed to the closet to retrieve a dressing gown. Kate had a beautiful body. She hadn't really gotten the pleasure of undressing Kate the night before because they'd fallen asleep first and then made love when they were already in bed. As Shaw watched Kate pull her hair over her shoulder and slip the gown over her porcelain shoulders, she felt a little cheated that she hadn't gotten to undress Kate.

"I'll be right back."

Kate slipped out to the laundry room and retrieved Shaw's clothes from the dryer. When she came back to the room, Shaw was propped up on her elbow smiling. The sheet had fallen to her waist, revealing her shoulder, chest, and torso. Kate committed the view to memory. A sudden wave of sensations washed over her, Shaw's hands against her skin, their bodies pressed together, Shaw's mouth on her breast, she was lightheaded and had to close her eyes until it passed.

"Are you okay?" Shaw got up and moved around the bed to where Kate was standing.

Shaw looked delicious wearing only her white Y-front underwear, and Kate had to fight the most overpowering urge to shove Shaw backward onto the bed and make love until neither of them had the strength to stand. She squeezed her eyes shut again in an attempt to tamp down her desire.

"I'm fine. I just…I can't believe we fell asleep and now we're having to sneak you out like we're still teenagers." She chewed her bottom lip as Shaw dressed.

"Don't worry about it. I'm the one who showed up drunk, standing in the rain. You must think I'm insane."

Hardly. Shaw sat at the end of the bed and pulled on her shoes. Then she stood up and, what now? Shaw looked as if she was going to kiss her but hesitated. Well, Kate wasn't waiting for her to figure it out. She tilted her head up and gave Shaw a lingering kiss.

Shaw briskly swept her fingers through her hair as if she was nervous. "I'll call you."

The phrase a woman least wants to hear as her lover makes tracks for the exit. Shaw reached for the door, but at the last minute she turned back and kissed Kate again. She felt Shaw's hands slip inside the dressing gown. Her skin tingled as Shaw swept them up the curve of her back and drew Kate's body to hers. The buttons of Shaw's denim jacket were cold against her flesh. Her lips were close to Kate's ear.

"I want to see you later."

"I want to see you later too." Kate pressed her lips to Shaw's. She tried to give Shaw a show of confidence as she quietly slipped out the front door when all she really wanted to do was cry. She'd given Shaw the one thing she rarely gave to anyone and she had no idea what that meant to Shaw.

Kate wiped at a tear trailing down her cheek as she put a pot of water on to boil for tea. She had to be okay with this. She willed herself to be okay with this. They'd made love. It didn't mean they were getting married. She repeated that silently. Maybe she should write that line in a notebook a hundred times. Maybe then she'd believe it. Sex didn't automatically lead to a relationship. She'd heard this from other people so she knew it was true. She simply didn't want it to be.

It wasn't Shaw's fault that she had to leave the way she did. Kate was the one living with her ailing mother. She was the one who wasn't free to do what she pleased or offer her time freely.

She exhaled slowly and tried to calm down. She and Shaw had made love and it was good. It was very good. For a first time, it was extraordinary even. She touched her lips with her fingertips. Her fingers carried Shaw's scent. She closed her eyes and allowed herself to relive their night together.

❖

It had rained all night. As Shaw eased the Jeep down the muddy drive, she could see that the creek was almost up over the culvert again. This would never work. What if Kate's mother needed urgent care at some point and the creek was too high to cross? This confirmed the plan she'd made with Jimmy to construct a proper bridge in place of the outdated culvert. Back when this had been constructed, the rains had no doubt been less erratic. With the climate shifting everywhere the way it had, hundred-year rains now happened every few months.

In four-wheel drive, she was able to traverse the swollen stream with no trouble, but she knew it would inevitably rain again and possibly be too high for Kate's Honda.

She'd gone to Kate's the previous night with the intention of talking with her about the bridge project and to tell her about the conversation she'd had with Addie. But then she and Jimmy had gotten carried away and she'd had a bit too much bourbon and showed up at Kate's tipsy and affectionate.

They'd made love.

She hadn't planned for that to happen, but she wasn't sorry it had. And she hoped Kate wasn't either. It was hard to read Kate's mood as she was leaving.

She decided to call Kate when she got back to the house and ask her out for a proper date. She wanted Kate to know she wasn't just using her as a distraction from her own restlessness. She owed Kate that much.

Shaw parked in the barn and trotted to the house. The ground was soggy and mud splashed up her pant legs. Damn, her phone was dead. She plugged it in and waited for it to build enough of a charge to call Kate. In the meantime, she'd make coffee and take a shower. Between her cathartic visit to the cemetery yesterday and sex with Kate, she was feeling energized and…happy. Yes, happy, for the first time in months. The lightness from the previous afternoon was still with her, and spending the night with Kate was the perfect ending to a highly emotional day.

Shaw towel dried her hair and dialed Kate's number.

"Hello?"

"Hi."

"Hi." If it was possible for someone's voice to sound shy, Kate's did.

"Hi." Shaw stupidly said it again. She didn't want sex to create some weird barrier between them. This confirmed the notion she'd had to take Kate out for a real date.

"You said that already."

"Sorry, I got nervous."

"I'm not sure that's possible." Kate was teasing her now. Good.

"Listen, I'm calling to find out if you're free for dinner tomorrow night."

"Why?"

"I'd like to take you out, for a nice dinner."

"On a date?"

"Yes, a date. I know I've possibly gotten this backwards by sleeping over before asking you out so I want to make that right."

Kate laughed. "Okay. Dinner it is then."

"I'll pick you up at six." Shaw paused. "And you should know that the creek is high again. It's not high over the road yet, but it does cover the road. If you need anything call me and I'll come get you or I'll bring something over for you."

"I'm sorry. I guess I'm going to have to call Greg. We need to address that. It's not good if we can't get across in the event that we need to for some urgent reason."

"Yeah, I thought the same thing, which is why Jimmy and I are going to replace the culvert with a bridge."

There was silence on the other end.

"Kate?"

"Yes, I'm still here. Did you just say you and Jimmy are building a bridge?"

"Yeah. I need a project. Jimmy needs the work. And you need a bridge. I hope you don't think it's too forward of me to suggest it." Kate didn't say anything. "Kate, let me do this for you and your mom."

"Shaw, I don't know what to say."

"You don't need to say anything. I had every intention of discussing it with you last night. That's part of why I drove over, but then…other things happened."

"Yes, they did."

"Don't overthink this, okay?"

"Have you been talking to Miriam?"

"No, why?"

"No reason." Kate's mother was talking in the background, but Shaw couldn't make out what she was saying. "I need to go."

"Okay, tomorrow night at six."

"I'll look forward to it."

Kate clicked off and Shaw finished getting dressed. She'd give Jimmy a call. As soon as the water went back down again, they'd tear out the culvert and start building. But there was no way construction would start by tomorrow; the ground was too wet.

She used her phone to search for a local car service. For the date she had in mind there was no way she was going to pick Kate up in her old Jeep. She needed something with style. She needed something with doors. Luxury Import Rentals in Asheville was just what she was looking for. These sorts of rental places would usually deliver a car for an additional service charge. Then she just had to figure out a place for dinner.

An incoming message alert flashed across the screen. It was Raisa. She clicked over and read the email, which, in Raisa's usual style, was brief and to the point.

It's a shitshow here. I need you back. Call me ASAP.

Damn. She checked her watch. It was early on the West Coast. Raisa must actually be stressed if she was already up doing email. Working with international clients did often require a response to emails at odd times. Maybe she'd had a conference call or something. She double-checked the time stamp on the message. Raisa had sent it just now, so she was definitely up.

Shaw dialed Raisa's cell.

"Thank God."

"Good morning to you too."

"Shaw, I've tried not to bother you, but I need you back."

"What's going on?"

"John Gordon and his fucking ego, that's what's going on." John Gordon was new to the company. He was a hard-core sales exec they'd hired from Manhattan. He was driven, and he usually got results, but Shaw had worried his style wasn't going to be a good fit at Red Rock.

"What happened?"

"I sent him to Tokyo to work with Akira on that big promotion with Dansai." Dansai was a huge ad agency. They brokered and managed a lot of food and convenience store promotions among other national accounts. These sorts of deals provided big exposure for companies trying to get a foothold in Asia. "He was supposed to have a face to face with the two head guys from Dansai. This was supposed to be a simple get to know you meeting, but according to Akira he gave them a full court press to discuss deal points and sign the agreement. Akira said the Dansai group was so insulted that they stood during the meeting and said good-bye."

"Oh, shit." That was bad. If you drove a Japanese company to rudely walk out of a meeting, then you'd stopped just short of an international insult. These deals didn't come together the same way Western business deals did. There'd be three meetings. The first meeting was always a friendly meet and greet, the second a discussion of the basic deal with lots of nodding and smiling. Actual deal specifics wouldn't be discussed until the third meeting. What John had done was a highly offensive breach of protocol and showed a glaring lack of cultural sensitivity.

"Akira was in tears when she called me late last night."

Akira in tears was like the first sign of the apocalypse. Nothing made Akira cry.

"Is this for the new animated feature?"

"Yes, the promotion is supposed to start in three months, but now, well, I don't know if we can get it back on track." Raisa paused. It sounded as if she were drinking something, probably too much coffee. "You can fix this, Shaw."

"How?" Standing barefoot, in boxer shorts, in her kitchen in Cooper's Creek, that seemed highly unlikely.

"Mr. Komori is going to be in New York next week. If you met him there you could fix this. You could smooth things over and get this promotion back on track."

"Raisa, I don't—"

"There's a lot of money riding on this, Shaw. I need your magic touch."

Shaw pinched the bridge of her nose and paced back and forth in front of the sink. In theory, she could be in New York by next week.

The question was, did she want to be? She could hear the stress in Raisa's voice.

"Can't Akira fix this?"

"No, she's tried. It's going to take an apology from someone at the top. That's either me or you, and you're so much better at winning people over than I am." That was true. Shaw could pull out the Southern charm when she needed to. She had her grandparents to thank for that.

"Okay, Raisa, I'll be there."

"Thank you."

"Tell Bethany to book the travel and send me the itinerary. Tell her she'll need to book the flight out of Asheville."

"How are you?" Crisis averted. Raisa had gotten Shaw to agree to what she wanted. Now she was asking how she was?

"I'm good. I'm better." She didn't want to go into everything with Raisa. She still hadn't quite sorted through all of it herself. "Listen, I've gotta go."

"Okay. I'll have Bethany send you details. Thank you, Shaw. I mean that."

"I know."

Shaw clicked off and slumped into a chair. If everything went smoothly, she would be ready to leave by next week anyway. It wasn't as if she could hide out here forever. The bridge project would either be finished in a week or well on its way to being finished and Jimmy could certainly wrap that up by himself.

And what about Kate?

What about her? Kate had a life here. She had responsibilities that were only going to become more demanding as her mother's health continued to decline. There wasn't anything Shaw could do about that. She had her own life to get back to in California. They'd made different choices that had led them down different paths. That was the way life worked out sometimes. That rationalization rang hollow and left Shaw feeling as if she were making bad decisions she'd later regret. That was the problem with bad decisions. Sometimes you were only sure after the fact.

CHAPTER TWENTY-ONE

Kate's mother had a rough day after Shaw left. Kate worried that her mother might be coming down with something. She knew that sometimes a small infection could be more dangerous to someone her mother's age, even something as routine as a urinary tract infection could cause disorientation.

All afternoon her mother had asked Kate to take her home. It took a while for Kate to figure out that her mother was talking about her childhood home, her grandparents' house. She tried to soothe her mother by repeatedly telling her that she was home, but nothing could redirect her mother's focus.

She seemed better today. A full night of restful sleep had done more good than anything Kate had tried the previous day. But she was worried that her mother might have another bad spell so she'd asked Miriam to stay with her for the evening so that she could go out to dinner with Shaw without worrying. Miriam was happy to stay over and she even brought Lara with her. Kate hadn't told Miriam that Shaw had spent the night and she didn't plan to. If this whole thing turned out to be nothing more than a fling then she didn't want her sister reminding her of all the things she should have done or could have done differently.

Kate was putting the finishing touches on her makeup in the bathroom. She could hear Lara talking with Miriam in the kitchen about what they'd have for dessert after dinner. Kate smiled as she applied lipstick. Lara always thought of dessert. She had inherited Miriam's sweet tooth for sure.

"How do I look?" Kate presented herself to Miriam and Lara. Her mother was asleep in her recliner and didn't budge when Kate spoke.

"You look great." Miriam regarded her with wide eyes. "I didn't even know you owned a dress like that. Even if I had that dress I couldn't wear it. I need to start working out." Miriam crunched on a carrot stick and shook her head. "Girl, Shaw isn't gonna know what hit her when she's sees you in that dress."

"Really, you think so?"

Miriam and Lara both nodded.

"You look pretty."

"Thank you, Lara."

She heard a car approach on the gravel drive and self-consciously smoothed the front of her dress. She glanced out the window but didn't recognize the car. She wasn't sure it was her ride until Shaw climbed out of the driver's seat. Kate was afraid she'd overdressed, but then she saw that Shaw was wearing a dark suit jacket and began to relax. She'd worn the right thing. She reached for her clutch purse.

"Okay, wish me luck."

"Good luck, but trust me, you don't need it." Miriam followed her to the door and whispered out of Lara's earshot. "And we're staying the night, so we won't wait up on you...you know, in case dinner goes really well."

Kate smiled and gave Miriam a hug.

"Thank you."

Shaw was looking down, adjusting the front of her jacket and was almost at the front steps when Kate intercepted her. When Shaw glanced up, the reaction on her face confirmed that Kate had made the right choice.

"Wow." Shaw stopped in her tracks. She was wearing a dark gray dress shirt open at the collar underneath a tailored black jacket. Her dark jeans were slim fit and made her look even taller. Black dress shoes rounded out her ensemble. She'd obviously packed at least some clothing that was neither plaid nor flannel.

"Thanks, wow to you too." Kate smiled.

"Kate, you, and that dress..."

"You like it?"

"Like it? That dress needs a safe word."

Kate laughed. She'd definitely made the right choice. They hadn't seen each other since the night they'd made love, and Kate wanted to make an impression. Based on Shaw's reaction, she'd achieved her goal. Shaw offered Kate her arm and escorted her to the passenger door, which she opened and held for Kate as she carefully slid into the leather seat.

"Where did you get this car?"

"It's a rental. I wasn't going to make you ride in the Jeep again." Shaw put the car in reverse and then turned toward the main road.

"I thought maybe we'd just drive my car." Kate didn't know much about cars, but she knew enough to know that this was a nice one. "What is this?"

"A Mercedes. Do you like it?"

"It's nice, but I feel bad that you went to this much trouble for a dinner date."

"After I showed up on your lawn practically drunk and water-logged I figured I should up my game." Shaw draped her arm over the steering wheel and smiled.

"Well, in that case, well done. Consider your game upped."

Twenty minutes later, Shaw parked on Main Street and they walked toward an old bank building that had been converted into a restaurant. Postero was an elegant place. This was the sort of place you brought a date to if you were celebrating an anniversary, or popping the question, or possibly trying to impress someone. Kate was flattered that Shaw had gone to so much trouble to make their night out seem special.

Shaw kept light contact as they entered the restaurant. She placed her hand at the small of Kate's back as they weaved between tables on the way to their seat, partly a gesture of protection and partly to establish visual connection. She was Kate's date. Yes, Kate was here with her. Every eye was on Kate in the emerald dress, as they crossed the room. It had taken Shaw's breath away the first moment she saw Kate step out of the house. The dress revealed a tasteful hint of cleavage, draping slightly at the waist and then fitting more snugly at the curve of Kate's hips. Gorgeous. Elegant. Jaw-dropping. And clearly a shared opinion based on the reaction of every man in the room. Kate seemed oblivious to the attention, which made her all the more attractive to Shaw. She pulled the chair out for Kate before taking her own.

"Thank you."

"For what?"

"For this." Kate draped the linen napkin across her lap. "For taking me out."

"Trust me, the pleasure is all mine." Shaw glanced at the wine list. "Should I order for us?"

"Sure, you probably know more about wine than I do."

"I don't know about that." Shaw glanced up from the list. "Red or white?"

"Red."

"Good choice. That's my favorite too."

Shaw ordered two glasses of some California Dry Creek Valley pinot that she was familiar with. She regarded Kate over the top of her menu. Kate was doing that adorable thing she did, biting her lower lip. Shaw had noticed that Kate did that when she was thinking and thought no one was watching her. Kate must have realized Shaw was staring because she stopped biting her lip and ran her tongue over it instead. The room felt suddenly warm. Shaw shook her head and grinned. Kate definitely had her number.

They ordered and then sampled the wine. It was good and Kate seemed happy with Shaw's selection. And then out of nowhere, Kate stiffened in her chair.

"What's wrong? Is something wrong?"

"My ex is here. Unbelievable."

"Where?"

"Over there, in the blue oxford shirt, short brown hair." Kate was intently studying the flower in the bud vase on their table as she gave Shaw the description.

Shaw tried to casually survey the room. She spotted Kate's ex on the far side of the restaurant. She was on a date with someone. Her date was a full-figured redhead, lots of cleavage, and teased hair.

"What's her name?"

"Karen."

"Hmm, Karen and Kate. Cute."

"It was more than a year ago now. Oh, good, it looks like they're getting ready to leave." A waitress delivered their check and small bag of leftovers.

"Too bad, I excel at annoying exes, mine and the exes of others."

"How many exes do you have?"

Shaw smiled but didn't answer. She wasn't falling into that trap. She leaned closer to Kate in a conspiratorial pose. "I'm pretty sure she saw you, and right now she's regretting every choice she ever made that resulted in losing you. Trust me."

Kate seemed pleased with that assessment.

Just then, their dinners arrived. Shaw watched out of the corner of her eye as Karen and her date stood up to leave. It looked as if Karen felt compelled to say hello. Across the table from her, Kate sat back in her chair no doubt preparing to put her good manners to the test.

"She's coming this way. I could manage to slosh red wine on her starched oxford shirt if you like."

"Shaw, you're incorrigible."

"Thank you."

Kate laughed.

As predicted, Karen stopped when she reached their table.

"Hello, Kate." Karen put herself between her buxom date and the table.

"Hello, Karen." Kate dabbed at her mouth with her napkin as if her perfect meal had just been annoyingly interrupted. "Karen, this is Shaw."

Shaw stood up and extended her hand to Karen. She was pleased to discover that she was at least four inches taller than Karen. Karen had a definite player vibe. Shaw disliked her immediately so she made sure the grip of her handshake was extra firm. Karen's date seemed harmless enough, but Shaw paid her hardly any attention.

"You remember Leslie." Karen introduced her date.

"Of course." Kate's response was neutral, but a chill issued forth from her side of the table.

"Well, enjoy your dinner." Karen nodded curtly to Shaw and let her gaze linger on Kate a little too long for Shaw's liking.

Shaw didn't take her seat again until Karen was almost to the door, staring her down the entire time she crossed the room. She sat down and took a sip of wine. "I'm pretty sure her night is ruined. So, you're welcome."

"I actually can't believe they're still together."

"When did they meet?"

"While we were still seeing each other."

"Oh." Shaw swallowed. "Well, she has more problems than bad fashion then. And what's with that haircut? Can someone tell her that the nineties are over?" Shaw teasingly pulled a carrot from her fork. She wouldn't normally make jokes about someone, but she had the sense that Karen had hurt Kate and that pissed her off. "And what's up with her date?"

"Leslie?"

"Lez be honest, she's about to bust out of that blouse. Those buttons are screaming to be set free."

Kate coughed into her napkin. "Stop making me laugh. You're going to make me choke."

Shaw hoped Kate's mood would rebound. This had to be one of the curses of living in a small town. No way to completely avoid ex-girlfriends.

"What does Karen do for work?"

"She's an attorney in the DA's office."

"She did sort of have that law and order vibe about her."

Kate laughed. "You're really witty tonight."

"I don't want her to ruin our evening so I'm pulling out my best material."

Kate covered Shaw's hand with hers. "Not a chance of that."

"Good."

Kate could tell that Shaw wanted to defend her honor where Karen was concerned, but it really wasn't necessary. Karen was old news. By the time Kate found out Karen was cheating on her with Leslie she'd already decided to break things off. She and Karen didn't share the same values, and she had long since grown tired of Karen's ego.

She'd watched Shaw just now. How she handled herself. She oozed the kind of confidence that she knew Karen aspired to. But Shaw wore it so effortlessly, like a well-fitted suit. Shaw was comfortable in her own skin and it showed. Plus, Shaw was so good-looking. Kate felt certain that Shaw was right. Karen's evening was ruined for sure. She couldn't help smiling.

"What's funny?"

"Nothing." Kate sipped her wine. The food was amazing, the wine was good, and the company was even better.

They ate quietly for a few minutes.

"I didn't get a chance to tell you that I set a date for my mother's funeral."

Kate set her fork down and focused on Shaw.

"It'll be Tuesday at three o'clock. The headstone will be delivered sometime before the service." Shaw cleared her throat as if she were nervous. "I'd love for you to be there if you can make it."

"Of course I'll be there."

"I probably wouldn't have done this if it weren't for you, so thank you for making the first call to Reverend Gilreath." Shaw took a few bites of food. "While I was looking around the cemetery I found Charlie's grave."

Kate waited for Shaw to say more. She could tell by the look on Shaw's face that it was hard for her to share these details.

"Addie happened to show up while I was there and, surprisingly, she suggested I bury Mom next to Charlie."

"Shaw, that's a really big deal."

"It is, isn't it?"

"Yes. I can't believe you didn't tell me all of this."

"Well, in my defense, I was a little distracted by our sleepover."

Kate felt her cheeks flame. She reached for her water. "Yeah, I've been a little distracted by that as well."

"Good." Shaw leaned back in her chair and grinned as she sipped her wine.

They were quiet again as they finished their food. A waiter cleared the table and left dessert menus. Kate wasn't sure she could eat anything else. She'd struggled to eat most of her main course. Every time she made eye contact with Shaw butterflies invaded her stomach overpowering her appetite for food. Her appetite for other delights seemed to be intact though. It was hard not to focus on Shaw's hands during dinner. The way she fondled the stem of her wine glass or held her fork. She had a flashback mental image of Shaw brandishing the welding gun, and the butterflies returned in force.

"How did you become interested in sculpture?"

They'd decided against dessert and ordered some after dinner tea instead. The waiter settled a teapot in the center of the table so that it could steep.

"I don't know exactly. I was always interested in all sorts of building toys as a kid. You know, everything from Lego to blocks to erector sets. I got my first set of real tools in second grade, and still have a few of them."

"Who bought them for you?"

"My mother." Shaw paused. "Thinking back, despite all our differences, she always encouraged me to be completely myself. Even when the person I was becoming seemed to annoy the shit out of her."

"She loved you."

"In her own way, I suppose."

Kate thought back to what Shaw had looked like as a kid. Adorable. It was impossible not to fall in love with that kid.

"So there you were, seven-year-old Shaw, toolbox in hand."

Shaw laughed. "That's a funny mental image. Thanks for that."

"You're welcome."

"I've always loved building things. I think I made my first actual sculpture out of small square sheets of plastic and glue in sixth or seventh grade. It was modeled after a windmill and it spun when you blew on it."

"What sort of things did you sculpt in college? You mentioned you were doing an installation when you met Raisa."

"Do you know Calder's work?"

Kate nodded. "He does the huge mobiles, right?"

"Yeah, and some static pieces as well." Shaw poured tea for each of them as she continued to talk. "Calder's mobiles are essentially the art of equilibrium. I wanted to explore that idea as my senior thesis, but I wanted to take it one step further. The sculpture I did as my final piece explored the precariousness of balance and the disorientation that follows when it's pulled away."

Kate sipped her tea. Shaw's eyes danced and her entire being seemed to glow as she talked about sculpture. Kate had never seen this side of Shaw. When she talked about art she seemed to open up.

Kate didn't want this conversation to end. She was falling for this Shaw, the Shaw who was talking about losing her balance.

"It sounds like high-minded art speak doesn't it?"

"Not at all."

"I guess I sort of embraced the notion that you make the work and it will change its appearance, based on wind and light, based on the viewer's perspective. Kinetic sculptures use simple air currents to bring life to line, color, and shape." Shaw looked at Kate and her eyes glistened. "There's something joyous and unpretentious about work that allows people to interact with it in a physical way. You know, art that isn't hidden away behind some gold rope or museum glass. I love it when people are permitted to participate in the physical space occupied by the work. Does that sound crazy?"

"No, it sounds beautiful. I wish I could see some of your sculptures."

"I think I have some pictures on my laptop. Even though I haven't done any work like that in years, I can't quite let go of the photos."

"Are any of the pieces still on display?"

"Only one, in my living room." Shaw grinned. "I think I might be my biggest fan, my only fan." She laughed.

"I doubt that." Kate looked around and realized that there were only a few diners left in the restaurant. Shaw had paid the bill and they'd been leisurely finishing their tea, but Kate was anxious for a little time alone with Shaw before the night was over.

CHAPTER TWENTY-TWO

S haw held the door for Kate. The snug fitting dress required that Kate swivel into the seat, giving Shaw a tantalizing view of her legs.

Dinner had been really fun. And talking about sculpture was invigorating. She felt as if she were back in college again, enlivened and inspired. It seemed Kate brought out the best she had to offer. She liked herself more when Kate was around.

She was reminded of something she'd forgotten. Something one of her professors was fond of saying. *That creativity gives voice to the things that are unknowable.* Now that she was older she knew that to be true. Things she hardly had a name for, feelings she couldn't articulate were sometimes easier to construct. What was it Addie had said to her at the gravesite?

The world is full of words and most of them don't mean much.

There was truth to that. Words had failed her so many times, her own words and the words of others. Maybe that's why Charlie had created things too. Maybe words failed him as well. There would never be any way to know that for sure.

The winding road into the mountains was dark. They only passed a couple of cars on the two-lane highway back to Cooper's Creek. Shaw reached for Kate's hand and their fingers entwined. Shaw wasn't ready for the night to be over, but she thought that maybe Kate needed to get home.

"Do you have time to stop by my place for a drink before I take you home?"

"Sure, Miriam is at the house and she's planning to spend the night."

Shaw glanced over at Kate, but Kate was looking straight ahead and gave no indication as to whether Shaw should read anything in to that statement or not. Shaw decided not to get her hopes up. The night had been great; if it ended with a drink and a good night kiss that was okay.

Shaw turned on the overhead light in the kitchen, but the bulb was too bright for the mood she was trying to create. She switched on a lamp in the living room and then turned the kitchen light off. The lamp offered enough illumination to find two glasses and retrieve the half-finished bottle of bourbon Jimmy had left behind after his last visit.

"This is really all I have to offer." Shaw held up the bottle to show Kate, who was standing near the window.

"Just give me a taste."

Shaw poured them each a little and handed a glass to Kate. Warmth from the first swallow eased slowly down her throat. She held Kate with her eyes, enjoying the contours of Kate's body in the form-fitting dress. She wanted to kiss Kate. She wanted to put her hands on Kate. She took another sip of bourbon and considered her next move.

"Do you know yet when you're going back to California?"

The question surprised her, but then again, it didn't. Kate obviously wanted to know where this was headed. Shaw had known from the beginning that Kate wasn't interested in casual sex. Even still, they'd had sex the night Shaw showed up at her house.

"Next week." Shaw sank onto the couch, leaving Kate standing near the window. For some reason, Kate seemed reluctant to sit down.

"That soon?" Shaw thought she heard a hint of disappointment, or did she imagine it?

"Raisa called with some emergency and I have to fly to New York next week to deal with it. Don't worry, Jimmy and I will finish the bridge project before I leave."

"I'm not thinking about the bridge."

Shaw savored the bourbon and imagined crossing the room to Kate. She'd stand so close that she could feel Kate's breath on her skin. She'd take Kate's glass and set in on the windowsill. She would hold Kate against her body and kiss her, open mouth, tongue searching, possessively claiming her. She'd feel Kate's hands at her waist, fisting her shirt, tugging Shaw firmly against her as if asking for more.

Shaw swallowed the warming liquor and imagined her fingers at the hem of Kate's dress, teasing it up over her thighs, slowly, methodically, until she felt the lace band of her underwear. She visualized sliding Kate's underwear down until she helped Kate step out of it. The hem of her skirt would still be gathered at the top of her thighs. Shaw imagined kneeling in front of Kate as she eased the dress up farther, exposing her sex. She'd begin to caress Kate with her tongue...

Heat flared between her legs and molten liquid flooded Shaw's core. She squeezed her eyes shut and fought the urge to massage her crotch. She was so fucking turned on and she hadn't even touched Kate.

When she opened her eyes, Kate was watching her. She shifted uncomfortably under Kate's intense scrutiny. Kate's face was flushed, her eye's heavy-lidded with desire as if she'd somehow known what Shaw had just been imagining.

Kate set her glass on the windowsill as if Shaw had conjured the action, and slowly approached the sofa. She kicked her heels off, gathered her dress, and straddled Shaw's lap. Kate filled her fingers with Shaw's hair and kissed her so passionately that Shaw thought for a brief moment she might spontaneously burst into flame. With one kiss, Kate owned her. When Kate released her, she sank back against the couch, completely smitten and wanting more.

Kate wasn't sure if Shaw was the sort of woman who always liked to make the first move, but Kate wasn't that sort of girl. She might not be the sort to chase for the sport of casual sex, but if she wanted someone, really wanted them, then she wasn't shy. She wasn't some pillow princess waiting on her back to be satisfied. She could tell by the look on Shaw's face that she was beginning to figure that out too.

"What were you thinking a minute ago, when you were watching me from across the room?" She swept her fingers through Shaw's hair and kissed her again.

"Um, I was thinking I'd like to have my mouth on you."

"Like this?" Kate kissed her again, deeply, and with her free hand began to unbutton Shaw's shirt.

"No, not exactly like that."

Kate kissed Shaw's neck and let her hands drift down the front of Shaw's shirt.

"Hmm, do you want to show me?"

Shaw nodded mutely. With one strong move, Shaw swiveled so that Kate was on her back across the sofa and Shaw was between her legs. Shaw kissed the inside of her thighs as she moved up her leg. When she reached the apex, Shaw teased with her tongue all along the lacey edge of Kate's underwear. Shaw hooked her fingers under the elastic and slowly eased the underwear down and off. Kate knew she was soaked and now Shaw would know it too.

Shaw sat back and took Kate in and Kate let her; she made no move to close her legs or cover her sex. Shaw unclipped her cufflinks and dropped them on the coffee table. Shaw could make the simplest task sexy. Shaw reclaimed her position between Kate's legs and began to caress with her tongue.

Shaw's touch was so exquisite that Kate thought she would come almost instantly. She pressed her sex against Shaw's mouth and fisted Shaw's hair to hold on for fear she'd climb right out of her skin from absolute ecstasy.

Just when she thought she couldn't hold on any longer, Shaw eased back, trailing wet kisses down each thigh. Shaw extended her hand to Kate and then reached to switch off the lamp. The click echoed loudly inside Kate's head.

It was one thing to make love to Shaw in a sleepy alcohol-induced haze. But this was different. She was willingly falling into bed with Shaw with full knowledge that Shaw was leaving in a week. And in this moment, right now, she didn't care. She wanted Shaw. She wanted all of her. Even if this was the only time she could have her. Shaw tugged her toward the bedroom and she offered no resistance.

The sheets were rumpled and Shaw had to shove random articles of clothing to the floor. The disheveled mess proved that this hadn't been a premeditated act, which Kate was relieved to discover. Shaw turned to face her. Her expression held a question: what next?

Kate finished unbuttoning Shaw's shirt and then pushed it off her shoulders. Kate ran her hands across Shaw's shoulders and swept them down her arms. Shaw had great arms, lean and muscled. Shaw was wearing a sports bra. She pulled it up and off with one swift movement. Kate worked at the front of Shaw's jeans. As she slowly lowered the zipper, she moved Shaw back until the foot of the bed hit her legs and she was forced to sit.

Shaw kicked her shoes off and her socks, then lay back and watched with an expression of wonder on her face as Kate unzipped the back of her dress and shimmied out of it. She tossed it over a chair along with her bra. She hesitated, allowing Shaw to get a good look before she tugged Shaw's pants down and off. She crawled up the bed, relieved Shaw of her boxers, and settled on top of her.

"I'm good at beginnings."

"What?" She feathered kisses along Shaw's jaw.

"I feel like I should tell you that I'm good at beginnings. It's what comes after that I have trouble with."

Kate was surprised by Shaw's confession.

"Do you feel compelled to come clean because I have you pinned to the bed nude?"

Shaw swallowed and looked away.

"I just…I don't want to hide from you. And…you might as well know the truth. That only seems fair."

The expression on Shaw's face tugged at Kate's heart. Shaw looked as if she was preparing for Kate to storm from the room because of this admission of perceived inadequacy.

"Shaw, I'm here because I want to be. You didn't trick me or ensnare me, although, I must tell you that cuff link move was sexy as hell."

Shaw smiled and seemed to relax.

"I care about you Kate. I don't want you to believe that I'm something I'm not. I don't think I could handle seeing disappointment in your eyes and know that I was the cause."

"Well, I don't know if you've been keeping score, but I'm on top at the moment. Is there anything you'd like to know about my motivations before I fuck your brains out?"

Shaw laughed and shook her head.

"All right then, I'm glad that's settled." She kissed Shaw's lips; she kissed her way down the center of Shaw's chest, and paused to pay particular attention to Shaw's nipples with her tongue before she insinuated herself between Shaw's legs.

She caressed Shaw's sex with her tongue. Shaw was close, but so was she. She rotated, straddling Shaw's chest so that Shaw could reach her. The invitation was immediately accepted. As she continued to work Shaw with her mouth, she felt Shaw slide into her with her fingers. She was coming. She was coming fast and hard and she wanted to bring Shaw with her.

Shaw's thrusts became more urgent. Kate felt Shaw's body tense and tremble beneath her. Kate fisted the sheet, turned her open mouth against Shaw's thigh, and cried out with release. Shaw eased out of her and she rolled onto her side breathing rapidly. She swept damp hair off her face. She was on her back with her eyes closed trying to bring her body back to earth. *Fuck, that felt good.* Soft kisses brushed her lips and caused her to open her eyes. Shaw hovered just above her smiling.

"Guess who's on top now?"

CHAPTER TWENTY-THREE

S haw teased Kate's fingers with hers. It was late. Shaw wasn't sure of the time. She didn't care for time except to slow its passing so that she could hold Kate as long as possible. Kate's head was tucked under her chin, her thigh across Shaw's. She pressed a kiss to Kate's hair.

"How are you?"

She sensed that Kate was smiling against her shoulder.

"That's a funny question to ask."

"It is?"

"After what we've been doing I think you know how I am. I'm very satisfied, thank you."

"I just want to make sure this was all…okay." Shaw entwined her fingers with Kate's and rested them on her chest.

"I'm okay, Shaw. Really." Kate propped up on her elbow and looked at Shaw. "For someone who's only good at beginnings, you worry an awful lot about what comes after."

Shaw smiled thinly. Maybe she was the one who wasn't okay with this. Wouldn't that be a switch? She made noise in her head worrying that Kate would read too much into this or be disappointed. Maybe she was the one who was reading too much into things. What was she hoping Kate would say? That this was the best sex she'd ever had? That she couldn't live without Shaw in her life? The minute a woman said those things to Shaw she'd bolt for the door. Kate wasn't saying any of those things. And Shaw was strangely disappointed by that fact.

She felt the sudden desire to be needed. Where did that come from? She tried to shake it off.

"Shaw, I know you have to leave in a week. I know this can't last. But that doesn't mean we can't enjoy each other while you're here." Kate kissed her lightly. "You'll be back at some point, right? Maybe you'll still be single. Maybe I'll still be single too and we can pick up where we leave off." She stroked the center of Shaw's chest with her fingers.

Kate's statement sounded so reasonable, so grown up. So why did the words make her feel so empty? For a minute, Shaw imagined several possible scenarios, one of which involved Kate with someone else. That didn't feel good on any level. What was going on with her? Was she falling for Kate?

It was as if by ensuring Shaw's autonomy, Kate had thrown down some challenge. Shaw wanted Kate to feel as if she couldn't live without her. She wanted Kate to desperately need her touch. She was looking up at the ceiling when Kate rolled onto her side away from Shaw. The loss of contact stirred something in Shaw.

"Maybe we should try and get a little sleep." Kate sounded drowsy, but now Shaw was wide-awake. She wanted Kate again.

Kate hoped she wasn't playing things too close to the chest. The truth was that she wasn't sure if she was okay with this situation or not. She was trying hard to be okay with it, but she couldn't know for sure just now if she actually was. She knew she was precariously at the edge of the cliff. One small shove and she'd fall hard for Shaw. She was trying to be present, to enjoy this time with Shaw, and still keep that deepest part of herself protected. The more time they spent together the harder her deepest self was to insulate.

Kate smiled into her pillow as Shaw kissed her shoulder lightly. Shaw swept her hair to the side and nibbled on her ear before moving to tease with her tongue along Kate's neck.

"Aren't you sleepy?" Kate didn't roll over. She hugged the pillow more tightly as she felt Shaw's hand drift down her spine. The tiny hairs on her arms stood at attention.

"No, I'm not sleepy just yet."

Shaw sucked her neck and pressed against her. She felt the hard points of Shaw's breasts against her back. Shaw arched into her, applying more pressure. She felt Shaw's hand on her ass now. Shaw insinuated her thigh between Kate's legs pushing them apart so that Shaw could gain access. Kate moaned when she felt Shaw's fingers at her entrance.

"Shaw…baby, I don't know if I can come again." She'd come twice already and was fairly sure she had nothing left, although what Shaw was doing felt extremely good. Her sex was still tender from her most recent climax.

"One more time. I need you one more time." Shaw's voice was low and husky next to her ear. She took special note that Shaw had used the word need, rather than want. Shaw's fingers thrust slowly in and out, and then she felt Shaw's thumb at the rim of her other opening. Slowly, gently, Shaw eased the tip of her thumb in while continuing to thrust with her fingers. She felt Shaw's weight against her back. Her face flamed hot and her heart pounded against her ribs pressed into the bed.

"Shaw, I'm not sure about—"

"Too much?" Shaw stilled her fingers. "What was the safe word? Did I hear you say *Flashdance*?"

Kate laughed. "Not on your life."

Shaw smiled against Kate's shoulder and pushed farther, she worked both openings as she began to grind her wet sex against Kate's ass. She was going to come again. In this position, Shaw was in complete control and she was bringing Kate to the edge with her.

"Oh, God, Shaw, oh…" She reached back and took a fist full of Shaw's hair and held on. Shaw was coming. She arched against Kate and groaned loudly as her body tensed, stiff and hard. Only for an instant did she slow what she was doing with her hand. As Shaw rode her climax against Kate's ass, she was coming too. Kate convulsed beneath the weight of Shaw's body. She'd never come that hard. She cried out and reached for Shaw's hand to still her.

She rolled over in Shaw's arms and pulled her into a searing kiss. She clenched Shaw's leg between hers and rode the undulating waves of her orgasm against Shaw's thigh. As she came down from her high, she clung to Shaw, pressing her lips to Shaw's neck, damp with perspiration.

"Was that okay?" Shaw whispered the question.

Kate kissed her. She let her head relax on the pillow and looked up at Shaw. "Yes, that was okay." She couldn't help smiling because okay was the last word she'd use to describe this night with Shaw. Amazing, illuminating, sexy, hot, transcendent, any of those would be more accurate than okay.

Shaw settled at her side and she repositioned Shaw's head to her shoulder so that she could stroke her back as they listened to the night sounds drift in through the open window.

CHAPTER TWENTY-FOUR

The sound of distant engine noise woke Kate. Probably a logging truck on the two-lane highway that wound its way through Cooper's Creek. Noises carried. Sound waves bounced off the granite in the hillsides and traveled up the hollows. Thunder was the same. It was always difficult to tell just how far away it was.

Kate looked for a clock but didn't see one. Beside her Shaw was still asleep. Kate fought the urge to kiss her shoulder, exposed as it was above the edge of the sheet. She pulled on Shaw's dress shirt from the previous night and went to the living room to retrieve her phone from her clutch. There was a voice mail from Emily but no messages from Miriam. That was a good sign. It was six thirty. Her body was trained to wake at this time for school. It seemed that even a night filled with sex wouldn't allow her internal clock to reset.

She was drinking a glass of water at the sink, looking out the window, when she felt Shaw's hands encircle her waist.

"Good morning." Shaw pulled her hair to one side and kissed her neck.

"Good morning to you too." She offered Shaw the glass. "I think I should take a shower before you drive me home. Do you mind?" She rotated in Shaw's arms. She was wearing a T-shirt and boxers and her hair looked adorably disheveled.

"I'll get a towel for you."

Kate was in the bathroom adjusting the water temp for the shower when Shaw returned with a towel and washcloth. Kate was still wearing Shaw's shirt. It hung to mid-thigh, but she hadn't buttoned it. She held the front together so as not to put everything on display.

"Should I join you?"

"No, you absolutely should not." Kate smiled, placed her palm in the middle of Shaw's chest, and playfully shoved her out the door.

"Really?" Shaw looked crestfallen.

"Yes, really. Now go make us some coffee. I need some caffeine before I face my sister." She blew Shaw a kiss and shut the door. She let the shirt fall away and climbed over the tall side of the tub and under the steaming spray. The original claw foot tub had been retrofitted with a shower curtain that wrapped around in a circle. The whole setup was quaint and charming.

There was no way she could let Shaw get in the shower. She was clearly unable to keep her hands off Shaw, and one thing would lead to another. She swept her fingers lightly over her sex. She was still aroused and tender. How was that even possible?

As the hot water pulsed down, she calculated in her head how many days she had left with Shaw. There was no way she'd let Shaw leave without having another night with her. But how could she pull that off? She'd have to at least tell Miriam something because she'd need her help if she wanted another night free.

She was toweling off when Shaw knocked softly at the door. She peeked out.

"Coffee?" Shaw held a mug out to her. "Cream, no sugar."

"How did you know?" Kate was puzzled.

"The morning you made me breakfast we had coffee." Shaw held Kate with her eyes, her gaze felt hotter than the coffee she held in her hand. "I pay attention." Shaw smiled and Kate's stomach fluttered.

Shaw signaled for Kate to stay where she was. She gathered Kate's things and reached around the door to deliver them. Kate seemed just the least bit shy this morning, which surprised Shaw a little after the night they'd had. Kate was definitely not shy in bed, and that discovery pleased Shaw. Actually, all of it pleased her. Kate's confidence as a lover and the shyness that followed, all of it was a big turn-on. It's probably just as well that Kate wouldn't allow her in the shower this morning because all she could think about was making Kate come again.

"Do you want me to make breakfast?" Shaw was standing outside the closed door.

"No," came the muffled reply. "I'll get something at home."

Kate opened the door. Her hair was damp, and droplets of water darkened the shoulders of the emerald dress from the previous night, the dress that had started all the trouble. Shaw really had no other choice but to make love to Kate wearing that dress. For a moment, Shaw felt woozy. She thought of Kate wearing that dress again, on a date with someone else, and the coffee suddenly turned her stomach.

"Maybe you should leave that dress with me."

"What?" Kate arched an eyebrow.

"I don't want you wearing that dress. It's dangerous. I should probably take charge of it, you know, for public safety."

Kate laughed.

"I'm serious."

"Shaw, I'll be careful. I only wear this dress for special occasions."

"Does that make me a special occasion then?" Shaw wrapped one arm around Kate and drew her close.

"Yes, Shaw Daily, you are most definitely a special occasion."

Kate waved to Shaw as she pulled away in the dark sedan. She tiptoed up the porch steps hoping she could get to her room and change before Miriam was awake. No such luck. Miriam leaned against the counter in the dimly lit kitchen, coffee in hand, grinning as Kate tried to sneak past.

"Good morning."

Kate stepped out of her heels and bent to pick them up. "Please hold all questions until I've had a minute to change clothes."

"Don't worry, I'm patiently waiting." Miriam's words followed her to the bedroom.

Kate dug through her dresser for a T-shirt and found jeans on a nearby chair. She pulled her hair back into a ponytail and returned to the kitchen. She poured coffee and waited for Miriam to pelt her for details.

"It must have been a good night if this is any indication." Miriam touched the back of her neck.

"What? No."

"Yes, right there." Miriam touched the spot again. "You, baby sister, have a hickey."

Kate quickly loosened her hair to cover it and shoved the hair tie in her pocket. "Well, that's embarrassing."

"At least it's in a spot you can easily hide." Miriam smiled and sipped her coffee. "So? Details? Quit holding out on me."

"Is anyone else awake?"

"Stop stalling."

"It was good." Kate sat down at the kitchen table and couldn't help grinning at Miriam.

"It, what it? The date? The sex?"

"All of it." Kate sighed and propped her chin in her hand. "I had a really good time. Shaw is...she's everything I'd imagined. Everything I've daydreamed she would be."

"Wow."

"I know."

"So, like, songbirds and angels singing?"

"Yes."

"Starbursts and electrical storms?"

"Yes. The best sex I've ever had."

"And?"

"And she's returning to California next week."

"So soon?"

"Yes, it seems some sort of crisis is going on with her work and she has to travel to New York next week to sort it out and then back to California." Kate took a long swig of her coffee. "So that's that."

"Just like that?"

"What am I supposed to do? I'm trying really hard to keep perspective about this. I followed your advice and went out with her, and now I'm striving to insulate myself from the disappointment I'm going to feel when she's gone."

Miriam reached over and affectionately put her hand on Kate's arm.

CHAPTER TWENTY-FIVE

All day Sunday Shaw was a mess. She'd dropped Kate off at her house early, and when she got back to her place, she couldn't relax. She had more coffee, which didn't help. She made breakfast, did the dishes, and then tried to lie down for a little while. They'd been up most of the night and she did feel drowsy, but after one minute facedown on the sheets her system was humming. The scent of Kate was all over the bed.

She looked at her phone about a hundred times and thought of calling or texting and ended up doing neither. Kate didn't ring her either, but she figured Kate was busy with her mom, Miriam, and little Lara. In contrast, Shaw had no distractions from flashbacks of the previous night's events.

After an hour of walking from room to room to inspect various random objects, she returned to the kitchen. She was looking out the window and her eyes settled on the birdbath.

She hefted the birdbath base and basin and loaded them in the back of the Jeep. She drove over to Kate's. No one was in sight so she circled Miss Edith's garden for a few moments before she settled on the perfect spot for her small, sculptural bird spa. She wondered how long it would take for one of them to notice it was there.

After she was satisfied with the spot, she jogged up the porch steps and knocked.

No one came to the door immediately, and Shaw was just about to turn and leave when she heard something on the other side. Miss Edith had one hand on her walker and one hand on the door.

"Hello there."

"Oh, I'm sorry, I was looking for Kate."

"Come in, come in." She put a finger to her lips. "Kate's asleep. Poor dear, she must have stayed up late last night."

Shaw felt her cheeks flame at the thought that Miss Edith had any idea what they'd been up to. In fact, the idea of hanging out with Kate's mother after what she'd done with Kate the previous night was rather unsettling. Still, what could she do now but follow Miss Edith inside?

"Maybe you could get that glass of water for me and carry it over next to my chair. This dang walker makes it hard to do anything for myself."

Shaw followed her to the chair and set the glass on a small lamp stand near Miss Edith's recliner.

"Maybe I should go." Shaw fidgeted and looked toward the door.

"Sit, sit. Talk to me for a minute. You only just got here." Miss Edith motioned with her hand toward the sofa.

Shaw obliged and sat down, but she didn't really want to. She rubbed her palms up and down her thighs with nervous energy. What the hell was her problem? Under Miss Edith's gaze she was as nervous as a long-tailed cat in a room full of rocking chairs.

"I hear tell your momma's funeral is gonna be Tuesday afternoon."

"Yes, ma'am."

"I'll be there if the Lord is willing."

"Thank you, but please don't go to any trouble on my account."

"Kate said she plans to attend. I'd like to be there too. I always liked Iris. She was a wild thing, always full of life. I'm sorry she had to leave us so soon."

It was an interesting experience to hear people talk about her mother. First, Addie had said things that implied she'd known things about her mother, and Miss Edith had known her mother in her youth. They both seemed to know an Iris that Shaw had never met, a young woman in bloom, full of promise and infused with life. Maybe if she'd met that Iris she'd have had more in common with her.

"What were we just talking about?" Miss Edith regarded her with an open, innocent expression.

"My mother's funeral."

"Right. I swear, my mind is scattered to the four winds these days." She reached for the glass of water. Her hand was so shaky that she had to use both hands to stabilize it long enough to take a sip. "It's bad when your mind goes while your body is still able. In my case both are suddenly feeble."

Shaw sat quietly. She studied Miss Edith's hands. Sinewy, knuckles distended, the skin sagging and marked with sun spots. She realized she had never spent much time with age. While she was feeling restless and confronted by her own approaching middle age, time from her perspective, seemed stretched in front of her forever. She wondered what it was like for Miss Edith. What it was like to know your life force was in a slowly decaying orbit.

"What does it feel like to get old?" The internal question burst out of her mouth before she could stop it. She immediately wished she could take it back, but Miss Edith showed no signs of offense.

"Age is an affliction no one can prepare you for. You come to dread time. Your body feels wounded, but you can't find the source of the hurt."

"I'm sorry. I didn't mean to seem rude."

"An honest question is rarely impolite."

Maybe Miss Edith was relieved on some level to have a frank conversation about what was going on in her life. Aging, sickness, death, all topics frequently sidestepped or tiptoed around. Rarely were these topics ever addressed head on, especially with those you were closest to.

"The edges of the present are sometimes blurry and out of focus, and I have these moments where I'm young again. It's all in my head, mind you. I know that after the fact, but I have no control over how my mind travels. I'm sure it's hard for Kate, bless her heart."

"I really appreciate the things you've said about my mother." Shaw picked at a loose thread on one of the sofa cushions. "You may not know this, but we never really got on very well."

"Mothers and daughters are a complicated thing." Miss Edith stared out the window as if she was looking at some far off place. "I don't think your mother ever figured herself out, which likely made it hard for you."

"I think I'm beginning to understand a little. I wish she'd talked to me about things."

"She may not have known enough to talk about it."

"But she could at least have told me about Charlie."

"True. I'm not sure why she wouldn't have told you. I suppose I thought you knew, but how could you?"

"What was Charlie like?"

"Charlie was special, I think. Maybe he left this world early because he wasn't meant to be here."

"What do you mean?"

"He was a sensitive, vibrant soul, dropped into a family that would never understand him."

"Why did my grandfather not want Charlie and my mother to be together?"

"I don't think it was anything more than the belief that Charlie's people were beneath Iris. That she could do better." Miss Edith let her head rest against the high back of the recliner. "If I've learned one thing in all my years of living it's that parents don't always know what's best for their children. No, sir, not by a long shot."

They sat quietly for a moment. Shaw wondered if Miss Edith was talking about the fact that Kate was gay. Maybe early on she hadn't understood or pushed Kate to take a more traditional path.

"Life is too short to spend too much time trying to figure everything out." She turned and looked at Shaw. "Make peace with your past. You can't audit life, all the hurts and slights and misunderstandings...the math never adds up. That's the advice of an old woman. Old women love to give advice that no one ever heeds." Miss Edith grinned.

Shaw smiled and nodded. She'd already taken the first step to letting things go with her mother. The day she'd stood and looked at Charlie's grave, something inside had shifted. She'd felt different, lighter, ever since.

"Charlie, would you be a dear and find something for us to watch on TV?" Miss Edith pointed toward the remote on the coffee table. "We can sit here and watch a nice show together."

And just like that the moment of lucid discussion gave way to the past. Shaw didn't correct Miss Edith. She simply reached for the remote and started surfing channels for something to watch.

❖

Kate heard voices in the other room. Fog slowly cleared from her head and she realized it was the television. She glanced at her phone. She'd fallen asleep for two hours. That had not been her intention. She chided herself for not setting an alarm. After she splashed water on her face she shuffled into the living room to see what her mother was watching. The scene that greeted her was a complete surprise.

Shaw was stretched out on the couch asleep and her mother was asleep nearby in her recliner. Some black-and-white movie starring Charlton Heston played in the background. How long had Shaw been there?

Kate knelt by the sofa and whispered, "Shaw?" Shaw didn't stir. She kissed Shaw's cheek and decided she'd start something for dinner. In the meantime, she'd let them both rest.

Kate was washing vegetables at the sink when she glanced out the window and saw the birdbath in her mother's garden. She braced against the sink as her stomach did a little flip-flop. Shaw had brought the birdbath she'd made for her mother's garden. The touching gesture caught her off guard.

Shaw Daily was turning out to be quite an unexpected surprise. Just when she thought she knew exactly what Shaw was up to Shaw would do something she didn't expect and could not have predicted. Finding her asleep while watching TV with her mother was one of those things.

For a minute, Kate allowed herself to imagine a life with Shaw in it. Sharing small, everyday joys like curling up on the couch to watch a movie, or sleeping in on Sundays. Family time. What if she and Shaw were a family? That possibility was too painful to consider, and as soon as it appeared she shoved it back. Those sorts of hopes would surely only end in disappointment, possibly despair if she allowed them to take root in her psyche. She needed to manage her expectations carefully or risk the consequences.

The vegetable stew was done and simmering on low by the time Shaw began to stir. Kate was standing nearby when Shaw shifted sleepily then jerked awake.

"Oh, no. I fell asleep." Shaw rubbed her eyes and shook her head as if that would dislodge grogginess.

"You did. I came out here and you and Momma were both asleep. It was adorable."

Shaw swiveled her legs and partially sat up. "I didn't mean to fall asleep. I guess..."

"That you were up half the night?" Kate smiled.

Miss Edith's eyes fluttered open. "Something smells good."

"I made a stew, Momma. Does that sound nice?"

"Yes, sweetie, that's sounds perfect."

"Shaw, do you want to help me set the table?"

"I should probably go. I—"

Kate glared at her.

"I mean, what was I thinking? Of course I'll stay so that you can feed me." Shaw grinned.

"That's what I thought you meant." Kate tugged her from the couch and handed her bowls and silverware, which she dutifully carried to the table.

CHAPTER TWENTY-SIX

Shaw stood off to the side as Jimmy worked the track hoe, a small excavator with a grapple bucket on the front that looked something like a crab claw. It was Monday, late morning, and the first phase of demolishing the old culvert was well underway. Jimmy was using the track hoe to dislodge the galvanized pipe and chunks of concrete, along with dirt and silt that had collected around the structure over the years.

Eighteen yards of concrete and four steel I-beams each about twenty feet long had been offloaded near the creek crossing. Shaw and Jimmy had figured and refigured the deflection on each beam carrying the weight of an average sized gravel truck. Nearly a mile-long driveway up to the Elkins place required seasonal grading and gravel. Shaw wanted to make sure they took that into consideration. This bridge would need to support more than car traffic.

They'd also designed the crossing so that it was higher, by five feet, to accommodate the hundred-year flood mark, which lately seemed to be a regular occurrence.

She'd brought welding gear from the shop down to the project site and was using a cutting torch to sever the rebar because the concrete saw wouldn't cut it. Shaw was as giddy as a school kid. Constructing the bridge was like bringing one of her erector set creations into existence on a life-sized scale.

When she paused for a minute, she noticed Kate standing on the other side of the creek. Kate waved and she waved back. She motioned for Kate to move downstream, away from the machine noise so that they could hear each other. Shaw had cautioned Kate that until the bridge was in place Shaw would have to run a shuttle for them across the creek in her old Jeep. There was a shallower water crossing a hundred yards downstream from where the bridge was being constructed that was easy with four-wheel drive. Kate had parked her Honda on the highway side of the creek so that once she was across she'd be able to leave or run errands. It would take a few days before the bridge was passable, so Jimmy had hired a couple of local guys to help with construction to speed the process because Shaw didn't want Kate to feel stranded.

She noticed that Kate had a small backpack over one shoulder. She was wearing shorts and a fitted T-shirt that looked so good it made Shaw's body temp go up a degree or two.

"Can you come get me?" yelled Kate.

Shaw nodded and in a quick minute retrieved the Jeep and eased it through the creek and back. Kate followed her to where Jimmy had just climbed down from the track hoe.

"Wow, this is a bigger job than I imagined."

"It probably looks like a big mess right now, but it'll begin to take shape." Jimmy took a long swig of water from a gallon plastic jug.

"I wondered if I could borrow Shaw for a few hours."

Shaw liked the sound of that request but figured she should stay and help Jimmy, although she wasn't that useful with the actual construction. She couldn't run heavy equipment and she had no experience pouring concrete.

"Please take her. All she's doing is standing around trying to supervise."

"Hey! I was just now cutting rebar. Did you see me cutting rebar?" Shaw looked to Kate for some backup.

"I did catch a glimpse of that from the other side." Kate smiled. "I've got this travel piece to write and I'm down to the wire to get it done. I'm going to hike a section of the trail out to Jump Off Rock just to refresh my memory. I was hoping you'd come with me." She tilted her head and looked sideways at Shaw. "But only if Jimmy doesn't need your help here."

"Please, go for a hike." Jimmy playfully shoved Shaw in Kate's direction.

"I'd love to accompany you on this walk in the woods. I'm at your service." Ignoring Jimmy, Shaw bowed and smiled.

"Great. I packed some water and snacks for us." Kate patted the small backpack.

"Okay, well, Jimmy try not to screw anything up while I'm gone. I'll be back to check your work later." Jimmy gave her a mock salute.

The air was warm and the sky peeking through the dense foliage overhead was cobalt blue. It was a beautiful day for a hike. Shaw had offered to drive. It was such fun to drive in the mountains, in a convertible. Traffic in San Francisco was so bad that she avoided driving whenever possible which, given her love for cars, was a tragedy.

Across from her, Kate was holding her gathered hair against the wind. She looked beautiful. Kate's proximity set off a deep ache inside.

"Would you let me pull over and make love to you on the side of the road if I asked?"

"No, I would not."

Shaw laughed. "Really? You'd say no to me?"

"We're not fooling around on the side of the road in a car with no doors."

"Oh, yeah, I guess I see your point."

"I do have my limits, Shaw Daily."

"And I was trying my best to find them Saturday night."

Kate swatted at her from the passenger seat.

The parking lot for the trailhead was five miles from downtown Hendersonville at the end of Laurel Park Highway. Kate gave Shaw directions as they neared the turnoff. Shaw's phone rang just as they parked.

"Hang on just a minute, I need to get this." She stepped a few feet away to accept the call. It was short. "Sorry, that was about the headstone for Mom's grave."

Kate looked away from the trail signage and gave Shaw her full attention.

"They'll deliver it in the morning so everything will be in place for the service."

"That's great, Shaw." Kate touched her arm.

"Yeah, it's sort of hard to believe tomorrow is Tuesday already." Shaw was painfully reminded that her time in Cooper's Creek was drawing to a close.

"You know you'll have to come pick Momma and me up tomorrow, since the creek crossing is under construction."

"Right, I won't forget." Shaw took a closer look at the sign next to Kate. The map showed three different approaches. "Which one are we taking?"

"All of them."

"All of them?"

"Don't worry, they're short. I wanted to walk all of them so I can accurately describe the level of difficulty of each in this article." Kate tugged Shaw by the hand away from the map. "Don't worry, we'll start out easy. I'll be gentle."

"It's not fair to flirt with me when you only just shot me down on the ride over." Shaw allowed herself to be lead to the trail.

The Blue Trail offered a casual walk. It was an easy hike out to the overlook. It probably only took them ten minutes to reach the viewing point. A couple of people were leaning against the railing taking selfies. The granite outcropping was huge and it offered a spectacular view.

"That's Hebron Mountain and over there is Mount Pisgah." Kate pointed out landmarks for Shaw. Even though Shaw spent time in the area as a child she was never able to identify the specific peaks. Maybe she'd have been able to pick out Mount Pisgah if pressed, but she wasn't sure.

Shaw leaned against the railing enjoying the vista. Behind her the couple who was there when they arrived chatted as they headed back toward the parking lot.

"Do you know how this place got its name?"

Shaw shook her head.

"There's an Indian legend about this rock. Supposedly, about three hundred years ago, a young Cherokee chief fell in love with an Indian maiden. They often met on top of the rock to spend time together and enjoy the view." Kate stood beside her, looking out at the rolling ridges, thick with hardwoods. "The young chief was called to war and his love told him that she'd wait for his return on their favorite rock overlook. When she received word that her young chief had been killed in battle, she climbed to the edge of the rock and jumped."

"Is that a true story?"

"I like to think it is." Kate turned to look at her. "Indian legend has it that sometimes, on moonlit nights you can see the woman's ghost on Jump Off Rock."

"Is that going to be part of your article?"

"Of course." Kate turned away and headed back down a different path. "Come on, we have two more trails to check out."

The Yellow Trail turned out to be moderately difficult and took about twice as long as the first path they'd taken. They saved the trail marked red for last and it ended up being the toughest. The route lead down a rock staircase into a thicket and then climbed back to the overlook. Shaw was winded and grateful for the water Kate had brought in her pack.

Kate was disappointed that on this last climb to the overlook they would have to share the view with three other people. The three young men looked as if they were somewhere between sixteen and eighteen, although she wasn't sure. They were joking around and shoving each other against the metal railing as if they were trying to scare each other. The boys were a bit rough around the edges. Probably local boys. They didn't give off a tourist vibe at all. Kate was reluctant to even step out on the overlook. She wanted to turn and go the minute she saw them, but Shaw had taken the water bottle and was leaning with elbows on the railing. She seemed to be ignoring the banter of male voices to her right.

"Are you ready to head back?" Kate was standing close to Shaw, keeping one eye on the boys, who seemed to be watching them.

"Sure, if—"

"Hey! Are you a boy or a girl?" One of the guys cut Shaw off. The other two laughed and punched his arm.

"Just ignore them." Kate kept her voice down and tried not to encourage them by looking at them. Shaw on the other hand rotated so that she was leaning back against the railing, facing in their direction.

"Are you a boy or a girl?" He repeated the question to more chuckles from his pals. He was scruffy looking, lanky with a beat up cammo truckers' hat. He looked to be about the same height as Shaw.

"Why, can't you tell the difference?" Shaw smiled, but he didn't. Behind him his friends laughed.

"Come on, let's go." Kate tugged at Shaw's arm. This whole situation was making her nervous, although Shaw seemed completely unperturbed by it.

"Why don't you find a real man?" That question was directed at Kate.

Shaw nonchalantly straightened, moved away from the railing, and stood in front of Kate blocking the guy's view.

"If we see one, we'll let you know."

Kate could tell by the look on his face that he was getting angry. She wasn't sure if he was mad at Shaw or mad because his friends seemed to be laughing at his expense.

"You want to start something?" He took a few steps toward Shaw.

"No, I wanted to enjoy a nice hike with a pretty view." Shaw stood her ground, casually tossing the water bottle back and forth from hand to hand.

"You've got a pretty view. Maybe you don't deserve her." He nodded in Kate's direction, and for the first time during the exchange, Shaw's demeanor shifted.

Shaw clenched her jaw muscle and handed the water bottle back to Kate. She took a step closer to the teen. Kate wouldn't have described the stance as aggressive, but definitely confident.

He looked back at his friends and then turned and adjusted his hat. He was fidgety where Shaw was still. After a minute, she relaxed her stance and smiled.

"Well, fellas, it's been nice talking to you. We're gonna hang out here and enjoy the overlook if you don't mind." She smiled and took a step back. Everything about her energy signaled *I come in peace.*

"Whatever." He looked annoyed but slightly relieved. Kate was sure she was the only one who noticed the tension in his shoulders release. Shaw had given him an easy out, and Kate was relieved to see that he was taking it. "Come on." He motioned for his friends to follow him back down the path.

He looked back at Shaw one more time. Whatever comeback he might have had in mind, it never came. He shoved his buddies toward the trailhead mumbling something under his breath that Kate didn't catch. Probably something original like calling them dykes, as if that were an insult.

Shaw stood where she was, watching until they disappeared from view.

"I can't believe you engaged with them, Shaw. That could have gone badly." Kate was impressed that Shaw had stood up to them, but at the same time she wasn't in favor of taking unnecessary chances.

"They were harmless." Shaw took another swig from the water bottle.

"How could you be so sure?"

"He was wearing his insecurity like a suit. It was all over him." Shaw brushed a loose strand of hair off Kate's cheek. "When you're the new kid in school every few months you learn a lot about social politics. Lots of people operate in the world by creating an us versus them scenario. No one wants to be alone and certainly no one wants to be an outsider, so even as kids people begin to create false groups, imagined barriers, to insulate themselves. The most insecure are the first to create cliques. If you let the leader know that you recognize yourself as an outsider and that you don't care, then you defuse the situation. You upend the paradigm."

"You must have had a hard time, Shaw."

"It wasn't bad. Some of the things I hated about moving around so much ended up building skills that have served me well." Shaw entwined her fingers with Kate's, brought them to her lips, and kissed them. "It's no fun if the rabbit doesn't run. I wasn't scared of them and that basically destroyed the game. Plus, I made his friends laugh. That's definitely a mood killer."

"Is this why you said you're good at beginnings?" Kate's heart ached a little picturing a young Shaw having to adjust to a new school every few months. She couldn't imagine having to start over with a new group of kids so often. She'd spent her entire school years, until she left for college, with the same group of friends.

"Oh, you remember I said that?"

"I remember everything."

"Thanks for that word of caution."

Kate laughed, but she wasn't letting Shaw off the hook. "What was it like moving around so much?"

"It was okay."

"Really?" Kate wasn't convinced.

"Some places were better than others. Some schools were easier than others to navigate, you know, in terms of social politics."

"But beginnings? I'm guessing there were lots of them."

"I realized at some point in high school that I'd never learned how to nurture a friendship beyond a certain point. I'd never had to. I never got a chance to. In college, when I started dating I realized I only knew how to build a relationship to a certain point. My first girlfriend was very frustrated by that." Shaw shoved her hands in her pockets and rotated to look at the view. "I wanted to be better. I wanted to let her get close. I just didn't know how." She turned and gave Kate a weak smile. "I suppose I confided that in you because I didn't want you to be disappointed."

"Shaw, nothing about you has been disappointing." Kate held Shaw's face in her hands and kissed her.

They took the less strenuous path back to the parking lot. Kate didn't want to cut the afternoon short, but she needed to get back to her mother. And she needed to write up her notes for the travel piece.

"Do you mind if we drive back now? I could make us some lunch when we get back to the house."

"If I didn't know this was some cultural imperative I'd swear you were trying to fatten me up."

Kate laughed. "It wouldn't hurt you to gain a little weight. Then I'd just have a little more to hold on to."

Shaw arched her eyebrows and grinned. She backed up and turned onto the main road.

"I was kind of surprised you left your mom for so long."

"She wanted me to go. I don't think she was feeling well, but she wouldn't admit it. I told her I wouldn't be long." Kate broke an energy bar in half and offered it to Shaw. "I think possibly she wanted some time to herself. She'd been living alone since my father passed away. I know she enjoys having me there, but I'm sure it's an adjustment if you're used to having the house to yourself."

Twenty-five minutes later, they pulled up in front of the house. Kate insisted that Shaw have some food before jumping back into the construction project with Jimmy. They'd made sandwiches and her mother had barely eaten, complaining of a headache.

Kate finally convinced her mother to take some aspirin and lie down. If she were getting sick they'd have to skip the funeral service the next day. Kate hoped they wouldn't have to miss it.

CHAPTER TWENTY-SEVEN

They'd made good progress on the bridge by Tuesday midday. The service at the cemetery wasn't until three so Shaw had most of the day to do what she could to help Jimmy and his crew. The plan was to pour the concrete late Tuesday afternoon. If the weather stayed warm and dry, the concrete would be set enough to drive on by Thursday.

Shaw had something special in mind for the end cap on the approach to the bridge. She'd spent a couple of hours working on it in the shop when there was nothing else she could do for Jimmy. Despite her best efforts, there was only so much she could do to be helpful. Most of the actual construction had to be handled by the guys who knew what they were doing. She'd done the schematic drawing for them to use as a guide and she'd provided the cash for the project. Kate hadn't asked how much it was costing and Shaw hoped she wouldn't. She knew Kate had no income at the moment, and she wasn't about to ask for money from Miss Edith. Shaw had the capital and was happy to offer it.

Shaw strapped the silver urn into the passenger seat and drove through the creek to pick up Kate and her mom. They must have heard her approach because they were already coming down the porch steps when she pulled up. Kate looked gorgeous as usual in a simple black dress.

She put a stepladder down by the passenger door to make it easier for Miss Edith to get in. This was definitely not ideal transportation for the elderly, but there was no other way to get across the creek at the moment. Kate helped her mother from the driver's seat, while Shaw half lifted her from the other side. Once they were across the creek they abandoned the Jeep and took Kate's car.

Shaw was a bundle of nerves once they arrived at the church. She knew she wasn't really expected to do anything except show up, but still a knot settled in her stomach that would not subside.

"You look nice." Kate put her hand on Shaw's shoulder. She'd only brought one dark jacket with her, and it was the same one she'd worn the night they'd had dinner.

"You look nice too. Thank you for coming."

As they stood waiting for the minister in the parking lot, other cars arrived. Jimmy and his wife, Anne; Miriam and the girls; and the last vehicle to park was the vintage pickup belonging to Addie Miller. Shaw was genuinely surprised by the turnout. Kate had been right. People did care enough about her mother to show up.

"I can't believe all these folks came." Shaw spoke quietly so that only Kate could hear her.

"Shaw, these people came for you."

"Hi, Shaw." Miriam hugged her and introduced her kids. They were adorable in summer weight Sunday dresses. "Greg sends his apologies. He's in Atlanta today and couldn't get back in time."

Kate took one of Miss Edith's arms and Miriam took the other. They abandoned her walker at the edge of the concrete surface of the parking lot and slowly made their way across the grass to the gravesite. Shaw carried her mother's ashes.

This whole scene was surreal. Not once in six months had she thought of planning a funeral for her mother. She hadn't known where to begin. She hadn't even been able to decide if she should scatter her mother's ashes or bury them. She owed Kate for making this happen. She glanced over at Kate and smiled after she delivered the urn to the minister. Kate kept one hand under Miss Edith's arm and reached for Shaw with the other. They held hands, in front of God and everyone present. The contact felt good; without it, Shaw feared she might get lost, or drift away, or run away. Any of those options sounded appealing at the moment as all eyes were on her.

She tried to focus on the urn-sized hole in the ground a couple of feet away from the headstone bearing her mother's name, Iris

Elizabeth Daily. It looked like nothing more than a posthole. Reverend Gilreath rested the urn on the ground next to the small dark round pit and looked up at those loosely gathered around the grassy space.

Reverend Gilreath nodded for the music to start. He'd asked a local high school boy to play a couple of hymns on the violin. The only hymn Shaw could think of when he'd asked what she wanted was the hymn they'd sung at her grandfather's funeral, "Amazing Grace."

The sound of the melody caused a knot to rise in Shaw's throat. She coughed and tried to swallow it down. Kate squeezed her hand.

The only scripture Shaw could recall clearly from her childhood in vacation Bible school was the twenty-third Psalm. Her mind drifted, past to present, sections of the passage took on different meaning hearing them now.

He leads me beside still waters;
He restores my soul.

She wasn't sure if she'd ever really heard the words before.

Amazing Grace and the Twenty-third Psalm were remnants from her past. Things she'd heard in her youth and traveled far away from. Things in this instance she found oddly soothing. Kate had been right. Funerals were for the living.

The minister was good. Probably better than Shaw had imagined he could be in a place as small and provincial as Cooper's Creek. He'd crafted a message that was sincere without feeling preachy or overly emotional. He'd somehow intuitively managed to strike a balanced tone between traditional religious belief and the secular language recovering believers used when they talked about faith.

She thought her mother would have approved.

"The past gathers in our memories so that we can visit it often." He spoke of a passage from a book written by an Irish theologian, John O'Donahue. "Our loved ones are never truly lost to us, as long as we remember."

So this is what closure felt like.

Everything came undone and Shaw gave in to grief. The pain in her chest was uncertain, vague. She wiped at a tear with the palm of her hand. She didn't want to cry. She hadn't intended to cry. Kate handed her a linen handkerchief and she took it, dabbing at the corner of her eyes.

She and her mother had never made peace. Never really understood each other, but were connected nonetheless. On some level, she assumed her mother was proud of her although she'd never said it out loud. And on some level, she loved her mother, didn't she? Yes, despite everything, the answer was yes.

If only her mother had confided in her and told her the truth about all of it. At least now she knew some of it. Thanks to Miss Edith and Addie, she at least had a partial picture of the past.

As she dropped a handful of dark earth over the urn, now sunk in the ground, she thought of her days in the mountains. She thought of her time with Kate, chats with Addie and Miss Edith. She thought of the boys they'd run into on their hike, rowdy, searching, restless, and lashing out. Thinking of them made her think of Charlie. If someone had just given Charlie a break when he needed it, maybe things would have gone differently. It was easy with hindsight to imagine how acts of kindness might have changed things for Charlie and her mother, and ultimately for Shaw. She was a product of the life her mother had been denied. She knew that now.

She felt the warmth of Kate's hand on her back as the urn was covered with soil. Her mother was finally at rest. In the place she most wanted but in all likelihood least expected to be, next to Charlie, forever.

Everyone quietly filed to the parking lot. Miriam hugged Shaw again, so did Jimmy and Anne. Shaw wasn't really in the mood to talk, which was just as well because she didn't know what to say anyway except thank you.

She helped Kate settle Miss Edith into the passenger seat and was just about to climb into the backseat when Addie spoke to her. Shaw shut the door and walked over to her.

"I brought this for you." Addie held out a small photo, yellowed and discolored from age. "I thought you might like to have it."

Addie had handed her a photo of Charlie and her mother. They were laughing and her mother had her arm draped across Charlie's shoulder. They were young and happy. Cooper's Creek General Store was in the background. Shaw swallowed, and for the second time that day, felt tears gathering. She swiped at them with the back of her hand. The emotion rising in her chest surprised her.

"Thank you." The words were half choked. She looked at Addie, knowing her eyes were rimmed with tears.

Addie hugged her. It was a stiff, awkward embrace, but it was a hug nonetheless.

"You're gonna be okay, Shaw." Addie patted her on the back and then released her. "Don't forget to bring your girl by the house. I have something to show you."

Shaw nodded. Addie obviously assumed Kate was her girl. She should be so lucky. She looked back at the car where Kate was standing in the open driver's side door patiently waiting.

Chapter Twenty-eight

It was late Thursday afternoon by the time Shaw finally set aside the welding gun and stood back to examine her work. She'd spent every hour since her mother's funeral working on a wind driven mobile that she couldn't stop thinking about. She'd started building it in the wee hours of the morning, that time between awake and asleep when she'd allowed her mind to drift.

Closure had opened something up and she'd felt an unfamiliar urgency to create. Working with her hands, forming the metal so that its own weight caused it to move when touched, she felt as if she were in college again. Joy. That was the feeling. Crafting an object for no other reason than because she had the vision of it in her head. Creation. Bringing into the physical world something from nothing.

She stood back with her hands on her hips and examined her work. The piece stood just above waist height. She hadn't had enough raw materials to build anything larger, and anyway, she wanted to be able to lift it into the Jeep by herself. She'd entwined thin metal strips to create the base so that the sculpture would be stable, but not too heavy. And then she'd mounted the moving parts by using small interlocking posts about the size of a wooden dowel so that they could be removed and then dropped back into place for transport.

Shaw loaded the piece and then stopped at the bridge on her way to Kate's. Everything was finished. Shaw walked around so that she could see the structure from both angles. It wasn't decorative by any means, but it had clean lines and it was structurally sound. Wing walls had been constructed upstream and downstream, angled back away from the creek to keep the dirt foundation from washing away. Shaw was pleased.

She'd invited Kate to drive over to Addie's. They hadn't gotten to see each other much since the funeral, except for a few meals they'd shared at Kate's house. Miss Edith hadn't been feeling well. Going to the funeral might have been too much for her since she was already a bit under the weather.

When she saw Kate trotting down the steps in her direction, her stomach started flip-flopping. Just from the sight of her. She'd never been around a woman that set her off so easily and so quickly. No matter what they were doing, no matter what Kate was wearing. Kate had such an easy grace about her, it slayed Shaw every time she was around her. She'd been aching to be alone with Kate, but the demands of Kate's caretaking seemed to continually conspire against them.

It was probably for the best that she was heading to New York Friday morning. The longer she stayed the more comfortable all of this felt and the more frustrated she was by not having time alone with Kate. She needed to get back to her life and let Kate deal with hers. And besides, Raisa needed her.

"What's that?" Kate pointed to the tarp in the back of the Jeep.

"Something I made for Addie."

"I never thanked you for the birdbath, by the way." Kate kissed Shaw on the cheek after she climbed in. "Momma loves it."

"I thought it would look best in Miss Edith's garden. Besides, there won't be anyone to see it if I leave it over at my grandparents' place."

"Oh, yeah, I guess you're leaving tomorrow." Kate gave Shaw a weak smile. If Kate was sad that Shaw was leaving she was doing a good job of not showing it. "I can't believe it's Friday already."

"Yeah, me either."

Addie was in the yard when they drove up. She must have just walked up from her garden, which was only partially visible from where they were standing. She leaned a hoe against the weathered siding of the house and stuffed worn leather work gloves in her back pocket. Shaw worried they should have called first, but she'd never gotten Addie's number. She wasn't even sure Addie had a phone. Addie didn't strike Shaw as the sort of woman who enjoyed idle chitchat. Although, Addie had definitely warmed a little toward Shaw since their first meeting when she'd threatened to get her shotgun.

"I hope today is okay. You said to come by, but we never settled on when." Shaw still gave Addie her distance and Addie seemed to appreciate plenty of personal space.

"Yep, today is fine. It's a pleasure to see you, Kate."

"Um, I have something for you." Shaw felt suddenly shy, but she went to retrieve the sculpture anyway. Addie would either scoff or politely accept the gesture or, who knows. It was hard to guess what her reaction to the gift might be.

"Do you need help?" Kate made a move to follow her.

"No, I've got it."

Shaw shucked off the tarp and carried the base over to an open spot of packed clay in front of the house where the high, wild grass hadn't reached. Then she returned with the two spiral arms that she dropped into the postholes in the base. She waited for a minute to see if there was enough wind to move the spirals. When she saw that they were going to be slow to start, she gave them a little nudge with her finger and then stepped away.

The moving curved shapes of the arms modulated into abstract shapes as they moved over each other. Lines, morphed into circles, which morphed into waves. The animated shadows cast on the ground were like moving pictograms of ancient cave drawings.

"Shaw, it's beautiful." Kate stood next to her. Kate seemed genuinely taken with the sculpture.

Shaw looked over at Addie, who'd moved closer but hadn't said anything. Addie was watching the pirouetting sculpture as if she'd just been spooked by a ghost.

"Addie, I made this for you, but if you don't like it I can—"

"There's something you need to see." Addie cut her off and then abruptly walked toward the barn.

Kate gave Shaw a questioning look as they followed Addie to the barn. Addie opened the large front door just enough to disappear inside. Loud creaking noises came from inside the barn. Shaw wasn't sure she should follow Addie into the dark interior so she didn't. After another minute, Addie returned and swung both sides of the large front doors open. She'd opened the large entrances at each end of the barn. Light and a gentle breeze passed through the cavernous space. It smelled of hay and dry earth. Shaw stepped closer as movement caught her eye.

There was a large metal structure visible as she stepped closer. Its two main components were made of oxidized metal mounted on a central fulcrum. Air currents brought the kinetic sculpture constructed of graceful spirals and ellipses gradually to life. The flat surfaces moved from darkness to light as they began to slowly rotate.

As the sculpture drew breath and stirred, it was as if Shaw was also breathing for the first time.

"Is this…" Her words died in her throat.

"Yes. Charlie made this." Addie crossed her arms and stood beside Shaw watching the sculpture slowly circle in the half-light of the open door. "It's been here, waiting, all these many years."

A sense of connection, a sense of belonging washed over Shaw. She looked at Kate who had covered her mouth with her hand. The wet paths of tears were on her cheeks. Shaw didn't have the language to explain the emotion that crowded her chest. It was as if Charlie had sent her a message of kinship from some other place, some place beyond knowing, beyond words. She couldn't explain it. The moving monument was like some secret presence of the divine, and in that instant, she knew she'd been loved.

Kate wanted to reach for Shaw. The drive back to her house had been deafeningly quiet and she was unsure how to breach the silence. She wasn't sure what Shaw needed. She'd been overcome by emotion seeing Charlie's sculpture so she couldn't imagine what Shaw must be feeling.

Impulse finally got the best of her and she reached over and stroked the back of Shaw's head.

"Are you okay?"

Shaw nodded. She turned to Kate and smiled, but both the gaze and the smile were distant, as if she were a million miles away. They drove across the new bridge and up the long drive. Kate wanted to thank Shaw for the new crossing, but now didn't seem like the right time for mundane topics.

"Do you want to come in for a little while?" Kate was hyper aware of the fact that Shaw was leaving the next morning. She couldn't decide if spending more time with Shaw would be more or less torturous.

"I should go home and pack."

"Okay." Kate didn't want to say more and give herself away. She didn't want to seem needy or emotional given all that Shaw must be processing at the moment.

"I'll see you tomorrow before I leave." The saddest expression passed across Shaw's face like a cloud in front of the sun. "I think...I think I just need to be alone right now."

"I understand." She leaned over and kissed Shaw lightly on the lips. "I'm here if you need to talk."

"Thanks."

Kate watched Shaw drive away before going inside. They'd had a magical three weeks. Their time together was more than she could have hoped for, but it was drawing to a close and they would each resume their lives. Shaw would return to the West Coast and Kate would remain.

"Momma, I'm home." Her mother didn't answer. "Momma?"

Kate checked the living room. She walked through her mother's bedroom and then she saw her mother's arm stretched out on the floor through the open door of the bathroom.

"Momma!" Kate ran to her mother's side.

She was unresponsive, but breathing. Kate frantically reached for the wall phone and dialed 9-1-1. Help was on the way. The rescue squad, deployed from the county's volunteer fire department, was ten minutes away. Kate pressed a damp cool cloth to her mother's face and tried to stay calm. She wasn't sure if her mother had fainted and if so, how hard she had hit the floor. There was no blood, but the injury could be internal. She shouldn't have left her alone. She'd known her mother wasn't feeling well. A million thoughts flashed through her mind as she waited so that ten minutes flew by in an instant. She heard the siren and ran to the door.

"She's in here!"

Two men carrying emergency gear met her at the door. She knew them both. One was Hank, her friend and fellow teacher. The other, Mack, was friends with her brother-in-law.

"Kate, are you all right?" Hank had a look of genuine concern on his face.

"It's not me. It's my mother. She's back here." They followed her.

"Do you know what happened?" Mack started to check her mother's vitals.

"I don't. I wasn't here when it happened, so I don't know how long she was unconscious. I don't know—" Her words ended in a sob. She covered her mouth and stepped back to give them room to work.

"Her heart rate is steady, but weak. I'm going to start fluids." Mack was talking to Hank. "Get the gurney."

Kate stepped aside to let Hank pass. After a moment, he was back and, using a backboard, they transferred her mother to the gurney. Her mother looked almost transparent: small and frail.

She followed on their heels and watched as they loaded her mother into the back of the EMT vehicle. The siren was off but the lights were still flashing. Hank turned to her as Mack climbed into the driver's seat.

"We'll take her to Hendersonville. You follow us, okay?"

She nodded.

"Kate, she's in good hands." He squeezed her arm.

Adrenaline spiked her heart rate as she followed the dust cloud of the ambulance down the long drive. With sirens blazing, they sped away on the two-lane main highway toward downtown Hendersonville.

Kate drove with one hand and rummaged in her purse for her cell phone with the other.

"Miriam?" She knew she probably sounded panicked, despite best efforts to remain calm.

"Kate, what's wrong?"

"Momma collapsed. I'm following the ambulance to the hospital—"

"I'm on my way...Greg!" She heard Miriam yell to Greg just before she clicked off.

Kate tossed her phone onto the passenger seat and tried to focus on driving.

CHAPTER TWENTY-NINE

Shaw threw T-shirts haphazardly into her suitcase. The howl of a distant siren echoed up the mountainside. She realized that was a sound she frequently heard in the city but rarely heard here, she'd hardly noticed its absence. She wondered absently what had happened. Probably some motorcyclist had taken a curve too fast. These roads were popular with cyclists.

She rolled jeans and stuffed them along the edges of her suitcase. She'd have to buy a dress shirt in New York before the meeting because she'd only brought one with her and it wasn't clean. The bed springs creaked as she took a break from packing and sat down. Packing hadn't been so urgent that she couldn't have stayed for a while at Kate's. It had just been a convenient excuse to escape. Not that Kate made her feel as if she needed to escape. So why had she? It was more habit than anything else. When Shaw needed to figure things out she was used to doing it alone. It never occurred to her until now how that might make Kate feel.

She picked up the phone and dialed Kate's number. No answer. When voice mail picked up she hesitated, then hung up without leaving a message. Kate was probably helping her mother get ready for bed. She'd give her a little time and then call back.

Restless and unable to complete the task of packing, Shaw strolled over to the shop. She'd almost finished one last small project for Kate. Something she thought only Kate would appreciate. She ran her fingers around the filed edge of the rounded arched shape.

It was getting dark outside. The light from the oversized shop door cast a long golden rectangle across the grass in front of the building. Fireflies flicked on and off at the edge of the yard. She pulled on the welding mask and gloves and began to work.

❖

Kate was in the waiting room at the ER when Miriam arrived.

"How is she? I left Greg with the girls and came right over." Miriam was out of breath. She dropped into the chair next to Kate.

"I don't know anything yet." She started to cry. "Oh, Miriam, I wasn't there when it happened. I was only gone…maybe an hour. And when I came back I found her."

Miriam put her arm around Kate's shoulders and drew her close. "Listen, this could have happened even if you were there. Don't go beating yourself up. There's no way any of us can be with her every minute."

"But I knew she wasn't feeling well. I shouldn't have left her at the house alone." Kate leaned into Miriam's shoulder. She was relieved not to be alone.

Alone.

She reached for her phone. There was a missed call from Shaw. Kate meant to call her right after she arrived at the hospital, but there'd been paperwork to fill out and she'd barely sat down when Miriam arrived. But Shaw was leaving tomorrow. The phone rang and rang and then voice mail picked up.

"Shaw, when you get this please call me." She didn't want to say too much in a voice mail.

"No answer?"

"No, she was going home to pack. She's leaving tomorrow."

"How's that going?"

"It's been going great. But all good things must come to an end."

"Must they?"

"Well, I think this one will." Kate sighed and shoved her phone in her purse.

A woman wearing scrubs under a white coat walked toward them. Kate saw the doctor first and stood up. She tried to read the news on the woman's face, but it was impossible. Beside her Miriam stood up too and took Kate's hand.

"Hello, are you Kate?"

She nodded. "And this is my sister, Miriam."

"I'm Dr. Renata. First, let me tell you that your mother is stable and doing well."

Kate felt the tension in her stomach release a little. She took a deep breath and waited for Dr. Renata to say more.

"Your mother has an infection which at her age can put a strain on her entire system. Her electrolytes were very low, along with her blood pressure. My best guess is that she passed out and then hit her head when she fell."

"Is she awake?" Miriam squeezed Kate's hand.

"She's awake, but very groggy. We're going to move her to a room shortly and when we do you'll be able to see her." Dr. Renata took the stethoscope from around her neck and slipped it into her jacket pocket. "We're going to want to keep her for one night, maybe two. Okay?"

Kate nodded.

"Thank you, Doctor." Miriam sank back into a chair.

"Do you want a coffee? I think now that we know what's going on I might need one."

"No, I'm fine. I'll wait here if you want to go to the cafeteria and get something."

As Kate walked down the hallway, she dialed Shaw again. This time she picked up.

"Shaw?"

"Kate, I was just about to call you. I got your message just now. I forgot to take my phone with me to the shop. Are you okay? You sounded...stressed."

"Shaw, Momma passed out and hit her head. I'm at the hospital."

"What?"

"She's okay, but they want to keep her for the night."

"I'm on my way. Where are you?"

"Shaw, you don't have to come. Everything is all right and there's nothing you can do anyway. I just wanted you to know where

I was…why I wasn't home. In case you changed your mind about coming over."

Shaw could hear the stress in Kate's voice, but she wasn't sure what Kate was trying to say to her. Did Kate want Shaw to come but was afraid to ask? Or did she want to be alone with her mother?

"Is Miriam with you?"

"Yes, she's here."

"Kate, I want to come be with you…unless you don't want me to." She decided to just ask because she couldn't figure out what Kate really wanted.

"I want to see you." Kate sounded like she was crying.

"Are you at the hospital in Hendersonville?"

"Yes."

"I'm on my way."

Twenty minutes later, Shaw burst through the sliding doors and strode across the waiting area to the desk. A young woman looked up as she leaned on the raised counter.

"Can you tell me what room Edith Elkins is in?"

"Shaw." Kate was still in the waiting area.

Shaw met her halfway across the room and swept her into a hug. She held on tight for several minutes, sinking her face into Kate's hair. She placed a kiss there before she pulled away, holding Kate at arm's length.

"I'm so sorry I didn't get your first call. I heard a siren from the house, but I never in a million years thought it was coming from your house."

"It's okay. There's no way you could've known."

"Is she okay?"

"Yes, they just moved her to a room and Miriam is with her." Kate led the way to the elevators.

They rode up to the second floor. Kate explained what had happened. She looked tired and worried. Shaw held her hand as they walked toward Miss Edith's room. Miriam looked up when they entered the sterile white space. Miss Edith was asleep, partially elevated on the hospital bed. She looked small and pale next to the stand of machines tracking her heartbeat and oxygen levels.

Miriam stood and gave Shaw a hug.

"Hey."

"I'm glad you came. I wanted to be able to say good-bye before you left."

Shaw swallowed. She really was leaving. It seemed strange to think of going back to San Francisco. She suddenly felt oddly unmoored, a woman with no country.

"Now that you two are here I'm going to go out in the hallway and call Greg. He's going to want to know what's going on."

Miriam left them in the room. Hospitals made Shaw uncomfortable. She assumed hospitals made everyone uncomfortable, but somehow others seemed to handle the discomfort more easily than she did.

"I'm glad you're here." Kate wrapped her arm around Shaw's waist and rested her cheek on Shaw's shoulder.

"Of course I'm here." She put her arm around Kate and kissed her forehead.

"Did you get everything packed?"

"Mostly." Shaw felt a knot in her throat. She hadn't even left yet. Why was she so sad? "I wasn't going to leave without seeing you."

"I had plans for you." Kate smiled. "I was going to do my best to convince you to sleep at my house tonight. Sleep being code for other things."

"Is that right? It wouldn't have taken much convincing. I miss being close to you." Shaw kept her voice low. She didn't want Miss Edith to hear her making a play for her daughter in her hospital room. That seemed like bad form.

Casual flirtation seemed to be erasing some of the stress from Kate's face. Or maybe having Shaw with her was actually helping. Shaw was reluctant to claim credit since caretaking wasn't what she would consider one of her strengths.

"Hey, you two sure look cute together." Kate shot Miriam a stern look. "What? You do. I'm simply stating the obvious."

Shaw dropped her arm from around Kate's shoulder. Feeling suddenly awkward in front of Miriam.

"I should probably go." The room felt crowded and she had the sense she was intruding. She wasn't family after all, and visiting hours would probably be over any minute.

"Don't leave on my account." Miriam took a chair on the other side of her mother's hospital bed.

"No, I didn't finish packing and I'm sure you two want some time with your mom." Kate looked a little crestfallen, but didn't try to stop her. "I'll call you tomorrow before I leave."

Kate nodded. They hugged briefly and then she left. Her footfalls echoed inside her head as she walked the long gleaming hallway to the elevator, and she couldn't help thinking she was making some terrible mistake.

Chapter Thirty

Shaw had a hard time going to sleep. All night she kept imagining what Kate was doing or where she was and replaying the hospital scene in her head. Why hadn't she stayed longer? Did Miriam's comment about them being a cute couple freak her out? Maybe. Probably.

She assumed Kate spent the night at the hospital because she never called Shaw. There'd been this slim glimmer of hope that Kate would call, but Miriam probably had to get home to her kids so Kate would have ended up staying with her mom.

By six a.m., she gave in and got up. She made coffee and headed down to the shop. She loaded the small sculpture for Kate into the Jeep and drove it down to the bridge and then set it just to the left of the approach side of the bridge where Kate would be sure to spot it as she drove across. Shaw spun slowly around and drew in a deep breath of the early mountain air. The grass was heavy with dew. The creek cut a rolling, glittering path across the bottomland, past Miss Edith's garden patch, and out of sight into the trees. For a moment, she considered recording the sound of the running water on her phone so that she could play it later when she was alone in her hotel room in New York.

Why was she being so morbid? She'd be back. It wasn't like she couldn't come back anytime she wanted. Her grandparents' place would always be here for her. She pulled her phone from her pocket and called Kate. She picked up on the first ring.

"Hi, Shaw." She sounded sleepy.

"Did you stay with your mom last night?"

"Yeah. She woke up around two a.m. and was a bit fussy. She was confused about where she was and kept trying to get out of the bed with the IV still attached."

"I'm glad you were there for her."

"Me too."

"Listen, I left something for you by the bridge."

"You did?"

"Yeah. You'll see it when you drive home. I hope you like it."

"Shaw…"

"Yes?"

"I'll miss you."

It seemed Kate wasn't going to beg her to stay. Kate wasn't going to make her feel guilty for not staying. Apparently, Kate wasn't going to make any demands on her at all. Normally, that was exactly the way she liked things. So why did she find this so disappointing?

"I'll miss you too."

"The doctor just got here so I should go."

"Okay, tell Miss Edith good-bye for me when she wakes up. I hope she feels better soon."

"I will. Good-bye, Shaw."

Kate clicked off and the sound of the call ending was like a sonic boom inside her head. Why did every simple gesture suddenly seem so final? She was simply flying back to San Francisco via New York, not leaving Earth's orbit. She drove back to the house and attempted to shake off the feeling of dread that was clinging to her shoulders.

She had forty-five minutes to shower and get dressed before the driver arrived to take her to the airport.

The door lock flashed green and clicked. Shaw leaned into it with her shoulder, pulling the rolling bag along across the threshold. Low recessed lighting greeted her in the entryway. She left the bag standing near the closet door and collapsed backward onto the bed, staring up at the ceiling.

There was that feeling again, the feeling that she was in the wrong place. That feeling that she was far from home.

The first leg of her flight was from Asheville to Atlanta. She was still in the South. The drawl of Southern accents could be heard intermittently as she passed through the terminal. The smell of Bojangles' chicken and biscuits confirmed she was still close to home. But when the aircraft door closed for her flight from Atlanta to New York, Shaw had the same sinking feeling she'd had walking down the sterile hospital hallway to the elevator, like a sinkhole in the pit of her stomach, telling her that she was making the wrong decision, but about which part? About her career, or Kate?

She'd gone to the mountains to recharge and reboot. She'd done that, right? So it was time to get back to her life. So why did all of this feel so wrong?

Shaw was only minutes into the trip when the flight attendant offered her a beverage. She opted for bourbon and Coke. One drink would take the edge off and hopefully settle her stomach. The alcohol would wear off before she needed to be on point in New York. She sipped the drink and absently flipped through the movie options on the console. Absolutely nothing held her interest. All she could think about was Kate.

Once on the ground, Shaw had gone straight from the airport to the dinner meeting with Mr. Komori from Dansai. It had been a relief to focus on something and get out of her own head for a couple of hours. The meeting went well. Basically, her goal had been to smooth things over. To assure Mr. Komori that top management at Red Rock did not approve of the pressure tactics applied during the last meeting and that, in fact, the salesman responsible had been relieved of duty. Mr. Komori seemed satisfied that things were back on the right track and that they had an understanding. That had been Shaw's mission and she'd succeeded.

She'd texted Raisa on her way to the hotel to let her know the status, then she'd sunk back into the deep leather seat of the town car and watched Times Square pass by her window.

She lay on the bed now, staring at the ceiling, replaying her thoughts from the ride to the hotel.

After two weeks in the mountains, New York City seemed like consumption central. Every square inch covered with concrete or flashing video ads or enormous billboards. Every space available dedicated to selling something—fashion, food, or happiness.

Auto-craving, that's what Shaw called it. A city built to serve those continually on the hunt for the one thing to make them content. Consumerism based on the carefully crafted illusion that life should be perfect. Materialistic, but not material. Shaw visualized the throng of people she'd passed on the sidewalk as they ate with one hand and talked on their phone with the other, walking briskly somewhere, laden with heavy briefcases strapped across their chests. She felt sad for them, sad for the world, and sad for herself.

Wasn't this exactly where she started? Wasn't this exactly what drove her to return to Cooper's Creek in the first place? Some search for deeper meaning? Hadn't she found it and walked away from it?

Shaw sat up, suddenly alert. If she stilled her mind on a granular level she knew her time with Kate had changed her. The dream hadn't reoccurred in more than two weeks. She'd felt happier with Kate than she'd ever felt, at ease, content. She'd felt loved. That was it wasn't it? Love.

Sitting on the edge of the bed, the room bathed in ambient light from the city outside the hotel window, Shaw unconditionally surrendered to love.

Shaw checked her watch. It was only six p.m. on the West Coast. She knew exactly what she wanted to do. She reached for the phone and dialed.

CHAPTER THIRTY-ONE

It had been almost a week since Kate's mother had been admitted to the hospital and things were getting back to normal. Her mother was much better, but Kate now knew she'd have to pay more attention to what her mother ate and also make sure her mother was getting plenty of fluids.

She'd been lucky this time, lucky that her mother hadn't hit her head on the sink as she fell. She'd gotten a lump on the back of her head, but the bathmat had cushioned her fall. Yes, she'd been very lucky.

"Momma, I'm going to go for a walk. Will you be okay for a few minutes?"

"I'm fine, sweetie. I won't leave this chair until you get back." Her mother was in her floral recliner looking at catalogs for flowers and bulbs. "You take your time."

Kate waved as she pulled the door to behind her. She felt like crying. She'd felt like crying all day. When she felt like crying and didn't want to give into it, sometimes a walk helped.

She crossed the creek and stopped near the sculpture Shaw had left for her. It was a turtle. As she had learned was Shaw's style, the sculpture wasn't a perfectly representational turtle, but more of an abstracted interpretation. In any case, Kate knew it was a turtle the minute she'd seen it. It was their turtle. The turtle they'd seen that first morning together that she hadn't seen since. She'd been giddy with pleasure when she first saw the sculpture and then promptly burst into tears. She took a seat on the arched shell and rested her chin in her hand.

Shaw had called several times, but they kept missing each other. Only once in the past week did they actually get to talk. Mostly it seemed Shaw had phoned to ask about her mother. They'd been cautiously casual. At least that's how it felt to Kate. Clearly, neither of them was going to admit they'd hoped for more time together. Or maybe she was the only one who'd wished for that. Maybe Shaw was fine. Maybe Shaw was happy and settled back into her life in California.

See, this is why Kate did not do casual sex. This is exactly why. She'd let things go too far with Shaw. She'd gotten invested in Shaw even when she knew Shaw was leaving. She had no one to blame but herself.

Shaw never made any promises to her. Shaw never said she loved her.

But…

But that didn't mean she wasn't in love with Shaw. And she had not allowed herself to admit it, not to herself and certainly not to Shaw. She definitely had no one to blame for her affliction but herself. They'd had their moment of glorious romance and the moment was gone.

Kate rotated so that she was facing the creek. Points of light bounced off the rippling water like loosely strung pearls as it wove among the rocks. She closed her eyes and let the sound of running water soothe her senses. The stream had so little to do and not a care in the world, its only chore was to join with the river in search of the sea.

She took a couple of deep breaths and opened her eyes. Just at the edge of the stream in front of her was the snapping turtle. He stretched his neck only slightly and regarded her with his wrinkled ancient eyes. She was frozen in place. This had to be a sign. She was taking this as a sign.

"Thank you!" She jumped up and jogged toward the house.

There was a light knock at Shaw's office door.

"Come in."

"You're still here?" Raisa sat down on the other side of the desk.

"I'm just sending some notes to Akira." Shaw made a few more keystrokes and then slid the wireless keyboard to the side. She leaned back in her chair and rubbed her eyes. This had been a long week and a long day.

"Did I thank you already for how you handled things in New York?"

"You did and you're welcome." Shaw slipped some paperwork into a folder and set it to the side of her desk. "Akira deserves half the credit. She laid all the groundwork before I got there."

"Even still. Thank you." Raisa picked up a pen off the desk and rolled it between her manicured fingers. "You're sure about this?"

"No, but I have to do it."

"You do seem different since you came back."

"I feel different." Something had happened to Shaw during her time in Cooper's Creek. She couldn't shake it and she couldn't explain it adequately to Raisa. Every time she tried it just sounded like some silly Hallmark made for TV movie. All she knew was that she had to go back to figure it out.

"I can't believe I'm letting you go."

Shaw laughed.

"Spoken like a jealous girlfriend."

"Maybe I am." Raisa smiled and tossed the pen onto the desk.

"I'm only a phone call away. Working with you on a consulting basis will probably be better for all of us. I'm too distracted to stay, but I can jump in for short assignments when you need me."

"I know. But it's not the same as having you here and being able to brainstorm late at night over takeout food."

"We can have takeout food separately, together. Just put me on speaker phone." Shaw leaned forward and rested her elbows on the desk.

While in New York she'd realized all she'd ever really wanted was contentment. Instead of looking for true contentment she'd participated in compulsive consumption and the sale of same or at least the promotion of that ethos. And she just couldn't do it any longer. She'd come to the conclusion that she was only going to get one life. That wasn't some esoteric idea; that was reality. She had one life and she wasn't going to waste another minute of it.

"You have an answer for everything."

"Not really. Not even close."

It was nearly seven by the time Shaw left her office. She took the trolley down Market to Dolores Street and then walked the rest of the way to her building on 17th, just down from the park. Normally, she'd stay at work until well past dark and then grab a bite near the office before heading home. But this evening she wanted to relish the things that made San Francisco unique. The refurbished vintage trolley cars that ran up and down Market, the lush palm trees that stood in line along the central median of Dolores, and the old Catholic Mission.

For some reason, the rock work of the Mission reminded her of the hike she and Kate had taken out to Jump Off Rock. For the first time since hearing the story Kate told of the princess, she realized this was her mom's story too. Her mom had never recovered from losing Charlie and spent the rest of her life jumping into things, never finding the one place that made her feel as if she belonged. At least, that was how Shaw saw it now.

When Kate had told the story, Shaw couldn't imagine anyone making such a drastic choice because of love. But that was exactly what she was doing, if not literally, then at least symbolically.

She was jumping off.

Taking a leap of faith.

She could only hope that Kate would be there to catch her when she landed.

CHAPTER THIRTY-TWO

Kate was a nervous mess on the flight to San Francisco. She'd chewed her nails and drank way too much Diet Coke. Every time the drink cart came by, she asked for the entire can. She should have just gone all out and added whiskey to the mix. Halfway through the flight, somewhere over Nebraska, she worried she'd made a colossal mistake. But now she was in San Francisco and she'd hate herself forever if she didn't see this through.

The cab stand was easy to find outside baggage claim. She'd gotten Shaw's address from Jimmy. And when she'd called Miriam to share her scheme, Miriam had readily agreed to load up Greg and the kids to stay at her mother's place for the entire weekend. Everyone had come to her rescue. All she had to do was ask.

San Francisco looked so foreign compared to Cooper's Creek. The deep blue green of the hardwoods in the Blue Ridge Mountains was missing from the dry landscape of the West Coast. They drove through hills covered in golden grass as they left the airport south of the city. And as the highway dumped them into the Mission District, narrow row houses pressed tightly together slid past her window.

She'd been rehearsing what she'd say. Every iteration sounded overly dramatic inside her head, and she had a hard time imagining how Shaw would respond.

Basically, she was in love with Shaw. She'd known it after the first night they slept together. Actually, she'd probably known it before that, but she wouldn't allow herself to go there. She'd tried so hard to hold herself apart, to protect her heart from falling, and she'd failed miserably. She had to tell Shaw the truth. What had gone unsaid between them was haunting her. Even if Shaw didn't feel the same way, at least then she'd know. She'd know the truth and could move on. As it was, she was stuck. She'd be comparing everyone she ever went out with in the future to Shaw, and the truth was she feared no one would ever measure up.

No, she was horribly, irreparably, and painfully in love with Shaw Daily. And she'd flown across the whole damn country to say exactly that.

The cab pulled up in front of a three-story building on 17th street. It was vintage, maybe early 1900s, with wood siding and tastefully painted gray with white and darker gray trim. Somehow, the building looked like Shaw to Kate.

She paid the driver and stood looking up at the façade. She'd eventually have to knock. She stood silently, gathering her courage.

Shaw had an armful of loose papers that she couldn't fit into her briefcase. The Realtor had couriered them over at the end of the day for signatures. She shifted the papers in her arm so that she could fish in her pocket for her keys. She wasn't really paying attention to where she was walking so when she rounded the corner she almost bumped into Kate.

"Kate?" Kate turned to look at her and smiled. She was holding onto a small rolling bag.

Shaw fumbled her keys, and in the process several papers fluttered to the sidewalk. Kate bent to help her gather them. When they stood up they almost bumped heads, and she was reminded of the first time they connected in the general store.

"Hi."

"Hi." Kate was in San Francisco. Shaw's heart was thumping in her chest from fear or joy or both. "I can't believe you're here."

"I had something to tell you."

"Maybe I have something to tell you."

"Me first." Kate stepped closer.

"Okay."

"I'm in love with you, Shaw Daily. I know my life isn't fully my own at the moment. I know I come with complications. But I still should have told you how I felt before you left. And you don't have to say anything, you don't have to do anything, I just—"

"My turn?" She cut Kate off.

Kate nodded.

"I'm in love with you, Kate Elkins. So there."

"You are?"

"Yes. And any part of your life that you'll share with me is worth my entire life without you in it. I'm sorry I didn't say that before I left, but I don't think I knew for sure how I felt until the plane landed in New York. Leaving you…it was like oxygen had been sucked out of my world, but I didn't realize it until I couldn't breathe."

Kate held Shaw's face tenderly in her hands and kissed her deeply. Shaw's hands were full and the urge to hold Kate was so powerful that she dropped her briefcase to the ground and drew Kate close. Papers crinkled in the embrace.

"Oh, I'm ruining these." Kate pulled away. "I'm sure I interrupted something important. Did you need to deliver these or something? And now they're all creased." Kate took some of the documents from her and started to organize them into a neat stack.

"They're from the sale of this place."

"What?"

"I sold it." Shaw nodded toward the three-story building. "It's a triplex and I rent out two of the floors. It seems I made a good investment when I bought this place because I just sold it for a little over three million dollars."

Kate arched her eyebrows and opened her mouth as if she was about to say something, but no sound came out.

"Are you all right?"

"Shaw, you sold your house? Why?"

"I thought it would give us some cushion."

"Us?"

"Yes, I thought…well, I thought while you're taking care of your mom that I could take care of us. We can set some of it aside for college for our kids…and I thought—"

"Our kids?" Kate cut her off. A look that was somewhere between joy and surprise on her face.

"Yes, children. Kate, however many you want."

Kate launched into her arms, papers flew everywhere, and they clung to each other leaving no space between their bodies. This was the kiss Shaw had been dreaming of ever since she'd left Kate at the hospital; a full body kiss, a kiss full of promises, a kiss without reservation. For the first time, Shaw held nothing back. She was all in.

"Get a room!" a bicyclist yelled at them as he passed by.

They both laughed.

"Maybe he's right. I do still have the keys to this place." Shaw dangled the keys.

Kate helped her gather up the documents again and they climbed the stairs to Shaw's apartment on the top floor. Once inside, Kate hugged her again and she was overcome by a sense of immediacy and belonging.

"What made you decide to come back to Cooper's Creek?"

"Besides being in love with you?"

"Yeah, besides that."

"I guess I decided I don't want to be an outsider in my own life any longer." She kissed Kate lightly. "And when I'm with you I feel like I belong. I feel like I'm home."

Tears gathered at the edges of Kate's lashes and one trailed down her cheek. Shaw wiped it away gently with her fingertip.

"Can I get you anything? I haven't been here, so there isn't much..."

"All I need is a glass of water, and you."

"Lucky me then, because I just happen to have what you need."

"Yes, you do. You are everything I need."

Shaw reached for a glass. She drew Kate's fingers to her mouth and kissed them as the water ran.

Shaw let Kate have the water, but once she'd finished drinking Shaw pulled her into another kiss. She would never tire of kissing Kate, but right now she wanted even more. She let her hand drift down the front of Kate's blouse. Kate moaned softly and squirmed in her embrace.

"Wait."

"What?"

"Just long enough for me to take a shower. I feel like I have the airport all over me."

"I'll get you a towel." Shaw ushered Kate to the bathroom with a fresh towel and reluctantly left her alone. When she heard the water running, she opened the door just a little. "Can I join you?"

"Yes."

Shaw quickly shucked her work clothes and got into the shower. Kate rotated to face her with lather in her hair. Shaw couldn't resist the urge to slide her hands up and down Kate's body, slick with soap. She kissed Kate deeply, insinuating her thigh between Kate's legs, braced with one arm against the shower wall, letting the steamy water wash over them.

"Don't do that." Kate smiled against Shaw's lips.

"Which part?"

"Any of it…not yet. For what I have in mind for you I don't want to be standing up." Kate teasingly escaped Shaw's embrace.

"In that case, this will be the quickest shower of my life."

Shaw watched Kate through the slightly foggy glass shower door as she toweled off. Gorgeous. And Kate must have known Shaw would watch. She turned partway to give Shaw an unhindered view of her shapely legs and ass.

Minutes later, they were both toweled off. Shaw led Kate to the bedroom, but it was Kate who tugged Shaw on top of her.

"You feel so good." She feathered kisses along Kate's neck and shoulder.

Beneath her, Kate began to move slowly against her. It had been days that seemed like months since they'd been alone together like this, and Shaw was afraid she wouldn't be able to go slow. It seemed Kate was sending her the same signal as Kate's hands put pressure on her ass, pulling Shaw firmly against her.

Shaw worked her way to Kate's breast and circled the hard point of her nipple before lightly rimming it with her teeth. Kate moaned and arched against her mouth.

"What was that safe word again? *Flashdance*?" Shaw's mouth was still on Kate's breast when she laughed.

"We don't need it."

"We don't?" Shaw hovered above Kate. She wanted to see her eyes.

"We don't need it because I'm never going to ask you to stop."

Liquid warmth flooded her body as she kissed Kate, luxuriously, tenderly. She'd made it past the beginning. With Kate in her arms she was ready for whatever came next. Whatever the future held, as long as she had Kate, Shaw knew she was home.

About the Author

Missouri Vaun spent a large part of her childhood in southern Mississippi, before attending high school in North Carolina and college in Tennessee. Strong connections to her roots in the rural South have been a grounding force throughout her life. Vaun spent twelve years finding her voice working as a journalist in places as disparate as Chicago, Atlanta, and Jackson, Mississippi, all along filing away characters and their stories. Her novels are heartfelt, earthy, and speak of loyalty and our responsibility to others. She and her wife currently live in northern California.

Books Available from Bold Strokes Books

A Heart to Call Home by Jeannie Levig. When Jessie Weldon returns to her hometown after thirty years, can she and her childhood crush Dakota Scott heal the tragic past that links them? (978-1-63555-059-7)

Children of the Healer by Barbara Ann Wright. Life becomes desperate for ex-soldier Cordelia Ross when the indigenous aliens of her planet are drawn into a civil war and old enemies linger in the shadows. Book Three of the Godfall Series. (978-1-63555-031-3)

Hearts Like Hers by Melissa Brayden. Coffee shop owner Autumn Primm is ready to cut loose and live a little, but is the baggage that comes with out-of-towner Kate Carpenter too heavy for anything long term? (978-1-63555-014-6)

Love at Cooper's Creek by Missouri Vaun. Shaw Daily flees corporate life to find solace in the rural Blue Ridge Mountains, but escapism eludes her when her attentions are captured by small town beauty Kate Elkins. (978-1-62639-960-0)

Somewhere Over Lorain Road by Bud Gundy. Over forty years after murder allegations shattered the Esker family, can Don Esker find the true killer and clear his dying father's name? (978-1-63555-124-2)

Twice in a Lifetime by PJ Trebelhorn. Detective Callie Burke can't deny the growing attraction to her late friend's widow, Taylor Fletcher, who also happens to own the bar where Callie's sister works. (978-1-63555-033-7)

Undiscovered Affinity by Jane Hardee. Will a no strings attached affair be enough to break Olivia's control and convince Cardic that love does exist? (978-1-63555-061-0)

Between Sand and Stardust by Tina Michele. Are the lifelong bonds of love strong enough to conquer time, distance, and heartache when Haven Thorne and Willa Bennette are given another chance at forever? (978-1-62639-940-2)

Charming the Vicar by Jenny Frame. When magician and atheist Finn Kane seeks refuge in an English village after a spiritual crisis, can local vicar Bridget Claremont restore her faith in life and love? (978-1-63555-029-0)

Data Capture by Jesse J. Thoma. Lola Walker is undercover on the hunt for cybercriminals while trying not to notice the woman who might be perfectly wrong for her for all the right reasons. (978-1-62639-985-3)

Epicurean Delights by Renee Roman. Ariana Marks had no idea a leisure swim would lead to being rescued, in more ways than one, by the charismatic Hudson Frost. (978-1-63555-100-6)

Heart of the Devil by Ali Vali. We know most of Cain and Emma Casey's story, but *Heart of the Devil* will take you back to where it began one fateful night with a tray loaded with beer. (978-1-63555-045-0)

Known Threat by Kara A. McLeod. When Special Agent Ryan O'Connor reluctantly questions who protects the Secret Service, she learns courage truly is found in unlikely places. Agent O'Connor Series #3. (978-1-63555-132-7)

Seer and the Shield by D. Jackson Leigh. Time is running out for the Dragon Horse Army while two unlikely heroines struggle to put aside their attraction and find a way to stop a deadly cult. Dragon Horse War, Book 3. (978-1-63555-170-9)

Sinister Justice by Steve Pickens. When a vigilante targets citizens of Jake Finnigan's hometown, Jake and his partner Sam fall under suspicion themselves as they investigate the murders. (978-1-63555-094-8)

The Universe Between Us by Jane C. Esther. Ana Mitchell must make the hardest choice of her life: the promise of new love Jolie Dann on Earth, or a humanity-saving mission to colonize Mars. (978-1-63555-106-8)

Touch by Kris Bryant. Can one touch heal a heart? (978-1-63555-084-9)

Change in Time by Robyn Nyx. Working in the past is hell on your future. The Extractor Series: Book Two. (978-1-62639-880-1)

Love After Hours by Radclyffe. When Gina Antonelli agrees to renovate Carrie Longmire's new house, she doesn't welcome Carrie's overtures at friendship or her own unexpected attraction. A Rivers Community Novel. (978-1-63555-090-0)

Nantucket Rose by CF Frizzell. Maggie Jordan can't wait to convert an historic Nantucket home into a B&B, but doesn't expect to fall for mariner Ellis Chilton, who has more claim to the house than Maggie realizes. (978-1-63555-056-6)

Picture Perfect by Lisa Moreau. Falling in love wasn't supposed to be part of the stakes for Olive and Gabby, rival photographers in the competition of a lifetime. (978-1-62639-975-4)

Set the Stage by Karis Walsh. Actress Emilie Danvers takes the stage again in Ashland, Oregon, little realizing that landscaper Arden Philips is about to offer her a very personal romantic lead role. (978-1-63555-087-0)

Strike a Match by Fiona Riley. When their attempts at matchmaking fizzle out, firefighter Sasha and reluctant millionairess Abby find themselves turning to each other to strike a perfect match. (978-1-62639-999-0)

The Price of Cash by Ashley Bartlett. Cash Braddock is doing her best to keep her business afloat, stay out of jail, and avoid Detective Kallen. It's not working. (978-1-62639-708-8)

Under Her Wing by Ronica Black. At Angel's Wings Rescue, dogs are usually the ones saved, but when quiet Kassandra Haden meets outspoken owner Jayden Beaumont, the two stubborn women just might end up saving each other. (978-1-63555-077-1)

Underwater Vibes by Mickey Brent. When Hélène, a translator in Brussels, Belgium, meets Sylvie, a young Greek photographer and swim coach, unsettling feelings hijack Hélène's mind and body—even her poems. (978-1-63555-002-3)

A More Perfect Union by Carsen Taite. Major Zoey Granger and DC fixer Rook Daniels risk their reputations for a chance at true love while dealing with a scandal that threatens to rock the military. (978-1-62639-754-5)

Arrival by Gun Brooke. The spaceship *Pathfinder* reaches its passengers' new homeworld where danger lurks in the shadows while Pamas Seclan disembarks and finds unexpected love in young science genius Darmiya Do Voy. (978-1-62639-859-7)

Captain's Choice by VK Powell. Architect Kerstin Anthony's life is going to plan until Bennett Carlyle, the first girl she ever kissed, is assigned to her latest and most important project, a police district substation. (978-1-62639-997-6)

Falling Into Her by Erin Zak. Pam Phillips, widow at the age of forty, meets Kathryn Hawthorne, local Chicago celebrity, and it changes her life forever—in ways she hadn't even considered possible. (978-1-63555-092-4)

Hookin' Up by MJ Williamz. Will Leah get what she needs from casual hookups or will she see the love she desires right in front of her? (978-1-63555-051-1)

King of Thieves by Shea Godfrey. When art thief Casey Marinos meets bounty hunter Finnegan Starkweather, the crimes of the past just might set the stage for a payoff worth more than she ever dreamed possible. (978-1-63555-007-8)

Lucy's Chance by Jackie D. As a serial killer haunts the streets, Lucy tries to stitch up old wounds with her first love in the wake of a small town's rapid descent into chaos. (978-1-63555-027-6)

Right Here, Right Now by Georgia Beers. When Alicia Wright moves into the office next door to Lacey Chamberlain's accounting firm, Lacey is about to find out that sometimes the last person you want is exactly the person you need. (978-1-63555-154-9)

Strictly Need to Know by MB Austin. Covert operator Maji Rios will do whatever she must to complete her mission, but saving a gorgeous stranger from Russian mobsters was not in her plans. (978-1-63555-114-3)

Tailor-Made by Yolanda Wallace. Tailor Grace Henderson doesn't date clients, but when she meets gender-bending model Dakota Lane, she's tempted to throw all the rules out the window. (978-1-63555-081-8)

Time Will Tell by M. Ullrich. With the ability to time travel, Eva Caldwell will have to decide between having it all and erasing it all. (978-1-63555-088-7)

A Date to Die by Anne Laughlin. Someone is killing people close to Detective Kay Adler, who must look to her own troubled past for a suspect. There she finds more than one person seeking revenge against her. (978-1-63555-023-8)

Captured Soul by Laydin Michaels. Can Kadence Munroe save the woman she loves from a twisted killer, or will she lose her to a collector of souls? (978-1-62639-915-0)

Dawn's New Day by TJ Thomas. Can Dawn Oliver and Cam Cooper, two women who have loved and lost, open their hearts to love again? (978-1-63555-072-6)

Definite Possibility by Maggie Cummings. Sam Miller is just out for good times, but Lucy Weston makes her realize happily ever after is a definite possibility. (978-1-62639-909-9)

Eyes Like Those by Melissa Brayden. Isabel Chase and Taylor Andrews struggle between love and ambition from the writers' room on one of Hollywood's hottest TV shows. (978-1-63555-012-2)

Heart's Orders by Jaycie Morrison. Helen Tucker and Tee Owens escape hardscrabble lives to careers in the Women's Army Corps, but more than their hearts are at risk as friendship blossoms into love. (978-1-63555-073-3)

Hiding Out by Kay Bigelow. Treat Dandridge is unaware that her life is in danger from the murderer who is hunting the woman she's falling in love with, Mickey Heiden. (978-1-62639-983-9)

Omnipotence Enough by Sophia Kell Hagin. Can the tiny tool that abducted war veteran Jamie Gwynmorgan accidentally acquires help her escape an unknown enemy to reclaim her stolen life and the woman she deeply loves? (978-1-63555-037-5)

Summer's Cove by Aurora Rey. Emerson Lange moved to Provincetown to live in the moment, but when she meets Darcy Belo and her son Liam, her quest for summer romance becomes a family affair. (978-1-62639-971-6)

The Road to Wings by Julie Tizard. Lieutenant Casey Tompkins, Air Force student pilot, has to fly with the toughest instructor, Captain Kathryn "Hard Ass" Hardesty, fly a supersonic jet, and deal with a growing forbidden attraction. (978-1-62639-988-4)